Large and
In Charge

Large and
In Charge

La Jill Hunt

www.urbanbooks.net

Urban Books, LLC
300 Farmingdale Road, N.Y.-Route 109
Farmingdale, NY 11735

Large and In Charge

ISBN 13: 978-1-64556-131-6
ISBN 10: 1-64556-131-3

First Trade Paperback Printing March 2021
Printed in the United States of America

10 9 8 7 6 5 4 3 2 1

*This is a work of fiction. Any references or similarities
to actual events, real people, living or dead, or to real
locales are intended to give the novel a sense of reality.
Any similarity in other names, characters, places, and
incidents is entirely coincidental.*

Distributed by Kensington Publishing Corp.
Submit Orders to:
Customer Service
400 Hahn Road
Westminster, MD 21157-4627
Phone: 1-800-733-3000
Fax: 1-800-659-2436

Large and In Charge

La Jill Hunt

Dedication

In loving memory of

Marshall Hunt Sr.
Lillian Hunt

And the double blessing God loved me enough to give:
Minnie E. Hunt and Martha J. Smith
Gone but never forgotten.

Special Thanks

To my family, friends, fans, readers, supporters, my SKs, beautiful sisters of Delta Sigma Theta Sorority Inc., and Carl and Martha Weber

Shout-out to the three very special people:

SanTara Cassamajor, for blessing me with your editing expertise, wisdom, comic relief, and encouragement.

Gerald Moore, for caring enough always to be honest and demanding that I live up to your literary expectations.

Kim "Got Books" Knight, for *everything:* love, friendship, sisterhood, and pushing me to be excellent in all things, not just with your words, but your actions as well.

Prologue

Devyn

"You look beautiful, sweetheart."

Devyn looked at her mother, who'd just placed the lacy, cathedral-length veil into her hair. "Mom, please don't cry. You promised."

"I can't help it. You're breathtaking," her mother sniffed.

"She's right. You are, Dev." Asha, her best friend of over twenty years, passed Devyn's mother a tissue. "That dress is absolutely perfect—everything is. The church, the bridesmaids . . ."

"Thanks to you." Devyn reached over and grabbed Asha's hand.

"Can't say I wish you had a different groom, but . . ." Asha smirked.

"Ash." Devyn gave her a warning look. "Not today."

Despite their decades of friendship, Asha not only declined Devyn's invitation to be her maid of honor, but she also refused even to be a bridesmaid. Her reason? Because she believed that when people accept their positions as members of the bridal party, they stand in solidarity with the bride and groom. And in doing so, they are declaring in front of God and the world that they support the marriage, which Asha absolutely did not. She'd voiced her opinion on more than one occasion about how she disliked Devyn's fiancé, Tremell Simmons, even before he put a ring on her finger.

Devyn and Tremell had dated less than a year before he popped the question on the biggest night of her career. She'd just walked the runway of her first designer show at New York Fashion Week and exited the stage where he was waiting for her on bended knee with a ring in hand and a photographer and videographer to capture it all. Asha felt that Tremell was using Devyn, who was known professionally as D'Morgan, and who was making waves in the modeling world, as a come-up. Tremell believed Asha was jealous of their whirlwind romance that was often displayed in the blogs and on social media. Devyn's followers and fans soon became his. Tremell was head over heels in love with Devyn and would accompany her when she traveled for work, despite his own schedule being full as he pursued his music career.

"She's right, you know." Scorpio, Devyn's matron of honor, turned toward the bride. The legendary cover model who mentored Devyn looked stunning in her chartreuse gown, custom-made by the same designer she'd commissioned to design Devyn's dress for both the ceremony and reception. "But so are you. Now is not the time for that conversation."

"I agree." Devyn's mother looked a little uncomfortable by the discussion the bridal party members were having.

"Well, considering he's about to be her husband, we probably shouldn't be having this conversation ever again. She has made her decision, and all we can do is support our girl." Chastity, also known as Chase, was the maid of honor who looked equally as beautiful as the other ladies. She put her arm around Devyn. "We got you, Dev."

Devyn looked at her small, two-person bridal party and sighed. "I get it. Tremell isn't anyone's favorite choice for me to marry. But he's my choice. He's not perfect, and neither am I, and for the record, none of y'all

are either, but I love the shit out of y'all. Sorry, Mom."
Devyn glanced at her mother.

"It's okay, sweetie." Her mother nodded. "Your foul
mouth is excused this one time."

"Like I was saying, I love Tremell, he loves me, and
despite the arguing sometimes—"

"Sometimes?" Asha groaned.

"Yes, occasionally." Devyn shrugged. "We make a good
team. He's going to win a Grammy one day, and I'm
gonna be right by his side when he does."

"Damn, he really is getting a good one," Scorpio whispered to Asha. "I hate to say this, but it'll be a miracle if
he even gets signed to a major label."

"I have faith in him." Devyn reached for the bottle of
Voss water on the dresser and took a long sip. She'd tried
to minimize how much she drank all day so she wouldn't
spend her entire wedding running to pee. Constant thirst
was something she'd had all her life, but it had been even
worse over the past few months, along with dizzy spells.
The stress of her rising career and planning a wedding in
a short time were wreaking havoc on her. *At least I'll be
able to relax on our honeymoon. The beaches of Belize
are only hours away.*

"You don't need his faith, boo. You're about to sign with
one of the biggest modeling agencies in the world and
be walking alongside me." Scorpio winked. Devyn was
grateful because she'd been the one to put everything in
motion for the contract she was signing as soon as they
returned from their trip.

Someone knocked on the door. Asha opened it, and
Devyn's uncle, who had agreed to escort her down the
aisle, stuck his head inside.

"I'm supposed to pick up a package and deliver it to the
sanctuary," he said.

"Julian, you look so nice." Devyn's mother told him.

"You do, Uncle Julian." Devyn agreed.

"Thank you. I do clean up nice, don't I?" Uncle Julian grinned as he displayed the diamond cuff links Devyn had given him as a gift.

"Ladies, I guess we need to get in place. Devyn, are you ready?" Asha asked one final time.

"I am." Devyn nodded.

Scorpio looked over at Asha and asked, "You guys made sure no outside press is here, right?"

Tremell wasn't thrilled about that but finally agreed when Devyn told him that she would not permit any press at the event, and Scorpio's security detail would be on deck to make sure.

"Of course," Asha nodded. "Security is in place and knows that the only photographers and videographers that have been signed off on are allowed. The guests have been instructed that there's to be no cell phone recording during the ceremony."

"Good." Scorpio nodded and headed out the door with Asha and Chase behind her.

Before Devyn's mother walked out, she paused, taking another long look at her daughter. "You are the best thing God blessed me with. Today is a day I prayed I'd see happen. Thank you."

"Mom, you're really being extra." Devyn wiped a tear from her eye. "And thank you because you are the best thing God blessed me with."

"Well, I'm glad he blessed me with both of you, but we kinda gotta get going," Uncle Julian walked in and said.

"I love you." Devyn's mom kissed her cheek, then pressed her forehead against hers for an extended moment, as she'd done so many times before.

"I love you too." Devyn smiled, fighting back the tears as she watched her mother walk out the door.

This is it. I'm getting married. This is really happening, Devyn thought as she stood beside her uncle in the vestibule of the church. The sound of the saxophonist playing "All of Me" faded, and the first chords of the "Wedding March" began. Devyn's heart raced, and the slight pain in her chest that she'd been ignoring for the past few days started to increase, along with slight dizziness. *Damn it. I should've grabbed my water.*

"You all right?" Uncle Julian gave her a concerned look.

"I'm fine. Just runway jitters." Devyn nodded. "I get them all the time before I walk."

Asha's nod signaled that it was time. The doors opened, and Devyn took a deep breath as she took her first step. The sanctuary pews were full of invited guests, most of whom Devyn didn't know. Unlike herself, Tremell came from a large family. She smiled under her veil at the sound of the *ooohs* and *aaahs* as she walked. Standing at the altar was her groom, looking handsome in his white tuxedo. Devyn could already picture in her mind how gorgeous their wedding photos would be. She glanced around, making sure she knew exactly where the photographer was located and was surprised that she saw three instead of two. But she continued. When she got to the front, she smiled at Tremell, who looked more nervous than she did.

"Who gives this woman to be wed?" the minister asked.

"I do," Uncle Julian proudly announced, then meticulously lifted Devyn's veil, kissed her, and whispered, "I love you."

He took his seat next to her mother on the front row. Devyn took Tremell's hand, and they faced each other. The sweat on his forehead was visible. He shifted his weight from one leg to the other.

"You're beautiful, Dev," he whispered. "Oh my God."

"Thanks, boo." Devyn gave him a quick, reassuring wink in an effort to comfort him.

"Dearly beloved, we are gathered here today to join together in holy matrimony Devyn Morgan Reynolds and Tremell Devaughn Simmons. Tremell, please repeat after me. I, Tremell."

Tremell swallowed and didn't say anything. Devyn frowned.

The minister repeated the vow, this time a little louder. "I, Tremell."

Devyn's heart pounded as she waited for Tremell to repeat the words.

Finally, he spoke, "I-I'm sorry, D."

Devyn lightly cleared her throat and leaned closer. "What?"

"I . . . I can't do this. I'm sorry." Tremell shook his head. The unison gasps from everyone were so loud that they seemed to bounce off the church walls and echo, followed by mumbling.

The reality of what was happening finally registered in her head. She refused to look away from Tremell, even though he no longer looked at her as he rubbed the back of his head nervously. *This fool is trying to jilt me. He's trying to leave me at the altar. Wait. No, the fuck he ain't.* She closed her eyes for a second, and before the cascading bouquet of dusty rose and ivory cottage roses in her hand fell to the ground, her fingers had formed a fist and connected with his jaw so hard, it nearly knocked him backward. His best man caught him, and as he regained his balance, she used the elbow of the same arm to strike again, then charged at him.

"Noooo!" the pastor yelled.

Devyn couldn't tell who was screaming and didn't care. She was too busy trying to tear off Tremell's head while maneuvering in the fitted gown. A pair of strong arms managed to pull her from the floor.

"Are you crazy?" Tremell screamed and scrambled to his feet. Blood oozed from the scratches on his face and fell on his white tuxedo jacket, creating what looked like crimson polka dots.

"Get off me! Let me go!" Devyn shrieked and continued to try to reach him. She was breathing so hard that she panted. Her chest was on fire. Tremell's groomsmen pulled him up and sheltered him while the minister quickly jumped in front of them.

"She's crazy! She's crazy!" Tremell yelled as he reached toward Devyn while his boys prevented him from doing so and guided him toward the side door. Total chaos erupted with people leaping out of their seats, shocked at what they witnessed and not knowing how to react.

Devyn lurched toward Tremell once more. This time, she was stopped by the pulling of her hair with the veil still attached. Enraged and determined to get free, Devyn turned and struck her captor with as much strength as she had struck Tremell moments before. Scorpio, the recipient of Devyn's blow, instinctively grabbed her to keep from falling, and they both tumbled to the ground. Within seconds, Scorpio's security guard yanked Devyn off and scooped Scorpio into his arms, carrying her out.

Finally, Devyn stopped. She turned toward the guests. The church was so quiet. The only thing heard was her heavy breathing. Her mother's eyes met hers, and despite wanting to rush into her arms and cry, Devyn decided to stand and handle this situation. She picked her crumpled veil off the floor, along with the tattered remnants of her bouquet.

After adjusting the lace on her head and straightening her dress, she proudly said, "There will not be a wedding today. Thank you for coming." Devyn then proceeded with the signature walk that she usually reserved for the runway shows, with her head held high, until she walked out the door. Asha and Chase were by her side within seconds, along with her mother and uncle.

"Devyn, oh my God! Someone call an ambulance!" Those were the last words Devyn heard as she crumpled to the floor in the church foyer and experienced a loss of consciousness.

Chapter 1

Devyn

Two Years Later

Devyn looked down at her Apple Watch for what seemed like the hundredth time in the past hour. This was her last class for the day, and she was beyond ready to go. Usually, the afternoon would quickly pass after lunch, but that wasn't the case today, most likely because the students were more rowdy than usual and because the classroom they were in was hot as hell, which didn't help.

"All right, settle down," Devyn said, her tone indicating that her level of patience was running low. "There is no need for all of these discussions. You've been given your assignment. Now, complete it quietly."

"This is too much work," one of the students groaned.

"And we haven't even gone over this stuff, Ms. Douglass. How are we supposed to know how to do this?" another one asked.

Hell, I don't know, Devyn thought as she looked down at the instructions that went along with the assignment she'd just given. Instead of saying the words she was thinking, she gave an empathetic shrug and said, "Just do the best you can. I'm sure Mrs. Hughes will go over the information when she returns next week."

"Next week? I heard she wasn't coming back until after Spring Break," a cute girl with a short bob and braces informed her.

"That's what I heard too." The girl sitting next to her nodded as she confirmed the information.

Within seconds, the complaints about the assignment quickly changed to a discussion about their teacher's absence. Devyn didn't know whether the rumors about why Mrs. Hughes was out were true, and she didn't really care. All she wanted was for the students to settle down for the remainder of the class, and somehow, someway, she needed to get some air.

"Enough! Now, settle down, do your work, and for God's sake, someone open the windows," Devyn pleaded. "It's burning up in here."

Nathan, one of the male students sitting closest to the windows, quickly jumped to his feet and honored her request. The slight breeze that entered the room was barely noticeable, but it was enough to bring a little coolness to the swelter that was the source of Devyn's growing perspiration. The class began to settle as quickly as the air did. She reached into the desk drawer where her purse was located and fumbled until she found a small pack of Kleenex and a compact. She removed some tissue and stared into the mirror as she dabbed along her forehead, nose, and the top of her lip.

"Stop, Nathan!"

Devyn put the mirror down and frowned as she tried to locate the voice. "What's the problem now?"

"He keeps leaning over and singing something about 'come and feel him.'" Clarissa glared at Nathan, sitting at the desk beside her.

Nathan innocently shook his head. "I wasn't singing."

"Well, he was rapping in my ear," Clarissa clarified.

"Nathan, why are you being disruptive?" Devyn sighed.

"I wasn't tryin'a be disruptive, Ms. Douglass. I was just tryin'a let her know *'I been wit' supermodels even before I was signed, and she tall and beautiful and beyond hella fine. But I had to let her go. I couldn't be tied down because chasing money was more important than me staying around. You tryin'a be wit' me, you betta show me just how much you wanna be by my side because it takes a whole lot for you to get on this ride. Now come and feel me.'*"

"That's my jam."

"You did that, Nate."

"He snapped on that jank."

While Nathan's classmates clapped and showed their enthusiasm, Devyn remained stoic, unmoved by his impromptu performance. She wasn't amused or entertained.

"Apologize to her. Now," Devyn told him.

"Awww, Miss Douglass, I ain't do nothing. I was just playin'." Nathan shrugged. "She just trippin'. It's just a song by this rapper named Touché. It's called 'Come and Feel Me.'"

"I don't care if it's a song. It's disrespectful. Apologize," Devyn repeated.

Nathan stared at Devyn for a moment, then cut his eyes toward Clarissa. "I'm sorry that you're so sensitive that you can't take a joke. That's why nobody wanna come and feel you."

Once again, the class erupted in laughter. Devyn closed her eyes and tried to count backward from ten, hoping that by the time she got to one, the profanity-filled tirade she was on the brink of releasing would be gone.

"Aye, what's going on in here?"

The noise in the class subsided as Officer Jeff Baker, the school security officer, walked in. Devyn slowly released the breath she hadn't realized she was holding as he approached the center of the classroom. He was good-natured and friendly, but the students knew not to play with him.

"I can hear y'all all the way down the hallway. I know you wouldn't be acting up like this if Mrs. Hughes was up in here, now, would you?" He looked around at the students. When no one answered, he repeated his question, "Would you?"

"No, sir," a few students murmured.

"That's what I thought." He nodded. Just as he was about to say something else, the ringing of the bell stopped him, and the class began shuffling and moving as they grabbed their belongings and got up to leave. "Wait, I ain't hear Miss Douglass say anyone was dismissed."

All eyes were on Devyn, including Jeff's. Devyn exhaled and told them, "Class dismissed."

"You good?" Jeff asked when the last student was out the door.

"Yeah, I'm fine. It's just hot in here, and they were a little out of pocket," Devyn explained. "I really could have handled it. But thanks for assisting. I appreciate it."

"I know you could handle it. You're one of the best subs we got around here. But you're right. This classroom is a furnace. Mrs. Hughes got low iron, so she keeps it warm in here. Not to mention, she's the only one with a key to the thermostat." Jeff pointed to the small case on the wall secured with a lock. "I'm surprised the windows weren't locked too. That's probably why the class was off the chain. They ain't used to getting fresh air in here."

"Well, if they plan on having me cover for her while she's out, they'd better hurry up and find another key," Devyn smiled. "You don't know how close I was to cussing them kids out today."

"Oh, I could tell. When I got to the door, I heard that li'l rap performance, and as soon as I saw your face, I knew you were not happy at all," Jeff teased.

"I was not," Devyn agreed as she gathered her belongings and stood. "I almost ran out of the room with them."

"I feel ya. Well, at least the day is over. You got plans for the weekend?" Jeff smiled.

"What? Isn't today just Tuesday?" Devyn asked, confused by his question and wondering why he was concerned about the weekend already. She barely knew what she was doing the next day, let alone the weekend. *Girl, don't even trip. You know the only weekend plans you have are the same ones you have every weekend: watch Lifetime movies, make herbal tea blends, and sleep.*

"Yeah, it is. But if you aren't busy, I was gonna invite you to a card party at the crib. It's gonna be fun. You should come," Jeff suggested. "I got someone for you to meet."

"I'm not really a card player, but thanks," Devyn shrugged as they walked toward the door.

"Fine. You don't have to play cards. Just come, have a few drinks, get a plate, and meet new people. My boy is a chef, and he's about to open his own spot." Jeff remained by her side as she walked down the hallway toward the school's front office to sign out.

"I'm good."

"I know. That's why I'm inviting you. I only invite good people to my crib, feel me? So, you should consider yourself special." Jeff winked at her. "And I'm not just saying that because you're gorgeous, and my boys would be impressed that you showed up and give me mad props. I really think you're cool people, Dev."

Devyn laughed. Jeff was one of the few people at the school that she liked. And it wasn't just because he also happened to be Black, another anomaly at their place of employment. He always checked in on the classes she worked in and made sure she had lunch. He always tried to set her up with a cousin, classmate, or homeboy that he just knew would be "perfect" for her. Devyn kindly declined each one. Jeff was an all-around nice guy, but she didn't know him well enough to trust him with her love life.

"Thanks, Jeff. You're good people too." Devyn reached for the door handle of the office but stopped upon hearing the haunting, familiar words.

"You tryin'a be wit' me ya betta show how much you wanna be by my side because it takes a whole lot for you to get on this ride. Now come and feel me."

Devyn looked down the hallway to see Nathan once again rapping. A couple of his friends bobbed their heads to the beat and served as his backup crew, laughing as they strolled away.

"You okay, Dev?" Jeff's voice came from over her shoulder. She'd been so caught up in her mind that she'd forgotten that he was there.

"Yeah, I'm fine," Devyn finally said. "I hate that fucking song."

Chapter 2

Asha

"I'm sure they didn't mean anything by it, Dev. It's just a popular song right now, that's all." Asha pulled into the parking lot of the Convention Center. "But I get it. You know I do."

"I'm not going to be able to do this much longer, Ash, I promise. Those kids are terrible, and it's hot as hell in that classroom. You know how bad I sweat now that I'm fat." Devyn reminded her just in case she forgot all about the extra twenty-three pounds Devyn's body now contained.

"Girl, shut the hell up. You're not fat." Asha shook her head even though they were on the phone, and Devyn couldn't see her reaction. She only had a few minutes to spare before she had to be inside for a meeting, and there was no way she was going to spend them trying to convince Devyn that there was nothing wrong with her weight. It would be a waste of time anyway. Her best friend was convinced that because she no longer weighed the one hundred and twenty-three pounds, she was obese. Of course, this was far from the truth, but Devyn refused to think otherwise. As far as Asha and anyone else with good sense could tell, there was nothing wrong with her body. Devyn was still beautiful, and though she was slightly larger than the average woman, mainly due to her stature, she still had a gorgeous, modelesque body that most women, including Asha, would love to have.

"I am, and we both know it. Look, I understand that Mrs. Hughes is going through a tough time with her divorce and all, but—"

"Wait, who the hell is Mrs. Hughes?"

"The chemistry teacher I'm subbing for."

"Chemistry? Oh hell, those kids gonna fail. You can't calculate how to tip 15 percent properly, and they expect you to teach them children formulas with chemicals? That's dangerous," Asha sighed. "Wait, she's going through a divorce? How do you know all of this?"

"Whatever. I'm a good tipper, and you know it. And I know because the kids told me all about it. She found out her husband was sleeping with her sister's hairstylist," Devyn explained. "She went to the salon and tore shit up when she found out."

"Oh snap, was she arrested?"

"If she was, they didn't mention it. So I think she wasn't."

"Probably not because Lord knows they would've spilled *that* tea right along with the rest of it," Asha laughed.

"Girl, they probably would've pulled up her mug shot and tried to show it to me. I kept telling them to stop talking and do their work."

"Whatever, Dev. You know your nosy ass was probably all ears while they were talking."

"Only for a second before they started with the dumbness and disrespect. They'd better be glad Jeff walked in when he did," Devyn commented. "He set them straight."

"Oh Lord, not the stalker."

"He's not a stalker, Ash. He just has perfect timing," Devyn told her.

"Because he's stalking you," Asha murmured as she looked toward the entrance of the building. Several young ladies were walking in carrying folders and portfolios. "Oh snap, looks like they're having a casting call."

"Who?" Devyn asked.

"I don't know. You want me to find out so you can come?" Asha asked jokingly but slightly hopeful that Devyn would be curious. She'd been subtly trying to encourage her friend to get back into her passion but hadn't been successful yet. Still, Asha wasn't going to give up.

"Hell no. I'm good." Devyn gave the same answer she always had when Asha mentioned modeling.

"I'm just asking because you were the one who said you needed to find something else other than substitute teaching."

"Well, that ain't the something I wanna do, and you know it."

Asha looked at her watch and saw that it was almost time for her appointment. "I gotta get inside to meet this client. We still meeting up for Taco Tuesdays at Pablo's?"

"See? You're such a bad influence. I just told you I was fat, and here you go inviting me to eat tacos and drink margaritas," Devyn teased.

"Who said anything about margaritas, heffa?" Asha laughed. "I'll see you at seven."

Asha ended the call and grabbed her laptop bag before hopping out of her Acura SUV. Her long strides across the parking lot allowed her to make it to the front of the glass door within moments. Being nearly six feet tall did have its benefits. Once inside, she looked around, expecting to find the client she was meeting but didn't see anyone. She ventured further down the corridor toward the ballrooms of the Convention Center.

"Miss Bailey, what brings you to our fine establishment today?"

Asha turned around to see Gail, one of the sales managers, walking toward her.

"Hey, Gail. I'm supposed to be meeting a client, well, a potential client, this afternoon. But I don't think they're here yet," Asha said.

"Oh, okay," Gail nodded.

Asha motioned toward the row of ladies sitting outside one of the ballrooms. "Casting call for an agency?"

"No, they're candidates for a beauty pageant," Gail told her.

"Beauty pageant?" Asha was surprised to hear that, especially in her line of work. Usually, her firm was the first to know about large-scale events in the area, and no one had mentioned anything about it.

"Yeah, it's a big deal, and the first time it's being hosted here this year. Miss Teen Elite." Gail imitated a sophisticated pose. She was an older woman in her late fifties who reminded Asha of Rose from the TV show *Golden Girls*.

"Miss Teen Elite," Asha repeated, glancing at the beautiful but nervous-looking young ladies waiting to be called inside.

"They've been lining up all day, I can tell you that much," Gail said as they went back toward the front of the building. "The woman in charge, Marcia Thompkins, is a piece of work. She has everyone around here stressed."

"I'm sure you say the same thing about me," Asha laughed. She'd worked with Gail on several occasions, and they'd bumped heads a time or two.

"We've had our moments, but working with you is always enjoyable. This woman isn't pleasant at all, and knowing that I have to deal with her for the next six weeks is giving me anxiety," Gail sighed.

"Yikes. Maybe it won't be as bad as you think," Asha suggested.

"Let's pray that it's not." Gail shrugged. "Do you need anything while you wait? Water or coffee? I have some snacks in my office."

"No, thank you. I'm fine," Asha told her.

"Grace!" a stern voice called.

Asha and Gail both turned around. A slender, blond woman dressed in a dark business suit walked toward them with precision and intensity. One look at her blouse tied at the neck in a perfect bow, long, blond tresses, a glammed face, bleach-white teeth, and the word "pageant queen" instantly popped into Asha's head. The only thing missing was a crown and sash announcing the title she probably held in her glory days.

"Oh Christ," Gail murmured, "Here comes Satan."

"I told you we'd need more chairs outside the room. I would hope you wouldn't expect my ladies to stand while waiting," the woman said, her voice as crisp as her blouse.

"Of course not, Mrs. Fisher. My apologies. I was just over near that area, and there were a few empty seats," Gail told her. "And it's Gail."

"Well, there aren't any now," the woman responded, then added, ". . . Gail."

"I'll call maintenance and have them bring some right away," Gail nodded.

"I need them now," the woman said before turning back around and walking away.

"Five weeks, four days, three hours." Gail closed her eyes and inhaled when she was gone.

"Damn, she is a handful." Asha gave a sympathetic look.

"It was nice seeing you again. Let me get these chairs before Cruella returns." Gail rushed off, and Asha took out her phone and dialed her office.

"Great Expectation Events, this is Libby," the administrative assistant answered in her bubbly voice.

"What's up, Libby? It's Asha. Did my four o'clock call?"

"No, I haven't heard anything. Sorry," Libby answered.

"Okay, thanks. I was just checking to be sure before I left." Asha exhaled. This was her last appointment for the day, and she wanted to get home in time to shower and change before meeting Devyn. She wanted to be comfortable while eating her tacos and drinking tequila.

"That's odd. When he scheduled the appointment, he was the one who specifically asked if you could meet him at the Convention Center instead of here at the office. Are you sure he's not there, and you didn't miss him?"

Asha went back to the front of the building. She looked around the lobby and then toward the front doors. The only person she saw was a maintenance man in grimy coveralls near the entrance along with a couple of other women, who, she assumed, were there for the pageant. "Yeah, I'm sure."

"You want his number?"

Asha checked her watch once more. It was almost four thirty. At this point, she was ready to go. By him not showing up, she had a chance to beat traffic and get home early. Knowing she had no intention of calling, she told Libby, "Sure, send it to me."

"Sending it over," Libby said.

"Thanks, Libby. See you in the morning." By the time the text came through with the name Max Transportation and the phone number, she was already out of the parking lot.

Almost forty-five minutes later, she pulled into the driveway of her town house directly beside a late-model pickup truck that she hadn't expected to be there. She stepped out of her SUV and called out for the owner of the truck.

"Sully? Are you here?"

A few seconds later, the gate leading to her backyard swung open, and Sully emerged, pushing her garbage can. "Yeah, I'm here. I thought you had a meeting?"

"I was supposed to, but it didn't happen. What are you doing here?" she asked as she watched him push the large plastic can with her address painted on the side to the edge of the driveway. When he finished, he walked over and kissed her cheek.

"I came to take the can to the street. And I wanted to make sure I put out those bags of leaves I raked this weekend to be picked up." Sully smiled.

"Oh, I forgot about those," Asha said.

"I figured you would. That's why I came to do it for you," he winked.

"Thank you, handsome. I appreciate it."

Calvin Sullivan wasn't someone Asha would've ever considered dating. He was attractive, hardworking, dependable, and the man could fix damn near anything. They'd met at the hardware store one Saturday afternoon. Not only did he help her find the tool she needed to fix her faucet, but he also repaired it, in addition to mounting her television, installing her ceiling fan, and painting the accent wall of her living room. He'd retired from the army, owned his own business, and was a deacon at his church. He was the most consistent man she'd ever met. She enjoyed spending time with him, and he was everything most women look for in a man. There was just one minor detail: at 51 years of age, Calvin Sullivan was a whopping twenty-three years older than she was. But for the most part, their age difference didn't matter to her, and he didn't seem worried about it either. They liked the same movies and restaurants. Asha wasn't a party girl like she'd been in her younger days and spent most of her time working. The only person she hung out with was Devyn, who was just as much of a homebody as she was these days. Unlike guys her age, Sully didn't require much.

"Well, since you're home, why don't you show your appreciation by letting me take you to dinner?" He grabbed her hand.

"Aw, I would, but I'm meeting Devyn for Taco Tuesdays," she replied. "I gotta get inside, shower, and change so that I won't be late."

"You look fine to me. Why you gotta change?" Sully asked, looking her up and down.

"Because as comfortable as this blouse and these slacks are, I need to put on something a little less boardroom and a lot more booyah," she laughed.

"I don't know what that means, but whatever. You and Devyn have fun. I'll talk to you tomorrow." Sully gave her a look of disappointment.

"Don't be like that. It's just tacos. We won't be out long. I'll call you when I get home. I promise." Asha put her arms around his neck. Because she wore flats, they were about the same height and stood eye to eye. She wanted him to see that he had nothing to worry about. He wasn't a jealous guy, but he seemed a bit bothered whenever she hung out with Devyn.

Sully nodded. "All right, just be careful. I'll try to wait up for your call."

"Good." She gave him a reassuring kiss.

Chapter 3

Devyn

Pablo's Mexican Bistro was packed. Since a gentle breeze was blowing and a decent amount of sunlight was still out, Devyn and Asha had opted to sit out on the restaurant's patio and feast on tacos, tortilla chips with white sauce and salsa, and a round of half-off happy-hour double-shot margaritas. The last thing Devyn needed was the enormous amount of calories she was consuming. Not only was she starving, but she also definitely needed a drink, in addition to a face-to-face girl chat.

"I'm telling you, he's into you," Asha said.

"He's not into me. First of all, he has a girl. Second, he keeps trying to hook me up with one of his boys. If he wanted me, he wouldn't be tryin'a do all that," Devyn said.

"It's a front. He's just saying that. He's not trying to hook you up for real. But then again, he might be. What does his friend look like?" Asha asked.

"Hell, I don't know. I ain't even ask. It doesn't matter because I ain't interested."

"In the friend or Jeff?" Asha raised an eyebrow.

Devyn reached across the table and took her glass. "Gimme this."

"What are you doing?" Asha gasped.

"Clearly, you're drunk," Devyn laughed.

Asha snatched her glass back and finished the last of her drink. "Now, you know I'm not drunk. I've only had one drink."

"I'm honestly surprised you even had that one. Hell, I'm surprised you even *wanted* to hang out tonight. You know how the deacon doesn't like for you to hang out with me," Devyn said, referring to Asha's boyfriend, Sully. Since they'd become a little more serious, Asha had become less and less available to hang out. Devyn knew it was because he didn't really care for her. "He must not know you're out. You're dressed cute too. And curled your hair?"

"You're trying to be funny." Asha gave her a snarky look.

"I'm not. I'm just saying that you're looking cute," Devyn commented. In addition to being surprised by Asha's suggestion earlier that they indulge in Taco Tuesday, she was equally shocked to see her best friend dressed in jeans and a cute top. Asha always dressed as if she were about to go into a corporate meeting: business suits, blazers, slacks, and heels. She also kept her shoulder-length locs pulled back. Tonight, they were hanging freely, framing her gorgeous face.

"You know Sully doesn't have a problem with you. And I figured you needed a night out after the day you had. You've been quite grumpy these days," Asha said, tucking a loc behind her ear.

"Grumpy? What the hell? Am I one of the Seven Dwarfs?" Devyn frowned.

"Maybe that was the wrong word. But I didn't want to use the word 'bitchy.'"

"Wow, I think I like grumpy better." Devyn's eyes became small as she looked across the table.

"Dev, you're my best friend. I know you better than anyone else on this earth." Asha picked up a chip and dipped it into the white sauce.

"Oh God, here we go . . ." Devyn groaned.

"The reason why you're in such a mood these days . . ." Asha continued.

"Please don't say it." Devyn pleaded.

"Is because you need some dick," Asha stated.

"I knew it." Devyn shook her head.

"It's been almost two years since your back has been blown out properly, Dev. That's a long time. And I know you've been through a lot. But you need—"

"What I need is another drink. And I'm gonna go get one." Devyn stood up, smoothing the front of her floral jumpsuit. She planned only to have one drink, but Asha was on one, and it was going to take more alcohol than usual to get through the evening.

"Señora, did you need something?" Miguel, their server, rushed over and asked.

"I was just gonna go get another drink from the bar," Devyn told him.

"Sí, I'll get it for you. It's no problem." Miguel nodded, then turned to Asha, "Another for you as well?"

Asha shook her head, "Oh no, I'm fine."

Devyn teased. "She's a lightweight."

"Whatever. I may be many things, but I ain't never been light nothing: light-skinned, lightweight, lighthearted. Besides, I came for the tacos, not the tequila." Asha pointed to the food in the middle of the table. "Now, stop trying to be cute and sit down and eat. People are staring."

Devyn glanced in the direction Asha was motioning, and sure enough, a guy was looking at her. She politely smiled back, then sat down and picked up a taco, taking a bite.

"So, about your dating dilemma," Asha continued.

"How can I have a dilemma when I ain't dating?" Devyn pointed out.

"That's my point. We're gonna fix that."

"But it's not broken. If I wanted to date, I would—but I don't. And it has nothing to do with what I went through. I'm over that. I just haven't met anyone I vibe with enough even to be interested in," Devyn explained. "Dating is the last thing I'm even thinking about right now. I have more important stuff to worry about than penis and the drama that comes with it."

"Really? Like what?" Asha asked.

"Like figuring out what it is that I'm supposed to be doing with my life. Something that's less stressful and gonna make me more money than this bullshit I'm doing now." Devyn immediately regretted her words as soon as she said them. She didn't have to look at Asha's face to know that they had probably stung a little, which she didn't mean to do. "I mean, don't get me wrong, Asha, I'm grateful for my job. But . . ."

"It's cool, Dev. I understand, and you don't have to apologize."

Asha's flat tone confirmed that Devyn had struck a nerve. Devyn hadn't meant to sound unappreciative. She wouldn't even be working if Asha hadn't heard about the job from a client and suggested that she apply since she complained about being bored. At the time, the savings she'd been living off of were dwindling fast, and she was still trying to figure out her next career move. Being a substitute teacher seemed to be a good idea and a way to put a little money in her pocket while figuring it out. But it definitely wasn't what Devyn enjoyed doing, and it was becoming harder and harder to go to work each day. Not only that, but she also wasn't any closer to discovering what it was she wanted or needed to be doing next.

"I do, and I'm really sorry. I'm not trying to be a bitch, but I'm just so . . ." Devyn tried to think of a word to describe her current state of mind.

"Unfulfilled." Asha found the word Devyn had been searching for.

"Exactly." Devyn nodded. She wasn't used to being in a rut. She'd spent her entire life maneuvering and positioning herself for success. Years of hard work, determination, discipline, and ambition had paid off—until she lost everything within a matter of days. Asha had been by her side through it all. Devyn couldn't ask for a better best friend.

"You went through a season of loss. We all go through that. Yours was longer and harder than most." Asha sighed. "But you've gained some things too. Like Fantasia says, sometimes you gotta lose to win."

Devyn thought about all the things she'd lost: her relationship, her dream job, her mother, and her health, all within a matter of months. The only thing she'd gained in the process was the house that her uncle allowed her to live in and thirty pounds that she didn't want.

"What exactly did I win? Remind me," Devyn said.

"It's all going to come together, Dev. I promise. It just takes time, that's all." Asha gave her a reassuring smile.

"I've given it enough time. I'm tired of being lost. It's like I'm searching for something, but I don't even know what I'm looking for." Devyn shook her head. "I don't even know what direction I'm supposed to face. I used to look in the mirror and know exactly who I was. Now, I don't even recognize the person on the other side."

"Devyn, you're still the same person. You're still beautiful, you're still smart, you're still talented, and God still has a plan for your life."

Devyn looked down at Asha's hand touching her arm. "I know. I just wish he'd give me a sign because right now, I feel like I'm all alone, stuck in a fog and can't see anything."

"You're not alone, Dev. You know I'm right here with you tryin'a help you figure it out. And God is gonna direct both of us to exactly where we're supposed to be."

"You think so?"

"I know so." Asha nodded. "You just gotta be open and willing to receive."

Devyn closed her eyes and lifted her hands, pretending to pray. "God, I'm open. Send me a sign."

"Compliments of the gentleman in the corner." Miguel reappeared and set her margarita on the table moments later.

"Well, that was nice," Devyn said. "Please tell him I said thank you."

"You can tell him yourself. He's standing behind you," Asha whispered.

Devyn turned around, expecting to see the guy she smiled at moments earlier, but it wasn't him. Instead, she found a lanky guy who looked like he wasn't much older than the students in Mrs. Hughes's chemistry class. "Oh, uh, hi."

"Hey, there, beautiful. I wanted to come over and make sure you got your drink," he said. "I'm RayQuan."

"I did. Thanks." Devyn hoped her dry tone would be a deterrent, but he remained where he stood.

"You are more than welcome. You've gotta be the most beautiful chick I've ever seen. May I ask you a question?"

After cringing at the word "chick," Devyn sighed and gave him the answer she knew he wanted to know. "Five-eleven."

"Damn, that's tall as fuck, ma. I love me an Amazonian woman." He nodded. "I guess you already knew what I was gonna ask, huh?"

"Yep."

"So, you think I could get your number?"

"I would, but I'm engaged." Devyn shrugged.

"Damn, that's too bad," RayQuan said, then turned his attention to Asha. "What about you? How tall are you, ma?"

"Six feet, but I'm going to have to decline that delightful offer as well," Asha said, looking quite amused. Devyn knew her friend was suppressing her laughter.

"Well, enjoy the rest of y'all night," RayQuan said, then walked off.

When he was gone, Devyn looked across the table at Asha's face, which was now red. "Go ahead. Let it out."

"You asked for a sign," Asha giggled.

Unable to keep her own straight face, Devyn joined in her friend's laughter. Within seconds, they were both shaking and dabbing at the tears that were streaming. Devyn was so caught up in the moment with her best friend that she didn't even think to turn around and make sure their young suitor was no longer in earshot until seconds later. She turned around in her seat and scanned the area nearby, relieved when she didn't see any sign of him. Just as she was about to turn back around, she noticed the guy who'd caught her eye earlier exiting the patio area. As she watched him, he turned around, and their eyes met. He smiled at her again.

"Do you know that guy?" Devyn turned to Asha. "I think I know him from somewhere, but I don't know where."

"What guy? Where?" Asha leaned over and looked past Devyn.

"The guy smiling at us. He's right by the door in the jacket."

Asha shrugged. "I don't see anybody by the door, Dev."

Devyn turned back and saw that he was gone. "That's crazy. He was right there."

For a second, Devyn considered getting up and going to see if she could find him. He seemed so familiar. But it was too late. He was probably long gone, and her free frozen margarita was melting.

***

Later that night, Devyn stepped out of her shower and stood in front of the full-length mirror behind the bathroom door. Instead of using her bath towel to wrap around her wet body, she used it to wipe the moisture from the mirror, then stared at her reflection. It was like looking at a stranger. Her face was the same, but the abdomen, which was once flat, now puffed out, and she could pinch mounds of skin on the sides. The once-perfect B-cup breasts were a full C cup, closer to a D, now. Countless hours of cardio that she'd been putting in lately had only resulted in her hips widening, buttocks tightening, and legs toning. No matter how hard she worked out, she couldn't get back to the perfect bikini body she used to have. The body that had made her almost famous was forever gone.

No longer able to tolerate what she saw, Devyn turned around and stared at the bathroom counter, which held the source of her contorted, fuller figure that also enabled her to live: her meds. The pills, prescribed by her physician, kept her alive, but they killed her dreams.

Devyn had never heard of Addison's disease until the doctors finally diagnosed her after she lay in the hospital for damn near two weeks after the wedding disaster. Her frequent nausea, fainting spells, constant thirst, and irritability that she'd been suffering from for a year prior were all a result of her illness. What she thought were panic attacks and chest pains brought on by stress were also symptoms that she ignored. Devyn was faced with the reality of never going back and doing what she loved: modeling. Because she was susceptible to blood clots, traveling on planes every week to get to even meet with design houses, let alone walk in runway shows, was no longer possible. The somber likelihood of having to be on oxygen in the future meant that her career was over.

Chapter 4

Asha

"Asha, Mr. Maxwell is here to see you." Libby's voice came through the phone intercom system.

"Maxwell?" Asha looked up from the team-building retreat proposal she'd been working on for the past hour. She'd promised the client, Dr. Reed, a prominent dentist with a large practice, that she'd have it submitted to him by noon for him to review. This would be the fourth time he'd hired their company to plan an event, and he'd specifically asked for Asha, which was why she was so meticulous. It wasn't anywhere near finished, and the last thing she wanted to do was stop, especially for someone who hadn't even bothered to show up for their previous appointment.

"Max Transportation," Libby whispered.

"I know who he is. I just wasn't expecting him. Give me a moment, please," Asha said. She'd sent a brief email to Maxwell Transportation regarding the missed meeting and invited them to reschedule and hadn't thought any more about it. In addition to finishing the proposal, Asha had a long list of other items on her agenda to complete for the day. She decided to tell Libby to have another one of her colleagues meet with him instead. "Libby, see if Paula can . . . Libby?"

"Yeah?" Instead of coming through the intercom, Libby's voice came from the doorway. Before Asha could say anything, Libby added, "You can come in, Mr. Maxwell."

"Thank you so much." The voice was deep, baritone, smooth, and perfectly matched the man that Libby guided into Asha's office.

Shit, Asha thought as she stared at him. He was tall, at least six foot three, about 200 pounds, with a nice build and a thick beard which made him ruggedly handsome. He wore khakis, a collared polo shirt with his company logo, and brown Cole Haan loafers. Even in his simple attire, he exuded sex appeal.

"Mr. Maxwell, I'm Asha Bailey." Asha stood and extended her hand.

"Nice to meet you, Ms. Bailey. I'm Benson Maxwell, but please call me Ben." He smiled, revealing bright, white teeth that were slightly crooked, but somehow perfect.

"Please, call me Asha." Asha motioned to the chair in front of her desk. "Have a seat."

"Thank you." Ben sat down.

Asha looked over at Libby, who was still in the office, staring just as hard at the handsome man as Asha wanted to. "Libby, I think we're good here."

Libby snapped out of her trance, blinked, and said, "Oh, no problem." Then she scurried off.

"Can I get you anything? Soda, water?" Asha offered.

"No, I'm good. I'm sorry to pop up like this. I did get your email about missing our meeting the other day. I wanted to apologize in person. When I saw you at the Convention Center, I thought you were there for the event with the other ladies," he laughed.

"You were at the Convention Center? I didn't see you. What other ladies?" Asha was confused. There was no damn way he could've been there, and she missed him.

"There were a bunch of ladies there. I held the door open for all of you when you walked out." Ben nodded. "You walked right past me."

"No, I would've remembered you," Asha told him.

"I had on coveralls because I'd been working in the garage all day. That's why I was late. One of my mechanics had to leave because his wife went into labor. I was finishing up a job that he was in the middle of when he left, which is why I ran late," Ben explained. "But I saw you."

Asha suddenly remembered passing what she thought was one of the maintenance men. She'd been so ready to leave that she hadn't even given him a second glance. "I'm so sorry. I can't believe this. And I'm flattered, but those ladies were beauty pageant contestants. That definitely isn't me."

"Hey, you looked like you fit right in with them to me." Ben shrugged.

Asha raised an eyebrow, taken aback by his statement. His demeanor wasn't flirtatious or facetious. He seemed sincere. Suddenly, finishing the proposal for Dr. Reed's retreat was no longer a pressing matter.

"So, Ben, what perfect event can I help you plan?" Asha grabbed a pen and pad, now more concerned with the client sitting in her office than anything else. By the time the meeting ended an hour later, Asha had a signed contract with Maxwell Transportation, a deposit for the event Ben was hosting, as well as an appointment to meet again.

"Oh my God, is he not the *finest* man you've ever seen?" Libby gushed after Ben was gone.

"Is that why you brought him into my office unannounced?" Asha leaned against the large desk that took up most of the tiny lobby area of Great Expectations.

Libby shrugged. "I did announce him, sorta. And you didn't tell me not to bring him in, and a man that good looking doesn't need to be announced. Besides, he said the two of you passed each other yesterday at the

Convention Center, so I figured you would be glad to see him again. I know I would be. Lord, he is fine. You didn't tell me he was that fine."

"I didn't even realize the guy I passed by was him. He didn't look like that," Asha confessed.

"What? Stop playing. Did he have on a mask? A helmet?" Libby's head tilted to the side, and she folded her arms, making Asha feel even more ashamed for not realizing who he was the day before.

"No, but he was dressed differently, and I was in a hurry to leave. I didn't really pay him any attention. But you're right. He is good looking. He's also quite interesting. He's hosting a benefit to raise money for Breast Cancer Awareness," Asha told her. "Buses for Boobs."

"What?" Libby frowned.

Asha chuckled. "I know. We're gonna have to work on the title, but Maxwell's transportation company mainly consists of charter buses. He also owns a couple of party buses and limos too."

"Ooooh, I get it."

"Like I said, it's a work in progress. It's gonna be nice, though. I'm excited." Asha stood up.

"I would be excited too. That man is fine. I didn't notice a ring, did you?"

"I didn't pay attention to that," Asha lied. Checking Ben's left hand for a ring had definitely been something she'd done, and she was relieved when she didn't see one. In addition to being tall, handsome, and a successful business owner motivated to raise money for charity, he was single. She had to do a little more research, but from what she'd learned and seen so far, he was *exactly* what she was hoping to find, maybe even better. Only time would tell.

"A man that fine has to have a woman, a girlfriend, or probably several. What do you think?"

"I think I need to get in here and finish this proposal for Reed Dental and get it over to him," Asha stated as she walked past Libby's desk and headed to her own office.

"Well, for the record, Dr. Reed is fine too," Libby called after her.

Asha retreated into her office and resumed working on the proposal, determined not to be distracted by thoughts of Ben Maxwell, and submit it on time. She'd just hit the send button with five minutes to spare when Mrs. Henderson, her boss, popped her head in while tapping on her door.

"Hey, got a sec?"

"Sure, what's up?" Asha asked, hoping she wasn't about to add another event to her already full schedule. Being one of the top event coordinators for the company was both a blessing and a curse. It allowed Asha to pretty much do her job without being micromanaged, but it also meant that when someone else dropped the ball, she was the go-to person to pick it up.

"Uh, I'm headed over to Gordon Hospital to meet with the board of directors in twenty minutes, but I was wondering if you could swing by the Convention Center and pick up the pending contracts for the car show next month. I'd be forever in your debt, and I'll bring you your favorite latte in the morning," Mrs. Henderson pleaded.

"No problem. I was just there yesterday. Had I known, I would've grabbed them for you."

"Thank you so much. And I'll make sure you have your Vanilla Chai, no whip, with almond milk." She winked before walking away.

Not that she needed one, but being tasked with picking up the contracts gave Asha an excuse to take her lunch break earlier than she expected. She'd planned to meet Sully at one of their favorite barbecue spots for a quick bite to make up for not calling when she got home the night before as promised. She had every intention of doing so, but between the alcohol from the margaritas and the overall fatigue from the day, she fell asleep. When she called him on her way to work, she'd apologized.

"I'm sorry, Sully. I was knocked out as soon as I got home."

"It's no big deal. I wasn't really expecting you to call anyway. I'm sure Devyn kept you out later than anticipated," he commented.

"Well, not exactly. I mean, I did get in later than planned, but that wasn't necessarily because of her. We both were talking," Asha told him, then suggested, "You wanna meet me at Jake's for lunch today?"

Sully didn't respond immediately, and for a moment, Asha wondered if he was going to decline the invitation until he finally said, "Sure, we can meet. How's one o'clock?"

"That's perfect."

"I'll see you there," Sully said.

Asha thought about stopping at the Convention Center to pick up the contracts before heading to the restaurant but didn't want to risk being late for her lunch date. She learned early on when they began dating that Sully was a stickler for time, a result of being in the military most of his adult life. The meeting time of one o'clock meant that he would probably be at the restaurant at twelve forty-five, at the latest. Sure enough, when she walked into Jake's with five minutes to spare, Sully was already seated in the dining area. What she wasn't expecting, however, was that he wasn't sitting alone.

"Damn it," Asha whispered. A mixture of disappointment and anxiety caused a knot in her stomach, and for a brief second, she thought about turning around and walking out the same door she'd just entered—but it was too late.

Sully's motioning hand in the air confirmed that he'd seen her. Instead of leaving, she took a deep breath and promised herself that she would only have to endure thirty minutes of what she anticipated was going to be orchestrated bullshit.

"Hey, baby." Sully stood as soon as she arrived at the table.

"Hey, honey." Asha gave him a quick hug, moving before he could kiss her cheek. She glanced over at the sour-faced woman sitting in the chair beside Sully. "Ingrid, I didn't know you were joining us."

Ingrid Sullivan was her father's only child, and as such, the apple of his eye. He was devoted to making sure she was well cared for and supported from the day she was born and continued to do so in every way possible: physically, emotionally, and financially. The fact that he was such a great dad was one of the things Asha respected about Sully, especially since she'd grown up without her father. But the relationship he had with Ingrid was also a thorn in her side. It had nothing to do with the fact that she was only a year younger than Asha. Nor did it have anything to do with her inability to keep a job or pay her own bills. Asha could even understand Ingrid not being too thrilled at the fact that she and Sully were dating. What irritated her the most about Ingrid Sullivan was that she was a selfish bitch whose life was one chaotic moment after another. Undoubtedly, her presence at the table meant a new crisis was so important that it had to disrupt their lunch plans.

"I didn't know he was meeting you either until we got here, and he asked for three menus." Ingrid's enthusiasm was just as nonexistent as Asha's. Her purple braids were the same color as the crop top that showed off her belly ring. Not long ago, she was in school to become a nail technician, but Asha hadn't heard anything about her finishing the program or that she was working in a salon. Undoubtedly, she most likely hadn't completed the course Sully had paid for, the same way he stroked a check for her to attend bartending, massage therapy, and whatever other schools she attended.

"I figured if I was going to have barbecue for lunch, I might as well enjoy it with both my girls." Sully smiled as he pulled the chair out for Asha.

She was going to point out to him that she wasn't a "girl," and neither was Ingrid but opted to ignore it. Although there was always an awkward tension between the two ladies, Sully never commented on it. It was as if he was oblivious to the fact that they didn't care for each other. He continued to act as if they got along great and looked forward to hanging out, and even tried to make it happen quite often, despite Asha's suggestion that he not.

Asha sat in the chair and picked up the menu, studying it as if she'd never been to the restaurant, which was one of her favorites. She'd been looking forward to a great meal. Had it been just she and Sully, she would've indulged in brisket, macaroni and cheese, baked beans, and homemade corn bread. Now, she wasn't even hungry.

"I hope you're paying for my food since you're the one who invited me here," Ingrid commented.

She must be talking to her father, Asha thought. *I damn sure ain't invite her ass nowhere.*

"Of course, I am. Lunch is on me," Sully nodded. "Whatever you want."

"In that case, I want a new car." Ingrid looked over at him. Sully laughed, but Asha knew Ingrid wasn't joking.

"I don't see that on the menu, so pick something else," he told her. "What would you like, Asha? Your fave, the brisket?"

"Actually, I think I'm just gonna have an appetizer. I've got to get to a meeting in a little while, so I don't have much time," she said. The waitress came over, and she quickly gave her order. "I'll just have some corn nuggets and a sweet tea."

"That's it? Are you sure?" Sully asked.

"Yeah, I'm sure," Asha nodded.

"Well, I don't know what I want yet, so you need to come back," Ingrid snapped at the waitress, sounding more like a 5-year-old than a grown woman.

Sully proceeded as if Ingrid's rudeness were nonexistent and placed his order. When the waitress was gone, he reached across the table and grabbed Asha's hands. "How's your day going so far?"

"Going really good. I finished one project and signed a new client today that I'm excited about," she told him.

"That's what's up. Congrats to you." Sully smiled. "I guess we need to go out to celebrate, huh?"

"We don't have to, but I won't say no if you want to," Asha laughed.

Ingrid's cell phone rang. She used her extralong, curved fingernails, which also had purple crystals, to take it out of her purse and answer without even excusing herself. "Hello. Yeah, eating with my daddy. I know. He better not try to hit me up. I'll get a restraining order and mess up those little coins he's lying to people about making now. I don't play about that gang-bang stuff, and you know what happened."

Asha glanced over at Sully. The slight frown on his face let her know that Ingrid's conversation concerned him. Had it been anyone else, the words "restraining order" and "gang bang" would be alarming for Asha, but she knew better than to even wonder about what Ingrid was discussing. The waitress returned with her basket of nuggets, and after a quick prayer, she pretended to be so engrossed in eating that she didn't even hear what was being said.

"Who's that?" Sully asked, interrupting Ingrid's conversation.

"Monee, calling about Bear," Ingrid said.

"Bear? What about him?" Sully turned his entire body toward his daughter.

"Monee, hold on. My daddy being rude," Ingrid said into the phone, then told Sully, "Someone said they saw him. I haven't seen or talked to him, though. Girl, I'm back. Wait, lemme just go outside so that folks won't be in my business."

"I swear, that's the last thing she needs to be dealing with right now," Sully said when Ingrid left the table.

I continued to be so focused on putting my straw in my tea that I didn't know what he was referring to. "Huh?"

"That no-good ex of hers, Bear. A troublemaker who left town awhile back after getting shot. I hope whoever it was that said they saw him is wrong. I don't want him anywhere near my daughter," Sully commented.

"I'm sure," were the only words Asha could think to say.

"Asha, I know you don't care for her, but she's a lot like your friend Devyn."

Asha nearly choked on her drink, wondering how the hell he would ever make the comparison of two people who were so totally opposite from each other, not only in physical appearance, but also in every other aspect as well. Devyn had class, style, elegance—hell, even manners. Ingrid possessed none of those.

Before she could stop them, the simple word escaped her. "How?"

"They're both young, beautiful, and trying to figure it all out. You say all the time how Devyn has a greater purpose that she just hasn't tapped into yet. I believe that for Ingrid. One of the reasons I invited her here today was so that maybe you could talk with her. But now, here comes this Bear mess." Sully shook his head.

Asha looked at her watch, then gasped, "Goodness, I gotta get to this meeting."

"What? Already?" Sully balked. "I haven't even got my food, Asha. You're the one who wanted to have lunch, remember?"

"I know, Sully. I told you my boss asked me to do something at the last minute. I wanted to see you and didn't want to cancel because I know how you hate that." Asha wiped her mouth and reached for her purse.

"Well, I meant what I said earlier. I want to take you out to celebrate your new client. And we need some quality time," Sully said, standing when she did.

"Sounds like you've got a date to plan, sir." Asha smiled and gave him a light kiss. "I've gotta go. We'll talk later."

As she walked out of the restaurant, she spotted Ingrid leaning against her father's truck, smoking a cigarette. Asha chuckled, thinking that Sully suggested that his misguided thot of a daughter was *anything* like her best friend who she loved more than anyone in the world.

Chapter 5

Devyn

"Have a great day, Miss Douglass. See you in a couple of months."

"Thanks," Devyn grumbled to the receptionist as she rushed out of the office. It wasn't her intention to be rude, but she was on the verge of tears and didn't want anyone to see them in case they started flowing. She made it to her car before the watershed began. Her sobs were silent as her head pressed on the steering wheel. The vibration of her phone interrupted her emotional breakdown, and she briefly looked at the screen to see who it was she was about to ignore. When she saw the name, instead of declining the call, she simply said, "Shit," before answering.

"How is my favorite niece in the whole wide world?" Uncle Julian greeted her. His voice was warm, full of joy, and sounded as if he didn't have a care in the world.

Not wanting to spoil the vibe, Devyn tried her best to compose herself before saying the response she always gave, "I'm your only niece in the world, Uncle Julian."

"But even if I had a thousand nieces, you'd still be my favorite, my Devyn," he laughed. "How are you, my love?"

"I'm good," she sighed.

"Liar. Now tell me the truth. What's wrong?" He said it with such conviction that Devyn looked around to see if he were lurking somewhere in the parking lot. Her father and mother never married, and right before she was born, he moved out of state and on with his life, which didn't include the daughter he left behind. Devyn found a father figure in her mother's twin, Uncle Julian, who she would spend every summer with.

"I mean, I'm just leaving the doctor."

"Is everything all right? Are you sick again? What's wrong? What did they say?" Uncle Julian's demeanor quickly changed to concern, and Devyn almost regretted saying anything. "Do I need to fly home?"

"No, no. I'm not sick. Well, you know what I mean. It was a routine checkup, but there are still no changes. I've been asking the doctor to take me off this medicine, Uncle Julian. They're killing me," Devyn said, her eyes filling with water again.

"No, darling, that's far from what they're doing. I know you don't like the side effects, but you know what will happen if you stop taking the pills," he responded. "We don't want that."

"Don't worry. I'm not gonna stop taking them. I don't want you to have to leave paradise because you need to attend my funeral. But I did ask about maybe having some plastic surgery done to help me—"

"Absolutely not, Devyn. That's not an option. Why would you even consider doing that?" he objected.

"I only wanted a little lipo and a tummy tuck, Uncle Julian. Get rid of some of this weight I've been trying to lose. I miss my body."

"Your body is fine. It's beautiful, just like you."

"Okay." Devyn knew that talking to him about this was just as pointless as talking to the doctor, especially since they were both medical professionals.

"How's the house? Everything still good?"

"It's fine. How's Bali and Ramon?" she asked. "He hasn't come to his senses and left you?"

A few months after Devyn's mother passed, Uncle Julian and Ramon, a retired pediatrician, who he declared was the love of his life, decided to move to Bali. He gave Devyn the keys to his three-bedroom loft overlooking a beautiful lake, a Toyota Prius, and his convertible Benz, all of which were paid for, and instructed her to take care of things and herself. The only thing he brought with him was his clothes.

Uncle Julian laughed. "Not yet. Bali is fine. We got matching tattoos last weekend, Devyn. I keep forgetting you don't have social media. We put the video on Instagram and got so many likes. I've got to send you pics. It hurt like hell. Do you have any tattoos? You probably don't."

"No, Uncle Julian, I don't, and I can't believe you do. And I won't believe it until I see it." Devyn laughed at the thought of her once-conservative uncle now getting tatted.

"Things we do for love, I guess. I transferred a little something into your account, so check it and make sure it's there."

"You didn't have to do that. I have a job now, remember?"

Despite Devyn insisting to Uncle Julian that he didn't need to send her a monthly allowance, he still did. Since he had no children of his own, he always treated her as if she were his daughter instead of his niece. She was appreciative but felt guilty. As she grew up, one of her goals was to one day spoil her uncle and mother. Now, her mother was gone, and he was the one spoiling her.

"Don't tell me what not to do. Promise me you won't use it on plastic surgery. You don't need to go under the knife to return to modeling."

"I promise," Devyn sighed. "It was just an idea, I guess, and a bad one. Honestly, although I loved modeling, it isn't what I want to do anymore."

"You have always been special, Devyn. And it's so much more than your looks. There is something in you that only you can give to the world and share with others. Sometimes in life, we think we're headed one way, then shit happens, God pivots us, and we are sent in a totally new direction. Stop looking back and move forward, sweetie."

"I love you, Uncle Julian. You are my most favorite uncle in the whole world." Devyn wiped the tears caused by the love and motivation she'd just received.

"That's because I'm your *only* uncle in the whole wide world, Devyn. I love you too. Speak soon." The call ended, and seconds later, she got a text with a picture of him smiling alongside Ramon, displaying the matching infinity hearts on their arms. Her uncle was right. His life had turned in a whole new direction, and he'd found happiness.

The pity party, disrupted by her uncle's phone call, was over. Devyn started the car engine and was about to head home when she got another text. This one from Asha, asking that she call her ASAP. Devyn instructed Siri to dial the number.

"Damn, that was fast. I figured you'd be in class," Asha told her.

"I had a doctor's appointment. I left school early."

"Everything okay?" Asha had the same amount of worry in her voice as her uncle when she mentioned going to the doctor. She hated that just the mention of an appointment sent her loved ones into panic mode.

"Yeah, standard checkup. Nothing's changed. Still stuck with the illness, but I'm still alive," Devyn said sarcastically.

"Cool. Wait, so, where are you now? Can you meet me at the Convention Center?" Asha's voice was low.

"Uh, yeah, I guess. What's going on?"

"I . . . We need your help. I'll explain when you get here. Come to Meeting Room B on the second floor," Asha said, then hung up.

Devyn arrived fifteen minutes later. The first thing she saw when she walked inside the lobby of the building was a small group of what had to be models. It was a damn setup. Obviously, there was an open call of some sort that Asha was trying to dupe her into participating in.

"This is that bullshit," Devyn mumbled as she walked past the group of beautiful women, toward the elevators, trying not to stare at their tall, slender, perfect bodies. As she rode to the second floor, she practiced the cursing out she planned on giving her friend in her head. Undoubtedly, Asha meant well, but Devyn had no desire to get back into the field that once brought her so much joy.

Unlike the first floor, the second floor of the building was empty. Devyn wondered if Asha had given her the wrong room number. The doors to Meeting Room B were closed. She paused before slowly pulling them open. She didn't see anyone in the large, empty space when she poked her head in.

"Good, you're here." Asha's voice came from the corner.

Devyn stepped in a little farther and saw her friend, along with three other women: two young, Black girls, and an older white woman. The white woman seemed to be consoling one of the Black girls sitting in a chair, visibly upset.

"What's going on?" Devyn asked.

"We'll be right back," Asha said to the ladies before grabbing Devyn by the arm and escorting her out the door and into the hallway.

"What am I doing here, and why is that girl crying?" Devyn's brows furrowed. "And this better not have anything to do with what's going on downstairs."

"It does," Asha said. Then before Devyn could object, she quickly added, "But it's not what you think."

"You don't even *know* what I think," Devyn retorted. "But, please explain. And before you start, you already know the answer if you're about to try to tell me about whatever they're casting for down there—"

"Devyn, can you please shut up for one second? No one is trying to get you to model. Those girls aren't even here for a casting call," Asha informed her.

"They aren't?"

"No. They're applying to be in a beauty pageant."

"A beauty pageant? What?" Devyn almost laughed. Asha had to know damn well that a beauty pageant would be the last thing she'd be interested in. "Why the hell would I enter a beauty pageant, Asha?"

"You wouldn't, but the two girls in there did. That's why I called you," she said. "For help."

"I'm so damn confused." Devyn shook her head. "Help with what? How do you even know those girls?"

"I don't. I came by to pick up some invoices from Gail, the white woman. We were talking when, all of a sudden, this girl came flying by, crying."

"The one sitting in the chair."

"Yeah. She runs into the bathroom, and her friend comes running behind her. And you know me." Asha shrugged.

"Your nosy ass ran in there to check on 'em." Devyn shook her head. "Asha, the Angel, always to the rescue."

"I just wanted to make sure they were okay. And the girl explained how she'd interviewed time and time again to be in this pageant, and the coordinator won't accept her. The coordinator keeps saying she isn't 'pageant ready.'" Asha continued. "The girl is gorgeous, Devyn. She showed me her application and her portfolio. There's no reason that woman shouldn't allow her to compete."

"Asha, that sucks, but what the hell does that have to do with you or me, for that matter? We are going to roll up in there and demand that they allow her in? This ain't our crusade, sis. It's a pageant," Devyn told her.

"No, that's not what I want. Come in. I'll let them tell you." Asha opened the door. They went back into the ballroom and walked over to the ladies. "This is my friend, Devyn."

"Nice to meet you. I'm Gail, one of the sales directors here, and this is Journi." Gail looked at the girl standing beside her, then looked at the young lady sitting in the chair and said, "And this is Dionne."

"Hi." Devyn nodded to all three.

"Well, I've kind of explained to Devyn a little bit of what's going on," Asha said.

Journi nodded. "I don't know why Ms. Thompkins is treating her like that. I don't even wanna be in the stupid pageant anymore. The only reason I was doing it was that Dionne asked me to do it with her."

"So, you got in?" Asha asked.

"Yeah. Barely. She told me they'd be in contact. Then she told me the competition was stiff, and I shouldn't get any high hopes of winning, but at least I'd have some pageant experience," Journi said.

"That's horrible." Gail shook her head.

"At least you got in. I didn't even get that. She keeps telling me I need 'training.'" Dionne sniffed. Even with her eyes puffy from crying and her tear-strewn face, Devyn could see how gorgeous she was. Her hair, piled high on her head into a perfect bun, showed off her high cheekbones, thick lashes, and pouty lips set against her smooth skin, the color of a perfect, frosted cappuccino.

"I'm dropping out anyway, so it's a moot point." Journi shrugged.

"You can't drop out. I won't let you," Dionne gasped and grabbed her friend's arm.

"Why should I be in a contest she already told me I'm going to lose?" Journi asked. "This whole thing is dumb, and she's a bitch."

Journi's comment caught Devyn off guard. She was just as gorgeous as Dionne, but with a more natural look and a tone slightly darker. It was apparent that she was the more vocal of the two.

Gail looked over at Devyn and nodded. "She's right. That woman is a bitch."

"I know you're disappointed, but maybe Ms. Thompkins is being selective," Devyn suggested. "I applied for a lot of jobs in the industry I worked in, and there were many rejections."

"I get that," Dionne said, "but she keeps saying that I need training."

"Okay." Devyn shrugged, still confused, "Then what's the problem?"

"None of the coaches around here will train us," Journi answered. "We've tried."

"I practiced so hard this time. You know I did, Journi," Dionne whined.

"Yup, every day, Di." Journi kneeled by her side and rubbed her back. "And you got better. I think she's just tripping. Your walk is perfect."

At the word "walk," Devyn realized why Asha had called. Sure enough, when she glanced over at her friend, she saw the smirk. Devyn went to shake her head, but Asha gave her a nod. Devyn inhaled deeply in preparation for whatever it was Asha was about to say.

"Dev, I mean, maybe you can have Dionne walk for you, and you give her some pointers right quick," Asha suggested.

Dionne lifted her head and looked at Devyn. "Could you? Please?"

"Sure," Devyn relented and shrugged.

When Dionne stood, Devyn realized they were the same height, and she had the same slim build that Devyn used to have and would give anything to get back. She studied Dionne as she went to the back of the room. They all turned around and waited.

"Ready?" Dionne asked.

"Whenever you are," Devyn told her.

"Okay." Dionne took a deep breath, then stepped toward them, looking more like she was in a parade than on a stage. She continued to the front of the room, twisted around, and stopped. "Hello, I'm Dionne Singleton, a junior from Garrett High. I enjoy modeling, uh, spoken word, and watching *Jeopardy*. I would like to be an anesthesiologist when I graduate from college."

"Yesssss, Queen." Journi clapped and cheered for her friend who gave a broad smile before walking back to where they were standing.

Devyn glanced over at Asha to see her reaction. Their eyes met, and Devyn knew they were thinking the same thing. Dionne was statuesque and beautiful, but she definitely lacked grace, poise, and elegance, all of which were required to compete in a pageant. Unfortunately, Ms. Thompkins was correct. Dionne needed work—and a lot of it.

"How was it?" Dionne nervously asked Devyn.

Devyn looked at Asha, hoping she'd answer, but she didn't. Not wanting to be the bearer of bad news and cause the girl to have another emotional breakdown, Devyn turned to Journi, instead, and said, "You're next. Let's see what you've got."

Journi looked surprised. "Me?"

"Yeah, she went, so, now, it's your turn." Devyn nodded.

Journi followed the same path that Dionne had earlier, first walking to the back of the room, then making her way to the front. Each step she took was intentional, and her head remained up, eyes forward and focused. She turned on one foot, then gave her introduction. "Greetings. I'm Journi Jacobs, a junior at Garrett High School. I enjoy reading, dancing, and fashion. I plan to become a political analyst for a major television news network."

"Okayyyy." Dionne beamed.

In addition to her overall presentation, Journi's walk, although not perfect, was better than Dionne's. There was an air of confidence and tenacity in her strides. But like Dionne, she still needed a lot of work.

"Very nice, ladies." Gail clapped. "You're both amazing. I think Ms. Thompkins is crazy."

"What do you think?" Asha whispered. "Be honest."

"I think they're both cute girls, but I don't know." Devyn sighed. "Dionne hunches her shoulder, and you can tell she's trying not to look down. She also has poor diction."

"Journi had a strut, though. It was a model walk." Asha's voice was low. "She mentioned she'd modeled a couple of times."

"I can tell that. But . . ."

"Were we that bad?" Journi asked.

Devyn saw that all eyes were on her. "No, not bad. Just . . . novices."

"This is pointless. So, Ms. Thompkins was right. I give up." Dionne wailed and threw her hands in the air.

"Wait, wait," Asha said. "You asked her for pointers, and you're not even giving her the chance to voice them."

The two girls looked at Asha, then at each other, then back at Devyn. For a moment, she just stared back at them. *How am I supposed to teach something that has always come naturally to me?* She took a minute to gather her thoughts, recalling everything she'd developed that helped her perfect her walk. *Posture, poise, personality,* she thought.

"Okay, Journi, you've been in fashion shows, huh?" Devyn asked.

"Yeah, a few. I just started modeling a couple of months ago," she said nodding.

"There's a difference in walking on a runway in a fashion show compared to walking on stage in a pageant. When you're on a runway, you're selling whatever you're wearing. That's what's on display." Devyn closed her eyes, composed herself, then made the same walk that the girls had done, but in such a manner that the black cardigan she wore seemed to flow with each step. She then did a quick turn while slipping the sweater off and tossing it over her shoulder, then momentarily pausing before she strutted back.

Asha, Gail, and the girls applauded with enthusiasm. Devyn took a slight bow.

"That was freaking awesome," Journi squealed.

"Thank you. Now, watch this." Devyn walked again, this time with shorter, yet graceful steps, shoulders back and her head turning from side to side while smiling. It was as if she were a finalist in the Miss Universe Pageant. When she finished, they all stared at her. "See the difference? When you're in a pageant, you're selling yourself, your personality. *That's* what you want the judges to buy."

"Ooooh," Journi and Dionne said simultaneously.

"That's deep, Dev." Asha nodded.

"Come on, let me show you." Devyn took the girls on each side of her and demonstrated. Fifteen minutes later, they'd improved tremendously.

"Now, do you see why I called you? I knew you could help." Asha nudged her as they watched the girls walk across the floor.

"They're still not all that great, Asha," Devyn sighed. "But they do have lots of potential."

"They're a hundred times better than they were. And look at Dionne. Her head isn't even looking down anymore," Asha pointed out. "You did good, Dev. And for what it's worth, you still got it."

"Thanks, Ash." Devyn leaned her head on Asha's shoulder, then announced. "Well, ladies, I'm glad we were able to help. It was nice meeting you, and we wish you the best."

"Goodbye, ladies." Asha waved.

"Wait, Miss Devyn, hold up." Journi ran over, followed by Dionne.

"What's up?" Devyn asked.

"I was wondering if maybe, you could train me for the pageant." Journi smiled. "I can pay you."

"And me too. I mean, I know I'm not a contestant in this one, but I still want to train so that I can be ready for the next one. Can you help me, Miss Devyn?" Dionne folded her hands as if she were praying. "Please?"

"That's sweet, but I'm not a coach. You two need to keep looking until you find someone who can help you guys," Devyn told them.

"We don't need anyone else. You're the one who can really help us. Look at what we've learned in these few minutes," Journi responded.

"This wasn't a class or a workshop." Devyn shook her head.

"It seemed like it to me," Gail interjected.

"Ladies, give us a minute," Asha said, then told Devyn. "Let's chat outside."

"Ash, before you even suggest it, the answer is no," Devyn whispered when they got into the hallway.

"Why not? You're good, and they need you. Plus, they're willing to pay. Check it, while you were teaching them, I Googled pageant coaching, and you wouldn't believe how much these chicks charge, Devyn. You can do this.

And you have pageant and modeling experience," Asha pointed out.

"Pageant experience? When?" Devyn frowned.

"You won Miss Black and Gold our senior year in college," Asha reminded her.

"That wasn't a real pageant, fool. That was a popularity contest on stage, and I was dating the president of the Alphas. I was gonna win regardless." Devyn shook her head.

"You can do this," Asha repeated herself. "Help them, Dev. I promise I got your back. Whatever you need. You know I wouldn't be pushing if I thought you couldn't do it."

As crazy as the idea sounded, something deep down told Devyn that Asha was right. Runway modeling was something she loved but could no longer do. But was it possible for her to teach?

"Fine. I'll try, Asha. But I'm not doing this by myself," Devyn warned.

"Dev, you've got me by your side, always." Asha hugged her.

Chapter 6

Asha

"I'm telling you, Sully, it was one of the most magical things I'd ever seen in my life. Devyn had those girls walking like professionals within minutes. And when she walked back in there and told them she'd be their coach, it was like they'd won the lottery." Asha grinned at Sully, who was driving. It was Friday night, and as promised, he'd taken her to dinner to celebrate, and now, they were headed back to his place.

"Sounds like it was quite a moment," Sully nodded. "I thought you said you had a meeting for work. That's why you left lunch early, remember? Devyn was at the meeting?"

"I told you I ran into the girls after the meeting with Gail. I called Devyn to come to talk to them," Asha replied. "She didn't plan to be there."

"Uh-huh, okay." Sully glanced over at her.

"I'm serious. That's what makes what happened even crazier, the fact that it spontaneously happened," Asha continued. "I'm so excited."

"I see. That's all you've talked about tonight."

He was right. Most of the conversation that she'd shared during dinner had been about Devyn, Journi, Dionne, and the incident at the Convention Center. Dominating the conversation hadn't been intentional, but she was ecstatic for her best friend who'd finally found a glimmer of hope after dealing with so much over the last couple of years.

"I'm sorry, Sully. I didn't mean to keep talking about it. That's selfish of me." Asha reached across the car and grabbed his hand. "I appreciate you taking me to dinner. I'm glad to be spending time with you."

His fingers intertwined with hers. "Me too. I got a bottle of that wine you like chilling for us to enjoy and a surprise."

"What is it?" Asha ran her hand up and down his arm.

Sully laughed. "You'll have to see when we get there. I think you're gonna like it."

"I always like the surprises you give me."

Asha tried to think of what it could be. Gifts were something she discovered that Sully enjoyed giving. From little things like sets of her favorite perfume to more significant tokens like the designer bag that she'd mentioned one day, or the new smart TV he'd gotten her for her bedroom. Asha never asked him for anything. Sully just did it.

"Home sweet home," he said when they pulled into the driveway of a four-bedroom, three-bath home that he lived in all alone. The first time she'd visited, Asha asked him why he had such a large house, and he answered that he enjoyed having a lot of space. Sully hit the button to open the garage and parked his Toyota sedan beside his work truck. Asha remained in the car after he got out and unlocked the door to his house. Being the true gentleman that he was, Sully liked to open her car door.

"Thank you," she said as she stepped out and followed him inside. They walked through the kitchen and into the den, where he turned on the television and handed her the remote.

"I'll be right back," he said.

Asha made herself comfortable on the sofa and took her cell phone out of her purse, making sure she hadn't missed any important calls or texts and checking her emails before going to her social media accounts. As soon as Sully arrived to pick her up for dinner, she turned her phone off. He often mentioned Asha having her phone, although he had no issue of Ingrid talking on hers while they were at lunch. She quickly responded to a few Facebook and Instagram posts.

"A'ight, put that phone away." He walked back into the den carrying two glasses of her favorite Chardonnay and a small gift bag.

"I know, I know." She laughed, putting the phone back into her purse.

After placing the two glasses on the coffee table, he handed her the gift bag. "For you, my dear, in honor of your new client."

"You do know that planning events for clients is part of my job, right? It's not a big deal and happens quite often. Dinner was enough," Asha told him.

"Just open the damn gift, Asha," he said.

Asha put the bag in her lap and slowly took out the soft tissue paper until she revealed a box at the bottom that she opened. Inside was a beautiful Swarovski crystal keychain in the shape of an "A" holding a key.

"What's this?" Asha looked over at him.

"It's a key," Sully smiled.

"To what?"

"To the house, silly."

"Wow, Sully." Asha blinked, not knowing what else to say. She knew they'd been spending more time together, but not to the point where she felt as if she needed a key.

"I just want you to know that you are welcome here anytime. You have full access," he told her, picking up one of the glasses and passing it to her. "You mean that much to me. Cheers."

"Cheers." Asha tapped her glass to the one he held and wished it were liquor she could gulp instead of wine. The passionate kiss Sully leaned over and gave her was a welcome distraction from her thoughts. Her body reacted to the warmth of his mouth. She quickly put her glass down and wrapped her arms around his neck, pulling him closer. He pressed against her for a moment as the kiss continued. Their bodies slid down until they lay on the sofa, him on top of her. Asha reached to pull his shirt up, and he suddenly sat up.

"Baby, hold up," he whispered.

"Oh." Asha adjusted her shirt that had worked its way over her stomach and tried not to show her disappointment.

"You know how these damn blood pressure meds mess with me, sweetie. I'd hoped they would've worn off by now, but just gimme a little while longer," Sully said, sheepishly.

"It's fine, Sully. We have all night." Asha rubbed his back, not wanting him to feel bad. It wasn't his fault that a side effect of prescription medicine sometimes prevented him from being ready to get it when she was. Sex with Sully was quite satisfying. It was just delayed and never spontaneous.

"We do, baby." He nodded. "I promise it'll be worth the wait."

"It always is. And besides, you know how much I love being in your bed," Asha teased. There was something about Sully's bed that made her get the best sleep every time. It was as if as soon as she got in it and her head hit the pillow, she was knocked out.

"Well, let's get you in bed then." Sully pulled her to her feet and into his bedroom. Asha took a quick shower and changed into one of the cute pajama sets she kept at his place. By the time Sully showered, she was asleep. Her slumber was so deep that she thought she was dreaming when she felt the soft kisses traveling from her neck to her collarbone. His hands went under her shirt and fondled her nipples, which quickly hardened. Asha's eyes fluttered open, and she arched her back and lifted her body so he could slip her shorts off. Her hands reached over, and she touched the small patch of gray hairs on his chest before caressing his nipples as her fingers made their way down the slight flab of his stomach. Sully covered one of her triple-D breasts with his mouth, sucking it gently while pinching the other one. Asha moaned. Her hand continued down his body until she found what she was hoping for. His manhood was at full attention, and she smiled with relief. *Good things come to those who wait,* she thought as she opened her thick thighs and welcomed him with her wetness. By the time their lovemaking was complete, Asha was exhausted as she snuggled against him.

"You okay?" Sully whispered, then kissed the top of her head.

"I'm great," Asha nodded, barely able to keep her eyes open. As she drifted off to sleep, she thought about the key he'd given her and why she didn't want to keep it.

Sleeping late was something Asha rarely did, even on the weekends. Sully's magical bed had her snoozing until well after ten the following morning. She woke up to the smell of bacon and coffee. The grogginess in her head was so strong that she felt like she was in a fog when she sat up. It took her a few minutes to get herself together.

"Oh my God, why didn't you wake me up?" She walked into the kitchen and asked Sully, who was already dressed and in the middle of cooking breakfast.

"Good morning to you too, beautiful." He handed her a cup of coffee.

"Good morning, and thank you," Asha said, taking a sip of the much-needed caffeine. "I gotta hurry and get dressed."

"Why? What's the rush? I thought you weren't working this weekend." Sully flipped over the bacon that was sizzling on the stove.

"I'm not, but I have stuff to do. Actually, I have a full day planned." Asha went over her to-do list for the day in her head. "And I forgot to put my phone on the charger last night."

Asha went into the den and grabbed her phone from her purse. As she suspected, the screen was dark, which meant it was dead. She took out the charger and plugged it into the wall, then connected it to her phone. It powered right up, and instead of an apple flashing on the screen, her own picture displayed. She then realized that her phone battery still had power.

Damn, I don't even remember turning my phone off.

Two text messages came through, one from Devyn and another from her hairstylist, Monya, confirming her appointment for the afternoon. If she planned on salvaging the rest of her day, she needed to hurry and get home.

"Ash, breakfast is ready," Sully called out.

Asha returned to the kitchen. "I don't have time to eat, Sul. I gotta get home and get my car. I have a hair appointment in an hour."

"I can just drop you off at the salon and come back and get you," he told her. Two plates with bacon, eggs, grits, and toast were on the table.

"Nah, you don't have to do that. It'll take me fifteen minutes to get dressed, and we can leave."

"I was gonna put some stuff on the grill later for us." Sully grabbed her by the waist and pulled her to him. He gave her a quick kiss. "If I let you leave and get into the streets, you won't come back and stay the night with me."

"Is that why you're Chef Sully this morning? To keep me here?" she laughed.

"Maybe. Is it working?"

"No, it's not. I *will* take some bacon and toast, though." Asha grabbed the meat and bread off the plate and gave him another kiss as she walked into the room to get dressed.

Chapter 7

Devyn

Saturday mornings were Devyn's favorite. She was an early riser, by nature, a habit inherited from her mother. Growing up, they would spend Saturday mornings curled up on the sofa, drinking warm tea and chatting. Devyn could talk to her mother about anything: boys, school, friends, dreams, and fears. When Devyn entered the world of modeling, her mother was her biggest cheerleader. Even when she was traveling for work, she would call her mom, and they would have their weekly "sips," as they called them, those moments when they would Stop, Inhale, and Process life's events. After her mother passed away, Devyn stopped drinking tea altogether. But after moving into Uncle Julian's home six months after the funeral, she began again the ritual they shared. It was peaceful, and she'd often journal while listening to jazz or blues music, her mother's favorites. It was a different type of "sip," but somehow, it made Devyn feel close to her mom.

After pouring herself a cup of her signature tea blend, then adding the perfect amount of sweetener and cream, Devyn grabbed her favorite blanket, Bluetooth speaker, journal, and headed to the deck. She adjusted herself on one of the cushioned, wicker sofas and enjoyed the view for a few moments while the voice of Calvin Richardson serenaded her as he sang about not being able to let go of his woman. Her mother loved the blues singer, and Devyn had grown quite fond of him too, especially since she avoided urban radio and hip-hop.

After taking a sip of her drink, she opened her journal and began writing her thoughts. There was plenty to write about. Since agreeing to coach Journi and Dionne, her mind had been all over the place. On the one hand, she was excited and interested in the opportunity to help the girls. On the other, she was terrified and hesitant. Modeling was one thing, but could she actually train someone else and be successful?

"What if I'm not good enough? I've never been a model," *Devyn said to her mother the day when she was approached about a fashion show by a casting director who spotted her in the mall. She'd just turned 19 and was a sophomore in college with aspirations of becoming a news reporter.*

"What if you are? What if you're better than anyone else who is a model?" Her mother shrugged. "You'll never know if you don't try. You're worried about what might not happen instead of the possibility of what will."

She had forgotten the conversation, but now, the memory came flooding back. Devyn heard her mother's voice so clear that it brought tears to her eyes. Her heart raced, and her hand, which held her mug, trembled. Devyn looked at the words emblazoned on the side: *"Faith not Fear."* The message was unmistakable. Devyn turned the page of her notebook and began writing. By the time she finished nearly two hours later, she had a clear head, a to-do list, and what she prayed was a good idea.

She checked her phone and saw that she had two missed calls. One from Asha, saying she'd stop by after her hair appointment, and another from her godsister, Chastity, affectionately known as Chase. Chase had just turned 25 and was a talented artist. The girl could draw, paint, and create anything. She was also the most comical person Devyn knew. Her texting so early on a Saturday had to mean one thing: she had something funny to share. Instead of returning a text, Devyn decided to FaceTime her as she walked back into the house.

"What happened now?" Devyn asked as soon as Chase answered.

"If you had social media, you would've witnessed the travesty I experienced last night as it unfolded," Chase said with an exaggerated sigh as she flopped back on her pillow with her hand dramatically draped across her forehead.

"Well, I don't, so, what's his name?" Devyn laughed. "And what site did you find him on?"

"Desmond," Chase answered. "And Instagram. He slid in my DMs."

"Oh God," Devyn groaned. "You should've known better."

"True, but he was on some real 'I dig your art, you're mad talented' type stuff. Nothing flirtatious or disrespectful, so I was like, a'ight; cool. So, we chatted for a couple of days. I checked out his page, and he looked decent, so when he asked to meet up for dinner, I agreed."

"You chatted for a couple of days? That's it? Chase, come on. You went out with a dude you barely knew, one you'd never even spoken to on the phone. Do you know how dangerous that was?" Devyn went into full big-sister mode. She respected the fact that Chase enjoyed the single life to the fullest, and she encouraged it, but she still wanted her to be safe at all times.

"Dev, at this point, I don't even give guys my number without checking them out in person first. Now, that is potentially dangerous. It takes too much energy ignoring calls and blocking numbers of guys you don't even like but who still insist on hitting you up because they can't take a hint," Chase explained.

"I guess," Devyn sighed, seeing how that could be sound reasoning.

"Anyway, I get to the restaurant, which he chose, by the way. A damn Chili's."

"I like Chili's," Devyn commented.

"I mean, it's a'ight, and as soon as he said it, I knew he was basic. And before you start, I've dated basic dudes before. But he ain't even ask me if I like Chili's. I woulda at least suggested Fridays. The drinks are better. Not only that, but you also know I always pay for my own shit on the first date. You taught me that," Chase pointed out.

"Good. At least you listen to some stuff I tell you. But continue."

"First of all, he's like ten years older than the pics on his IG. I don't know if they're old pics or what. But dude was much grayer, and he's bigger," Chase said. "Not only that, but he also needed a haircut, and a shave, and some new Tims because the ones he had on were rocked over."

"Chastity, stop," Devyn laughed. "As someone who's gained weight recently, I'm offended."

"Naw, Dev, you don't understand. I didn't even recognize him at first. He had to walk over and introduce himself. He was *that* unrecognizable. Your ass still looks the damn same. You're just a little thicker. You're still a bad bitch. You just also have horrible body dysmorphia. But this ain't about you, Devyn. It's about me and this horrible old man. I felt like I was on a date with one of Sully's friends," Chase giggled.

"Chastity, now you know you're dead-ass wrong for that." Devyn tried not to laugh, but she couldn't help it.

"He had the nerve to order a strawberry daiquiri, and he sipped it with a straw. Then after telling me about how his ex's mom, sister, and her friend all tried to sleep with him, he proceeded to ask me if I had cute toes."

By the time Chase finished telling how the date from hell had ended, Devyn was crying tears of laughter. She could only imagine how the story played out on Chase's social media. Moments like this almost made Devyn wish she still had her own accounts that were verified and had thousands of followers at one point. She'd deleted all of them in an effort to erase that part of her life shortly after the video of the wedding brawl went viral: the rumors, the trolls, the cyberbullies, the sadness, the anger, and most of all, the heartbreak that she felt.

"And this is why I have no desire to date," Devyn told her.

"You've got to kiss some frogs before you finally find your prince," Chase shrugged. "Enough about me, though. What the hell do you have going on? What are we sipping on today?"

Devyn held up her mug. "Sipping on tea and contemplating the latest craziness that Asha has gotten me into."

"Oh Lord, please don't tell me she's got you dating an AARP member too." Chase rolled her eyes.

"No, Chastity, she's not. She talked me into coaching two young ladies for a beauty pageant." Devyn wrinkled her nose and squinted as she waited for Chase's reaction.

"A beauty pageant? Like Miss USA, Miss Universe, *that* kind of pageant?" Chase turned her head as if she were straining to hear.

"Yes, not quite that big, but, yeah," Devyn nodded.

"I. Love. It." Chastity sat up and clapped. The large satin bonnet on her head slid to the side, revealing what looked like a shaved scalp.

"Chase, your hair!" Devyn shrieked, noticing that the long, shoulder-length tresses that Chase wore her entire life were gone.

"What? Oh, again, if you had social media, you would've seen this." Chase took the bonnet off, fluffing the long curls on the other half of her head. "You like it? Cool, huh?"

"I think I've gotta get used to it," Devyn replied, still shocked at the dramatic change in Chase's appearance. Even with a half-bald head, the girl was still gorgeous.

"I think your being a coach is such a dope idea. I'm here for it, sis."

"Really?"

"I mean, why not? You taught me how to walk in heels and pose for pictures. That's why my selfie angles have always been on point," Chase laughed.

"True. I don't know. I want to do it, but I'm still trying to figure it all out. The two girls I'm working with are paying me one-fifty an hour, three hours a week. I ain't mad at that at all."

"You probably could've gotten more, Dev. Pageants are big business, and people pay big bucks to win," Chase told her. "And you can do runway training too. You have plenty of experience, and you're an industry vet. I know once those girls realized who you were, they freaked out."

"Whoa whoa whoa. They didn't know who I was. As far as they know, I'm just Miss Devyn. And you know if I do this, I want to remain low-key. That's not changing. But we'll see what happens after I try it out. It's funny because the day this all happened, Uncle Julian said how sometimes we have to pivot in life and change directions."

"Pivot? It's perfect. Pivot Runway and Pageant Coaching. I'll start working on the logo today. I already have an idea. What else do you need me to do to help? I'm excited." Chase clapped again.

"Calm down, ma'am. I said I was still trying to figure it out. It's a thought for a side hustle, not a business, Chase."

"It will be, trust me. It'll only be as big as you allow, Dev."

Devyn heard the charm of the alarm as the front door opened and closed. She knew exactly who it was. There was only one person other than Uncle Julian who had the code and key to the house.

"Dev, where you at?" Asha's voice came down the hallway.

"In the kitchen," Devyn answered.

"Who is that? Is that Asha? Hey, Ash," Chase waved.

"Hey, Chase," Asha waved over Devyn's shoulder at the phone. "What kinda trouble are you just getting out of? I saw your fruity guy date story. You are hilarious."

"I just told Dev about it," Chase said.

"Another frog bites the dust," Devyn teased.

"Someday, my prince will come. Well, at least, I hope so," Chase added. "And yours too, Dev. Asha ain't gonna be the only one around there with a boo. All three of us will be cuffed up."

"I just told her the other night she needed some penis in her life. I'm working on something, though. Don't worry, I got her," Asha winked.

"Oh, really? She didn't tell me about the potential penis. She only told me about the pageant coaching stuff, which I think is perfect for her." Chase gave a thumbs-up. "I'm for the penis plans too, though. Good job, Ash."

"Goodbye, Chastity," Devyn said. "I love you."

"Love you too, Dev, and you, Ash." Chase blew kisses before hanging up.

"She is so funny," Asha said.

"She is. What the heck were you talking about? What are you working on?" Devyn leaned against the kitchen island and folded her arms.

"I'll let you know soon, but I promise, you'll like it," Asha winked.

"I thought you had a hair appointment?" Devyn said, noticing Asha's locs that, although neat, didn't look freshly twisted.

"I was late and had to reschedule. I overslept again this morning while at Sully's. That man's bed has magical powers, Devyn, I swear. I be knocked out." Asha reached for one of the mugs hanging on the rack.

"It ain't his bed, and you know it. Every time you spend the night, he gives you a good ol' dose of Dickquil." Devyn's joke caused both of them to burst into laughter.

"I can't stand you. Where are your special brew bags? I know you got some," Asha asked.

Devyn reached into the cabinet and passed her the jar of tea bags that she'd filled with a custom blend. Asha put one into the mug and filled it with hot water from the kettle on the stove.

"I needed this," Asha said, taking a sip. "I was so groggy when I woke up. You're joking, but I get the best sleep at his house. Don't get me wrong. The sex was decent too . . . once we were finally able to have it."

"His rising to the occasion still on delay, huh?"

"Yeah. But I got another gift last night."

"What was it? A Birkin bag? Gucci watch?" Devyn asked playfully, knowing that the only person Sully would spend that type of money on was his daughter.

"This." Asha held up a small, shiny object.

"Is that a key? To the crib?" Devyn's mouth gaped open. "Oh, damn. I knew y'all were getting serious, but not like that."

"It's not like that. I don't want this."

"Does this mean you have to give him a key to your house?" Devyn asked.

"I'm not giving him a key to my house. That's not happening." Asha shook her head. "I mean, don't get me wrong, Dev. Hanging out with Sully is nice. He's nice. But that's all I want and need in my life: nice."

"I get that, but I think giving you a key means he wants something serious, Asha. And honestly, I know what you said, but you deserve more than something that's just 'nice.'"

"Whatever. I like nice." Asha exhaled and tossed up her hands. "Anyway, did you talk to Dionne and Journi? What did you all come up with?"

"We agreed to a price, and we're supposed to start this week. That's about it. But, Asha, I don't even have a place to coach them. Maybe this isn't something that can happen right now." Devyn felt the fear slowly returning that she'd released earlier while she was on the deck.

"It's happening. I told you I got you, Dev. This isn't something you gotta do alone. I have a connection over at the main library. I can call and reserve the auditorium or one of the performance rooms for you to use until we find something a little more permanent. Problem solved, see?" Asha smiled and sipped her tea. "This is the bomb."

Devyn looked at her friend in amazement. Sometimes, it was like being best buddies with Superman because she always came in and saved the day, no matter what.

Chapter 8

Asha

When Asha was motivated, she was unstoppable. She'd spent most of her weekend researching the pageant industry, and what she discovered was shocking. It was a billion-dollar industry. She knew it was profitable but had no idea the amount of money it generated. Entry fees alone could cost a contestant anywhere from $500 on up. Some of the larger-scale pageants cost in the thousands to enter. In addition to the profitability, she also discovered something else: a lack of diversity.

"They don't want to coach us because they don't want us to win," Journi said. "They'll take our money and let us compete, but they ain't tryin'a help us get the crown. Not for real."

"They're scared. Last year, Black women won Miss Teen USA, Miss America, Miss USA, and Miss Universe. Now, they're trying to do whatever they can to stop us," Dionne added.

"Makes sense," Asha said. "Nothing like good ol' systemic racism. It's everywhere else, so why wouldn't it be in the pageant industry?"

The four of them sat down on Sunday afternoon at Starbucks to have coffee and chat. One of the things Devyn wanted was everyone to be on the same page when it came to their expectations, and Asha agreed.

"Well, at least, now, we have a coach." Dionne's words sounded more like a question than a statement. "I mean, we do, right?"

Three sets of eyes looked at Devyn, including Asha's, who already knew the answer.

"Yes," Devyn nodded. "Actually, you have *two* coaches. Miss Asha and me. She'll be part of the process as well."

Hearing Devyn include her in the plans had come as a surprise, but a welcomed one. Asha had committed to supporting her friend in whatever way she needed, and she meant it. Besides, it was an opportunity for her to be a part of something she knew would be big. Probably bigger than what either one of them expected.

"She's right. We're a team." Asha nodded to show her support.

"Miss Asha is an expert when it comes to public speaking, media training, professional etiquette, and things of that nature. She's a PR beast and event planner by trade," Devyn bragged.

"*That's* what's up, Miss Asha." Dionne smiled.

"So, when do we start?" Journi asked. "Because I'm ready."

"Me too," Dionne nodded.

Devyn set a schedule for the week. After the girls left, Asha and Devyn remained at the coffeehouse for another two hours, developing a layout and weekly sessions plan. Devyn tried to downplay her excitement, but Asha knew her relaxed demeanor was a way of protecting herself in case things didn't work out. Devyn's biggest fear was enduring another fall from grace like the one she'd previously suffered. Asha was determined not to allow that to happen. She was going to make sure this venture was just as successful as Devyn's former career—if not more.

***

"Don't tell me, you're working late again," Sully said when he called to tell her he'd arrived at her house to take her to the movies on Friday night and discovered she wasn't home.

Asha looked at her watch and was surprised to see that it was seven thirty. She'd been sitting in the corner of the Panera Bread for nearly three hours without even realizing it. She intended to stop on the way home to grab her favorite green tea and a pastry and check out the logo samples that Chase sent over. Before she knew it, however, she'd whipped her iPad mini and portable keyboard out of her bag and began working.

"Oh, damn, honey. I didn't even realize it was that late. I'm sorry," Asha apologized. "Chase sent over some ideas. I tweaked them and then started working on the website. I guess time got away from me. I'll pack up and be right there."

"No, don't rush on my account. By the time you make it home, it'll be too late to get to the movies."

Sully's disappointed voice made Asha feel even worse than she already did. It was bad enough that she hadn't seen him since leaving his home the Saturday before, nor had they really spoken at length. After working her regular job and then assisting Devyn with coaching the girls, her time was limited. The week had flown by. Not wanting Sully to feel neglected, she accepted his invitation to the movies.

"Maybe we can catch a later showing," she suggested.

"I already got the tickets. It's fine. I'll go ahead without you."

"Sully, I feel horrible. I got so caught up in—"

"I know. I get it. But we were supposed to go to the movies since you're working all weekend. Besides, I thought you said Devyn wanted this coaching thing to be low-key. Now, you're talking about logos and websites. I guess she changed her mind," Sully commented.

"No, that's what she said, and she hasn't changed her mind yet. When she realizes this is something she loves and has potential for success, she'll change her mind. And when she does, everything will already be set up," Asha explained. "I'm just being proactive rather than reactive."

"I think you're doing a little too much, too fast, for something that might not even work," Sully told her.

Says the person who still pays the cell phone bill for his grown-ass daughter who won't work, Asha thought as she rolled her eyes.

"No, I'm not doing too much of anything. I'm supporting my best friend and her talent. To see ourselves as others see us, what a gift it would be. Isn't that how the poem goes?" Asha asked him, trying not to sound annoyed by his comment.

"Well, I'd love to see myself with you after I leave the movie. Do you think that's possible?" he asked.

"That is a possibility. I will definitely be home by the time the movie ends. I promise."

"Or how about you can just go to my place and be waiting for me?" he responded. "I mean, after all, you do have a key."

Asha was grateful that he couldn't see her face. After careful consideration and much deliberation over the past few days with Devyn, and even on the phone with Chase, Asha decided to keep the key to be polite and not cause any confusion. She reasoned that Sully giving her a key didn't mean she had to use it. It was a nice gesture, but she didn't even want to be in his house without him being there.

"You know I'm not spending the night, right? I have to be at the event venue for the conference super early.

But you're more than welcome to come to my house for a little while. We haven't seen each other all week, and I'd love to get a hug." Asha hoped the last part would encourage him to agree to her counteroffer.

"Just a hug?" Sully asked. "I don't get to spend any quality time with my baby this weekend, and all I get is a hug?"

"And a kiss," Asha told him.

"I mean, I guess I can swing by for a moment. I'll text you when I'm on my way," he said.

"Have fun, and I'll see you later," Asha told him, relieved because now she had some additional time to work on the site she was building.

"Pivot? Looks interesting. What is it?"

Asha turned around to see Ben Maxwell smiling as he looked over her shoulder at her iPad. His presence so caught her off guard that she didn't respond immediately but finally managed to simply utter, "Uh, oh . . ."

"I didn't mean to startle you. I just wanted to say hello." His dimpled grin was the perfect setting for his perfect teeth, and Asha tried not to stare too long, but it was a struggle. He had on another polo shirt with his company logo, but instead of khakis, he wore jeans that looked as if they were designed just for him, along with a pair of black Nikes.

She finally forced her eyes off his exquisite physique long enough to notice the tray of food in his hands and pointed to the empty seat across from her. "Well, hello, there, Mr. Maxwell. Please feel free to join me."

After placing the tray on the table, he sat down. "Are you sure you're not too busy? I don't want to interrupt you if you're working, especially on my event."

Asha smiled. "Nah, this isn't your event, although I have been putting some ideas together for our meeting next week. I think you'll be pleased."

"Better than 'Buses for Boobs'?" he asked.

"*Definitely* better than that," she laughed.

"I don't know. That's gonna be hard to top," he said, picking up one of the chips on his plate and popping it into his mouth. He looked at her empty plastic cup and the plate of crumbs left from her cinnamon roll that she'd already devoured, then asked, "Did you eat already? You want me to get you something?"

"No, I'm fine. I've been here for a little while, actually," she told him.

"Come on. You can't let me sit here and eat by myself. I'd feel rude," he said.

"You're not being rude. Please, eat," Asha said. "But I will get a refill on my tea."

She walked over to the beverage station and filled her cup with ice, then tea. When she returned to the table, he'd placed a few chips and half of his sandwich on her plate.

"It's Bacon Turkey Bravo," he told her.

"You don't have to share your food with me, Ben. I told you I'm fine," Asha laughed.

"But I'm not. And since you won't let me buy you your own, you'll have to share mine."

As they began eating and after making small talk, they became fully engrossed in their conversation. He was just as engaging and entertaining as he'd been the first time they'd spoken in her office, and he was just as fine. He told her how he'd started his business with one limo that he purchased from an auction. He worked as the driver until he saved enough to hire an employee and buy a second vehicle. Within five years, in addition to five limousines, his fleet included party buses, town cars, and charter buses. He was a self-made man. Asha was impressed even more.

"So, you pretty much created an empire because you wanted to surprise your mom for her birthday? Unbelievable." Asha sat back in her seat.

"Yeah, she used to tell me the only time she ever got to ride in a fancy car was for her mother's funeral. She never got to ride in a limo for something good, like her birthday. So, when I saw the car at the auction, that's all I thought about. I wanted to make that dream come true for her. And I ended up making way more than that," he nodded.

"Incredible. I'm sure she gets all the limo rides she wants now, huh?" Asha asked.

"She would if she were still here. She died two years ago . . . breast cancer." Ben looked down at the table.

"That's the reason the fund-raiser is so important to you," Asha said softly.

Ben nodded. "It is."

"Don't worry. I will make sure it's as special as I know she was to you. I promise," she told him.

"I'm going to hold you to that because my mama was something else," he said with a half smile. "But I know you're going to make something amazing happen. That's why I hired you. You came highly recommended."

Asha wasn't sure whether he meant her personally or the company she worked for, but either way, she knew the event she planned for Maximum Transportation was going to be one of the best she'd ever handled.

"Wow, no pressure, huh?" she smiled.

"What's up, Ben?" An attractive young woman walked over and spoke, then politely turned and smiled at Asha. "Hi, how are you?"

"Hey, Nadia, what's up?" Ben nodded at her. "Asha, this is my friend, Nadia. Nadia, this is Asha. She's the event planner for the fund-raiser we're sponsoring in honor of Mama."

"Nice to meet you, Asha," Nadia smiled.

"Same here."

"Event planner? I'm glad to hear that. I was afraid he was gonna try to plan it himself, and it would end up being something like Boobs, Beer, and Barbecue or some mess," Nadia laughed.

"Damn, I shoulda thought of that. That sounds like fun." Ben snapped his fingers.

"Well, I've gotta go. You know we're working around the clock getting everything ready for the Culture sneak peek next weekend. You're coming, right?" Nadia asked Ben. "This is gonna be big."

"I wouldn't miss it for the world," he told her.

Nadia looked over at Asha and said, "You should come too and bring a friend. Give her the details, Ben."

"Will do, Nadia," Ben said.

"Then I'll see you both next Saturday." Nadia waved as she left.

Asha had no idea what she'd been invited to, and she didn't care. She was going. The window of opportunity she'd been waiting on was open, and she was ready to take it.

"So, what is this that's happening on Saturday night?" she asked.

"It's a sneak peek for a new business venture a friend of mine is opening. I could try to explain it, but really, it's something you should see for yourself. Nadia is right. It's gonna be big, and Saturday night is gonna be fun: music, drinks, food. As a matter of fact, there's gonna be a cooking demo. You down?"

"That does sound like fun. I'm definitely down. And it sounds like something my best friend Devyn would enjoy too." Asha clapped. "She's amazing: smart, beautiful, talented, and she likes to cook. And guess what?"

"What?"

"She's single. I mean, unless you aren't . . ." Asha said in a way to make sure he understood what she was saying.

Ben gave her a strange look, then said, "Aren't what? Straight? No, I am definitely hetero."

"I was gonna say single." Asha blinked. She'd been so focused on his looks, personality, career, and marital status that she'd never considered questioning his sexual preference.

"Oh, I'm definitely single too," Ben told her.

"Good. I mean, not that it wouldn't be good if you weren't because I don't judge. But I'm just saying it's good that you're solo, and she's unattached. You're both free at the moment." Asha found herself babbling for some reason.

"It's cool. Invite her to come along. The more, the merrier. If she's everything you say she is, I, uh, look forward to meeting her. What's her IG? I can go ahead and follow her."

Asha paused. "Uh, she kinda doesn't do social media, so no IG, FB, Twitter . . . none of that. She's really private."

"None at all?" He frowned.

"No, it's a long story. But I can show you a pic. I'm not kidding. She's gorgeous. As a matter of fact, you asked me about Pivot, the website I was working on when you walked up. That's the business that she's starting. She's a pageant coach." Asha took out her phone and pulled up a photo that she'd taken with Devyn. Photos were a rarity for her friend now, but after sharing two bottles of wine one girls' night, they were both tipsy, and she'd convinced Devyn to smile while she took a quick selfie before she could object. It was a cute picture even though Devyn's half-closed, inebriated eyes made her look sexy. Asha looked drunk. She immediately wished she'd had a better one to show him, but it was the most recent one she had of her friend. *This isn't about you, Asha. It's about Devyn. He's looking at her in the pic, not you.*

"Damn, she is beautiful," Ben said, taking the phone from Asha.

"I told you." Asha nodded excitedly.

"Give her my number. Maybe we can hang out sooner than next weekend if she's not busy coaching beauty queens." Ben returned her phone.

"I think maybe it would be easier if you just 'happen' to meet her at the event."

"Uh-oh, I got a feeling Devyn doesn't know you're trying to play matchmaker." Ben shook his head.

"I plead the Fifth. It'll be our little secret," Asha smirked. Suddenly, her phone rang. Sully's name and number appeared on the screen, and she was shocked to see that it was almost ten o'clock. "Oh, snap, I didn't realize it was this late."

"Late? It's not even close to midnight, Cinderella. But I didn't realize we've been here this long, either." Ben began picking up their trash and putting it on the tray.

Asha stood and packed up her belongings. "It has been quite enjoyable, but I've definitely gotta go. I'll see you next week at our meeting."

"I'll bring the tickets for Saturday when I come," Ben told her. "You sure you don't want me to walk you out?"

"No, I'm good. I appreciate the offer, though."

Asha thanked him again before hurrying out the door and into her truck. She instructed Siri to call Sully as soon as she turned on the ignition and prayed that he wouldn't be too pissed at her. Not being home one time was bad enough, but twice in one night was downright disrespectful. She knew that Sully was probably pissed and deservedly so.

"I'm on my way right now, Sully." She told him as soon as he answered the phone. "You're not gonna believe this. I'm still at Panera. I ended up—"

"Don't worry about it, Asha," Sully interrupted her. "I'm already halfway home now. Finish working on your Devyn stuff. I'll talk to you later."

Before Asha could say anything else, he hung up. She considered just going over to his house to apologize and tell him what happened in person but didn't want to risk being talked into spending the night. She had to be at the Marriott at the crack of dawn to make sure things were in place for the Regional Realtor Conference she was handling. After getting home, she tried to reach Sully again, but he didn't answer. Knowing that he preferred talking instead of texting, Asha left a voicemail and hoped he would understand.

"Sully, I'm so sorry. Tonight was a total bust, twice. My fault. It's been a pretty busy week, and I've done a crappy job of balancing my time. I appreciate you making an effort. I'm gonna do better. Hopefully, we can chat some time tomorrow or at least before the weekend is over. Good night."

Although she felt bad for missing the time with Sully, Asha was still excited about the fact that she'd run into Ben. He was just the kind of guy Devyn needed in her life. They seemed perfect for each other. Getting them in the same place at the same time so they could meet was one thing. Convincing Devyn to give Ben a chance was going to be another. She just hoped Devyn wasn't lying when she said she was open to dating again because as far as Asha could tell, Ben Maxwell was more than "potential penis"—way more.

Chapter 9

Devyn

Devyn stood in the middle of her closet and stared at the racks of clothes. For the past hour, she'd been trying to come up with an outfit that was not only slimming but also stylish, by her standards—getting dressed to go out used to be simple. Her favorite "go-to" ensemble was always form-fitting jeans, a crop top, a colorful blazer, or a kimono of some sort, and whatever pair of heels that struck her fancy. Now, her form didn't look right in any of it. Everything made her look bigger than she already was. It was useless. Just as she decided to call Asha and cancel, her phone rang.

"Stop standing in the closet and get dressed."

"I'm not standing in the closet," Devyn lied and wondered if her friend had some kind of sixth sense that alerted her sometimes.

"Whatever, Devyn. I know you better than you know yourself. Grab something cute and stop overthinking this. You just told the girls that fashion is not about what you wear, but how you wear it. Take your own advice, Dev. It's not that serious," Asha told her. "And before you even think about trying to back out—don't. You're coming."

"I don't understand why I have to go. Don't you think you and Sully should be going to this alone? I'm not trying to be a third wheel," Devyn pointed out.

"I already explained, the tickets were given to you and me originally, but I decided to invite Sully to come along to make up for last weekend."

"Does he even know I'm coming?" Devyn asked, moving from the section of clothes that she knew were her former size to the ones that were her current.

"Of course. Ben, I mean, Mr. Maxwell, knows you're coming," Asha said. "I told him about Pivot, and that's when he invited us."

"Not him. I'm talking about Sully. You know he doesn't like me," Devyn sighed.

"Stop saying that. Yes, he knows you're coming, and he's excited."

"Now, who's lying?" Devyn laughed at the thought of Sully being thrilled about her tagging along with them. He could hardly stand the fact that Asha talked to her on the phone when she was at his house. That man was clingy. She couldn't understand how Asha didn't see it.

"Whatever, Devyn. Just be ready by six o'clock. Ben is sending a car, so we'll pick you up on the way."

"A car service? Why can't I just drive? This is too much. I have nothing to wear, for real. Oh God," Devyn groaned.

"Don't go bothering God with this nonsense. He has more important things to worry about than you whining about jeans that used to fit you like a glove," Asha snapped. "It's a cooking demo, not the damn prom. Just look cute, and I'll see you by six."

"Fine," Devyn exhaled.

"And Devyn? Tonight is going to be fun," Asha said. "Now, I need you to promise me something."

"What?"

"No black," Asha said and hung up.

Devyn looked at the black dress she'd just taken out, then reluctantly put it back. Asha's call did make her feel a little better. It also made her see that maybe she was ridiculous and a bit selfish. She'd been so caught up in her own vanity that she didn't even appreciate the fact that Asha had included her in an event that her client invited her to attend. Devyn wanted to show Asha that she was just as supportive as her best friend had always been.

Devyn was satisfied with the look she pulled together two hours later, which consisted of plaid, printed crop pants, a gorgeous bell-sleeved blouse, and Valentino ankle booties that she'd had for years but never worn. Her makeup was natural with a dramatic red lip, and she added extra length to her hair so that her sleek, side ponytail hung down to her waist. She put items into a black clutch that was the final touch of her outfit when Asha walked into her bedroom looking equally as chic in black jeans, a leopard print top, and black Giuseppe Zanotti stilettos.

"Oh shit, Devyn, you look amazing." Asha's mouth dropped. "Your hair, your makeup, those shoes . . . everything."

"Wow. I must look hella bad on the regular these days." Devyn smiled and turned around to give Asha a full view. "You look cute too. I'm stealing those shoes when you take them off."

"We can switch," Asha nodded. "I can't believe how good you look, Dev. I mean, you always look beautiful, even in all of that damn black that you wear, but it's good to see . . ."

"The old me?" Devyn asked, picking up a pair of black-framed glasses off the coffee table and slipping them on.

"I don't know what that even means, because you've always been you," Asha replied. "Now, come on, so we're not late."

"I'm ready. And I figured you were right. I can't encourage and advise the girls on fashion and appearance if I'm

looking like a trash bag. As a matter of fact, take this."
Devyn passed Asha her cell phone and posed.

"You want me to take a pic? Stop playing." Asha grabbed
the phone and began snapping. "Wait, we need a selfie."

"I thought you said we were gonna be late? Isn't Sully
waiting?" Devyn laughed as she leaned into the frame
with Asha and smiled.

"He can enjoy sipping champagne in the back of that
stretch Escalade a little while longer. He'll be all right."

Devyn's head snapped around. "A what? Why?"

"It's the car Mr. Maxwell sent for us. I told you he owns
a transportation company," Asha said as they walked
out the door. The driver of the limo greeted them as he
opened the door, and they climbed inside. As Asha stated,
Sully was sitting in the rear, sipping champagne and
listening to Anita Baker.

"I was wondering if y'all were ever gonna come out," he
said.

"Oh, stop acting like you haven't been in here enjoying
the wait." Asha took her seat beside him while Devyn sat
on the opposite side.

"Hey, Devyn, you look nice," Sully said. His compliment took Devyn by surprise.

"Hey, Sully, you look spiffy yourself." Devyn used a
word she felt a man of his generation would appreciate,
referring to his dress pants and sweater vest. Although
she and Chase gave Asha a hard time about her "seasoned" beau, there was no denying that he was handsome
in a Blair Underwood kind of way. Devyn could imagine
that he was probably quite a catch in his prime. Someone
who would wine and dine women and take them to see
Anita Baker in concert.

"Where is this event being held?" Devyn asked as the
limo pulled away from the house.

"Over near Dockside at a place called Culture," Asha
said as she poured them both a glass of champagne.

"East or West?" Devyn's eyes widened. There was a huge difference between the two locations. Both areas were predominantly Black communities, but Dockside East was considered middle class, and Dockside West was not a place where one would want to be caught after dark, especially in a stretch Escalade.

"East, I think." Asha shrugged.

"Hell, I hope so." Sully sat up and looked out the window.

"Why Calvin Sullivan, let me find out you're afraid of the hood," Asha teased. "Isn't that your old stomping ground?"

"First of all, I ain't scared, and, yeah, I lived near the West for a little while. I'm also no fool. I prefer to be safe, not sorry, in the East," Sully told them as he straightened his watch.

Devyn had to agree with him. She was relieved when they took the exit that led them toward the East Side. They continued on the main street past the Target, Whole Foods, and other brightly lit, high-end commercial businesses near the neighborhood filled with large brick homes and newer schools. Instead of stopping, they kept driving, closer and closer to the side of the city they were hoping to avoid.

"I think we're going to the West," Devyn said, just before the limo turned into a fairly crowded parking lot. There was a colorful sign out front that read *"Culture."*

"No, this is still the East," Asha said.

The driver pulled the limo to the front and opened the door. Devyn looked at the familiar building. "Wait, isn't this the old bank building?"

"It is." Sully nodded as he took Asha's hand. "It looks like someone bought it and remodeled it. Did a damn good job too, looks like."

They joined the crowd of about forty or so other guests that had already arrived. Everyone had the same reaction and were surprised to see that the building had been repurposed into a unique space that looked like a cross between an art museum and a minimall. Gorgeous paintings and artwork lined the walls that separated the doors of large, open spaces. Obviously, the new owner had put a lot of time and creativity into the end result. Servers were wearing black T-shirts with the same Culture logo as the entrance sign offered wine and signature beverages while people explored the venue. A live band played a mixture of jazz and R&B as people posed for pictures in front of a backdrop. The atmosphere was casual, yet classy.

"This is dope," Devyn commented as she admired the marble floors and bright lighting.

"It definitely is," Asha agreed.

"I need to find a restroom. The champagne we had on the way over has made its way through me," Sully announced. "I'll be back."

As soon as he walked off, Asha turned to Devyn and gave her a warning look. "Don't even joke about it."

"I wasn't going to say anything," Devyn smiled innocently, deciding not to comment about weak bladders being a sign of old age.

"I don't see Ben anywhere. Let me text him and let him know that we're here."

While Asha set off to find her client, Devyn maneuvered through the crowd to explore a little more. She ventured down to the back of the building and ended up in what had to be the pièce de résistance of the establishment: a windowed room that contained a beautiful state-of-the-art culinary studio. Inside was filled with large tabletops that could hold about twenty people and enough space for more tables, if needed. The kitchen itself was loaded with commercial equipment: a convection oven, two compartment sinks, prep tables, and small glassware galore. An archway led to a virtually stunning dining room that was connected next door. The large entryway into the space held display tables of perfectly mounted aprons for those who would be participating in the cooking class.

She was so caught up in staring at the high vaulted ceilings and hand painted windows that she inadvertently bumped into what initially felt like a brick wall. She was knocked backward, and the hard fall was stopped midair by a pair of strong hands.

"Oh, damn." She gasped and instinctively grabbed the arms that reached for her. "I didn't even see you."

"Somehow, I find that hard to believe."

Devyn glanced up at the man that could only be described as "brawny." He was tall, chocolate, and his voice was just as seductive as his familiar smile. Everything about him was captivating. He was at least six foot seven from Devyn's estimation and had to weigh 300 pounds, easily, but he wasn't fat. He was muscular and solid. Big and sexy. As she stared at him, Devyn became painfully aware that she wasn't the only one. From her peripheral vision, she could see several other women looking in their direction, and for a good reason. This man was straight eye candy. Devyn didn't realize she was still in his arms until she felt his hand move slightly.

"I'm serious. I didn't." She smiled back at him. "I was too busy admiring this place."

"Yeah, it's pretty impressive, huh?" He nodded, looking around. "You sure you're okay?"

"I am," she nodded.

"Good." He steadied her before relaxing his hand.

"We need you in the back," one of the servers walked over and said.

"A'ight, gimme a sec," the guy told him, then returned his attention to Devyn. "Duty calls, but maybe we can chat a bit more later?" He raised an eyebrow and shrugged slightly.

Though he was polite, Devyn noticed the hint of urgency in his voice and replied with a simple, "Sure."

"That's what's up," he told her, finally letting go of her hand as he backed away, then turned before hurrying to wherever he was headed. Devyn tried to keep her eyes on him as long as she could, which was relatively easy due to his height.

"There you are, Dev. I've been looking for you." Asha's voice made her finally turn around. "Ben is somewhere waiting on us, and Sully is probably having a fit because he can't find us."

"My bad. But, Asha, I just ran into the finest man in the world." Devyn gushed as she grabbed her friend by the arm.

"Where? Was he tall and fine?" Asha gasped. "Brown skin with perfect teeth?"

"Yes, hella tall and hella fine," Devyn grinned.

"That's who we're here to meet. That's Ben Maxwell. I was gonna introduce you to him." Asha sighed. "See, I knew you'd like him. Oh my God, I'm officially excited."

"I knew you were up to something when you kept insisting that I come with you tonight. You ain't slick, Ash," Devyn said.

"I had to get you here some kind of way. But aren't you glad I did?"

"I am." Devyn laughed and hugged her.

"Wait, here he comes now."

Devyn was giddy with anticipation and couldn't remember the last time she'd been this excited to meet a guy. They hadn't been formally introduced, but if Asha had already given him her stamp of approval, then he had to be special.

"Mr. Maxwell, so nice to see you. This is Devyn Douglass, my best friend."

Devyn stared blankly at the man she didn't recognize that was shaking Asha's hand. He was good looking, no doubt, but he wasn't the same guy she'd seen earlier, that was for sure. She and Asha had been speaking about two different men.

"Nice to meet you." Ben smiled and held his hand toward her.

Devyn reached out and shook it, hoping he didn't see her slight disappointment. "Likewise."

"I'm so glad you guys were able to make it. Where's your boyfriend?" Ben asked Asha.

Devyn looked around, hoping to find the man who turned out not to be Ben Maxwell, but she didn't see him anywhere.

"He's around here somewhere. Why don't the two of you get acquainted while I see if I can find him," Asha said. "I'll be back. Dev, you're in good hands with Ben."

"I'm sure." Devyn smiled nervously, then, in an effort not to seem rude, said, "Thank you for the invite and car service. This place is incredible."

"You're welcome. It's a pretty dope spot. My friend Nadia and her brother have created something really special here. I figured you guys would enjoy checking it out," Ben replied. "Asha told me about your new coaching business, Pivot. Congratulations. I think that's really cool. Were you in a lot of beauty pageants?"

"Actually, just one," Devyn told him. "In college."

"I'm pretty sure you won." He smiled.

"I did, but I admit, it was rigged."

"From what I'm looking at, I'm pretty sure you would've won anyway. You definitely are stunning." Ben stared at her.

Devyn knew his compliment was genuine, but for some reason, instead of feeling flattered, she felt flat, partly because she was slightly distracted by discreetly looking for her mystery man and wondering where the hell Sully and Asha had disappeared to.

"Thank you." She tried to sound sincere. Her watch vibrated and displayed a notification for the text that she'd gotten. Devyn frowned as she read the small font, then took out her phone to make sure she'd read it correctly. "I'm sorry, Ben. I need to go and check on Asha."

Devyn apologized and rushed off in search of her friend. Somehow, she knew they wouldn't be coming back. Something was wrong.

Chapter 10

Asha

"Sully, baby, please tell me what the hell is going on," Asha pleaded and touched his shoulder.

"Asha, I told you, I'm out of here. If you wanna stay, that's on you." Sully shook his head.

"I don't have a problem leaving with you, but at least let me know why it's so abrupt. Are you sick? Did something happen?" she asked.

"No, I ain't sick. And, yeah, a lot of shit happened. I can't believe I agreed to come to this bullshit in the first place." Sully began to walk away.

"Asha, what's wrong?" Devyn rushed out the front door and toward her. Although justified, her question made Asha even more upset than she already was because she didn't have an answer.

"Sully wants to get out of here. So, I guess we're going," Asha shrugged.

"Why?" Devyn frowned. "And how are we leaving if we didn't drive?"

Asha closed her eyes for a moment, realizing that Devyn was right. They'd been chauffeured to the event, courtesy of Ben Maxwell, who was probably inside thinking she was the rudest person on earth.

"Sully, can you please come here so we can talk about this like adults?" Asha yelled.

Sully paused but made his way back to where she and Devyn were waiting. The front door opened again, and Ben walked out.

"Hey, is everything okay?" he asked.

"Yes, but Sully's not feeling well." It was a lie but sounded a hell of a lot better than admitting that she didn't know what was going on. She continued. "I'm sorry, but we're gonna have to leave."

"Oh, wow. I'm so sorry. I'll call the driver and tell him to get back here as soon as possible," Ben offered.

"You don't have to do that. I can call an Uber." Sully glared at him.

"It's no problem. He's not far at all." Ben reached for his phone.

"Don't bother. I can get my own ride." Sully raised his voice, and Ben took a step back.

Asha's face became hot, and had the hue of her skin not been the color of deep caramel, she was certain that her blushing cheeks would be very noticeable. She was confused, frustrated, angry, and most of all, embarrassed. Not wanting the turn of events to deter the potential romance between Devyn and Ben, she tried to offer some suggestion.

"Dev, you don't have to miss this great event. Stay with Ben and enjoy." Asha lowered her voice so Sully wouldn't hear.

"No. We came together, so we leave together. Girl code." Devyn shook her head.

Asha turned to Ben. "I'm so sorry. Thank you so much for the invitation and your hospitality. I wish—"

"Hey," Ben touched her shoulder, "I understand. It happens. I hope he feels better."

"Thanks." Asha nodded, grateful for Ben's understanding. She hoped that Devyn noticed the level of concern he demonstrated.

"Devyn, it was nice meeting you," he said and shook her hand.

"Thanks, you too," Devyn told him.

Ben went back inside just as a Ford sedan pulled up. Sully opened the back door and waited as Asha and Devyn got in. Then he sat in the front seat with the driver. They were quiet the entire ride. When they arrived at Devyn's house, Asha walked her to the front door.

"Are you sure he's okay? What the hell happened?" Devyn asked as she unlocked the door and stepped inside.

Asha punched the alarm code. "I don't know, Dev. I've never seen him this angry. Something set him off. That's why I didn't pressure him into staying."

"Yeah, he's pretty upset. Well, call and let me know how things go." Devyn hugged her. "I'm here if you need me."

"Thanks. I'm sorry stuff went down the way it did, but at least you hit it off with Ben," Asha smiled.

"Uh, about that—"

The face Devyn made indicated that she was about to say something Asha didn't want to hear. "Oh, hell no, Devyn. You said that he was hella fine. Don't let whatever Sully has going on make you—"

"No, it has nothing to do with Sully, Ash. The dude I was talking about wasn't Ben. He was someone else. Another impressive male specimen." Devyn shrugged. "Quite impressive."

"He couldn't have been more impressive than Ben. No way. That's not possible." Asha refused to think whoever the guy Devyn talked to was any comparison.

"This man was all that, and then some. There was something about him. We vibed. I can't explain it."

"I don't know who he could be, Dev. But I do know that Ben is interested in you, and you should give him a chance," Asha told her. "He is a great catch and the kind of guy you deserve. Good dudes like him don't come around very often. Keep that in mind."

Asha hugged her once more before leaving. When she got back to the car, Sully was now in the backseat. She got in and slid beside him. He still seemed bothered, so she stayed quiet. If he didn't want to talk, then neither did she. When they got to his house, she wasted no time getting out of the vehicle and rushing to her car, parked in his driveway.

"Where are you going?" he called out to her.

"Home." She unlocked her door and opened it.

"You're not staying the night?"

"Why would I do that, Sully? You acted like a complete ass and embarrassed me in front of my best friend and new client, who went out of his way to invite us. You insisted on leaving an event that everyone was enjoying with no explanation. You've been giving me the silent treatment since we left. Do you *really* think I want to come inside right now?" Asha lashed out.

Sully gave her a solemn look. "I'm sorry. You didn't deserve any of that. I owe you an explanation and an apology. Can you please come in so I can give you both?"

Despite her aching feet, growling stomach, and mounting headache, Asha wanted to hear what Sully had to say, so she closed her door and followed him into the house. When they got to the den, she sat and waited for him to speak.

"You want something to drink?" he asked.

"No, I'm fine." Asha shook her head and folded her arms.

Sully took a deep breath. "I truly apologize for the way I acted tonight, Asha. You know me well enough to know that I'm a laid-back guy. I don't upset easily, let alone get angry. I don't bother anybody. There's only one person in the world who I would go tooth and nail for, and tonight, that almost happened."

"What are you talking about, Sully?" Asha was still confused because no one bothered or said anything to him from what she could recall.

"When we got to Culture, I knew there was something familiar about a couple of people. I couldn't place them at first. Then when I saw that bastard walking past with that grin on his big-ass face, I nearly lost it. That's why I ran in and out of the rooms so fast. I wanted to make sure it was him. And it was. He looked right at me, had the nerve to nod, and then said something smart." Sully's eyes were full of anger. "Seeing him standing there with that smug-ass look on his face, I felt like someone opened an old wound and poured salt on it. The sting came rushing back like it never left. All I could think about was my daughter. I couldn't be in the same damn room with him. I was gonna lose it."

"Sully, who did you see, and what does this have to do with Ingrid?" Asha asked.

Sully looked over at her and said, "Bear."

"Bear? Who the hell is that?" Asha had no idea who he was talking about.

"He is Ingrid's ex. The guy who ruined her life," Sully explained.

Asha remembered the conversation they'd overheard Ingrid having at lunch. The news of her ex being in town bothered him. She didn't think much about it, but it was obviously more serious than she would've considered. She'd never seen Sully so enraged.

"I guess they had a pretty bad breakup, which left you with some ill feelings about him." Asha's statement could've easily been a question considering that she really wasn't sure. "But don't you think you're being a little irrational? You're acting like this guy tried to kill someone."

Sully looked directly into her eyes and said, "He did. He tried to kill Ingrid."

His words and tears rendered Asha speechless. She was shocked at the revelation and felt terrible that he'd had to face this guy. A part of her felt responsible for putting him in this situation, even though she hadn't done it intentionally. Not knowing anything else to do, Asha stood up, wrapped her arms around Sully, and hugged him tightly.

"I'm sorry, honey," she whispered. "I didn't know."

"I know you didn't. I could not be in that place another moment while all those people celebrated for that monster. Oh God, I know someone is going to tell Ingrid I was there. She's going to be so upset." Sully sighed. "I've gotta get to her."

"Yeah, it's probably best that you do. There were a lot of photographers there, and I'm sure people are gonna post on social media, if they haven't already," Asha told him.

"Damn it. You're right. Asha, I feel bad about the way I behaved. I would never act like that under normal circumstances. I hope you know that." Sully touched her face.

"I know, Sully. It's fine," Asha smiled.

Sully kissed her. "Stay the night, please."

"I'm not sure, Sully," she told him. "I'm starving. We didn't eat anything but hors d'oeuvres, remember?"

"I'll get food. I need you tonight, Asha."

"I'll stay," she told him after he promised to pick up wings from her favorite spot. As soon as the door closed behind him, she wasted no time calling Devyn to update her on what he'd shared.

"Shut the hell up! A killer? Do you *really* believe we were at a party with a potential murderer? And when did all of this happen? How did he try to kill her? Like, did he shoot her or stab her? Did he go to trial?" Devyn quickly fired off the questions, and Asha didn't have any answers.

"That's what he said, and I don't know the details. I mean, I know this is gonna sound crazy, but I didn't see anyone there that looked like a murderer. Did you?" Asha thought back to the faces of the people who'd been at the event.

"Uh, I don't think killers have a certain look, Asha. Do you know how many fine men are in jail for murder?" Devyn laughed. "And why don't you know the details? Did you ask questions?"

"No. I think I was too shocked to ask anything. I just let him talk."

"You suck, Asha," Devyn groaned. "When he gets back, I'm gonna need you to ask questions."

"Okay, I will, but on one condition," Asha told her.

"What?"

"You go on a date with Ben."

"A date? What happened to just think about it?" Devyn asked.

"You want the details or not?"

"Fine. One date, Asha."

"Yessss," Asha squealed.

"Don't get too excited. I'm only agreeing because I wanna know what Sully was talking about, and if I don't agree, then you probably wouldn't even ask," Devyn sighed.

"You're right. However, if it will get you to go out with Ben, I'll ask Sully whatever you want," Asha laughed.

"Whatever. I'm going to find something to eat. I'm starving because we didn't get to stay and indulge in our culinary delights that we were supposed to prepare."

"Talk to you tomorrow. And I'll make sure that Ben has your number," Asha told her before hanging up.

Since Sully still hadn't made it back, Asha decided to shower and get ready for bed. Her headache was getting slightly worse. She opened the medicine cabinet in search of something to help. There were several bottles of prescription medicine and vitamins. She wasn't a pharmacist, but she recognized that most of the drugs were for blood pressure and high cholesterol. Asha shifted through them until she found a bottle of Aleve and took two. She got into Sully's comfortable bed and turned on the television. Within minutes, she was fast asleep.

Chapter 11

Devyn

"Dionne, you've got to stop slumping," Devyn yelled, forgetting for a moment that they were in a library meeting room. She quickly lowered her voice and said, "What is up with your shoulders?"

It was her second week of coaching, and although both girls showed some improvement, they had a long way to go. Asha had to work late, and in her absence, Devyn decided to focus on stage presence. They'd spent most of the past hour practicing poise and confidence while being centerstage.

"Oh, my bad." Dionne straightened her back.

"Thank you. Much better," Devyn nodded.

"She does that to elongate her torso," Journi explained.

"What?" Devyn turned and frowned.

"Lengthening her body. That's why she kinda folds her shoulders in like that." Journi demonstrated the awkward stretch Dionne was attempting, looking just as ridiculous.

"I don't understand," Devyn said, still confused by the explanation.

"I mean, she's tall and has long legs, but her torso is short. The technique makes her look longer."

Devyn looked from Journi, then to Dionne, who now stood beside them. "That's the dumbest thing I've ever heard. Where the hell did y'all get that from?"

"YouTube," the girls said simultaneously.

Devyn held her head down, and despite her effort to suppress her laughter, a giggle slipped out.

"What's funny, Miss Devyn?" Dionne asked. "The girl on Top Model said every great model has a signature walk. Something that makes them stand out. My shoulder hunch is mine."

"No, sweetie, your shoulder hunch is horrible," Devyn laughed. "Your torso is beautiful, just like the rest of your body. Embrace it, boo. There is no need to elongate anything. Head up, shoulders back. Let's perfect your basic walk before we develop anything else."

"Fine," Dionne sighed.

"Good, now, try it again," Devyn instructed, then watched with pride as Dionne demonstrated a much-improved walk. Her praise was instant. "Yes, *that's* what I'm talking about."

"Can I ask you a question, Miss Devyn?" Journi said.

"Yep, ask away," Devyn shrugged.

"We know you used to model. Miss Asha said you don't like to talk about it. But did you have a signature walk?"

When she made her official decision to coach, one of the things she insisted on with Asha was that none of her past modeling experience was to be disclosed or discussed. She'd put that part of her life behind her and had no desire to revisit it. However, she was slowly discovering that some things were necessary for her to be an effective instructor. *It's not like you haven't demonstrated a walk for them already. Just show 'em what you got and act like it's no big deal.*

"I did," she finally said.

"Oh, really?" Dionne elbowed Journi. "We wanna see."

"You've seen me walk." Devyn shrugged. "Now, come on, let's get finished. We've only got about ten minutes left before we gotta get outta here."

"But we haven't seen your signature walk," Journi said. "So, go ahead, Miss Devyn."

"Like you said, we only got ten minutes. Unless it was so long ago that you forgot . . ." Dionne taunted. "Maybe that's why she doesn't like talking about it, J, because she doesn't remember. She is kinda old."

"I know what y'all are trying to do, and it's not gonna work." Devyn shook her head.

"All we're trying to do is see what you were working with back in the day. *If* you were working with it, that is," Journi smirked.

Devyn exhaled. "Fine. If you'd like to use the remainder of your coaching session to watch me walk instead of working on your own, that's on you. It's your dime."

"We definitely do," Dionne nodded. "And I know the perfect song."

"Gimme those." Devyn pointed to the three-inch heels on Journi's feet that she'd been practicing in as she slipped off the Uggs she wore. Journi quickly complied and kicked them off for Devyn to put on. They were a little snug, but nothing she couldn't stand. One thing seasoned models knew was even if the shoe doesn't fit, you still had to wear it.

Music began playing on Dionne's phone. Devyn strutted to the front of the room like she was in a designer show during Fashion Week in Milan. Her body was fluid, her steps purposeful yet graceful. Eyes forward, hips swayed, shoulders squared, and then she hit it, the thing that made her walk unique and distinctively hers: the pivot move at the end of the runway. She had perfected it after weeks of practice when she first started modeling. Devyn posed briefly, turned, and strutted back in the direction she'd walked from. The girls were screaming and clapping as she approached. She also noticed Journi's phone pointed directly at her, breaking another one of her cardinal rules: no unauthorized photos or videos.

"Uh-uh, put it down. You know the rules," Devyn sternly warned.

"I know, I know," Journi whined as she quickly put the phone away.

Devyn returned her shoes and told them, "That's it for today. I'll see you guys next week. Work on those intros. Oh, and Miss Journi?"

"I know. Less Marcus Garvey and more Michelle Obama," Journi said, matter-of-factly.

They exited the library, hugged, and said their good-byes. Devyn got into her car and took her phone from her purse to call Asha and update her on how the session went. That's when she noticed she had a missed call and voicemail from an unknown number. As always, she opted to read the transcription before listening, but after seeing the first few lines, she hit the *play* button to hear what was being said.

"Hello, Devyn. This is Ben Maxwell. Asha said you gave the green light for me to call, so I'm reaching out. Feel free to give me a call back at this number when your schedule permits. I look forward to talking to you," Ben's voice stated.

Devyn recalled the conditions of the agreement she and her bestie made regarding Ben being given her information. Clearly, he now had her number, but Asha still hadn't even asked Sully to divulge any more details. Someone wasn't keeping up their end of the bargain . . . If Asha expected her to entertain the idea of Ben Maxwell, she was going to have to find some kind of incentive to trade or offer in return.

"Oh, I'm gonna lay her out for this one," Devyn said as she hit the *call* button and started the car. "She didn't even give me a heads-up. She's about to owe me big time."

"Hello?"

Devyn was caught off guard by the voice that answered the phone, which was much deeper than the one she expected to hear. "Uh, hello?"

"Devyn?"

Devyn looked at her phone and saw that it wasn't Asha's number she dialed. She'd accidentally called someone else. "Yes, uh, hi, uh, Ben."

"Hi. How are you?" he asked.

Devyn grimaced. "I'm good."

"I guess you got my message. I almost didn't leave a voicemail because most people don't check them these days. Guess I was wrong."

Devyn didn't know how to respond, so she simply said, "I guess so."

"Well, I was wondering if you weren't busy this Saturday night, would you like to hang out?"

"Together?" Devyn asked.

"Yeah, we didn't get to enjoy the cooking demo at Culture, and there's another one this weekend. I figured we'd check it out. It would give us a chance to get to know one another," Ben told her.

"I, uh . . ." Devyn stammered, caught off guard by his sudden invitation. She'd expected a simple phone conversation or two before having to decide if she wanted to go out on an actual date. He wasn't wasting any time, though, and she needed to think about it. "Can I get back to you?"

"Sure, no problem," he said.

"Okay, cool. I will let you know." Devyn told him, then for good measure, added, "We'll chat later tonight. Is that okay?"

"I look forward to it," he told her.

There really wasn't a reason why Devyn couldn't go out on a date with him. It wasn't like she had a social calendar full of events to attend on Saturday night. She definitely didn't have multiple suitors blowing up her phone or knocking down her door, although that was by choice. Ben Maxwell was the first guy to formally ask her out on a legitimate date since her ex. Come to think of it, she couldn't recall Tremell ever asking her out. Their entire relationship had been a whirlwind from start to finish. They met one night at an after-hours club, sparks flew, and they became inseparable.

"What's the issue?" Chase asked later that evening when she called and told her about Ben's phone call. "You said he seemed nice the other night. And from what Asha told me, he's not hard on the eyes either."

"There's no issue, not really. And he is nice and quite attractive. She ain't lying about that. I just don't know if I'm ready to go on a date with anyone. Being in a relationship isn't—"

"Whoa whoa whoa, Grasshopper. Slow your ass down. Who said anything about being in a damn relationship, Devyn? This dude asked you on a date. He ain't get on one knee, did he?" Chase yelped.

"No, Chase. You're trying to be funny," Devyn sighed.

"I'm not. The reason you're freaking out is that you're putting all this pressure on yourself. Just because you go on a date with a guy doesn't mean you're obligated to anything."

"I get that."

"Dev, you know what your problem is? You've only dated three guys in your entire life: one in high school, one in college, and the asshole you almost married. For some reason, some kind of way, you somehow ended up in long-term relationships with them. But that's not how dating normally works, Devyn. Most people date to have fun. That's it. Dating is about having a good time," Chase said.

"I know what dates are, Chastity," Devyn told her.

"Then go," Chase said. "I know Asha has been building him up in your head like he's the perfect guy and a great catch. I'm not saying that he's not. But that shouldn't even matter to you right now. She's saying all of these amazing things, I believe, so you'll be motivated to go out with him. She doesn't mean to pressure you and probably doesn't even realize it. That's just Asha. We all know she wants nothing but the best for her BFF Devyn. Hell, at this point, we are just glad you've gotten to a place where you'll even consider dating anybody. We're not tryin'a marry you off. We just tryin'a help you get some dick."

Devyn laughed so hard that she almost choked. "Chase!"

"What? I'm serious. It's been a long time since you've been manhandled, has it not? And, no, I'm not saying that's why you should go out with him either. But you can't get penis from someone you don't know. Well, you can, but you know what I mean." Chase giggled. "And for the record, even if you wanna get penis from him on the first date, that's fine too. Go for it."

"I thought talking to you would help me get some clarity. Now, I'm even more confused," Devyn laughed.

"You're scared, and that's fine. Whether you go out with Ben, someone else, or no one at all, it's up to you," Chase said softly. "Take the pressure off yourself. As a matter of fact, you know what you should do?"

"What?" Devyn asked.

"Take a 'sip' and then decide," Chase answered. "You know that always works."

Devyn smiled. "You're absolutely right. I swear, sometimes I wonder who's the oldest because you are always the wiser one."

"What can I say? It's a gift. Now, the next issue at hand is this website for Pivot that Asha and I have been so diligently working on. What's the holdup? I thought coaching was going well."

"It is, and I am really enjoying it. I'm just not ready to pull the trigger yet. I'm getting there. I appreciate all your hard work. I owe you both," Devyn said. "And not just for the business and logo stuff. But for always being there when I need you. It's been a rough past couple of years, but y'all have stuck it out."

"We're family. Besides, it's practice for when I do meet Mr. Right. I'll have plenty of experience dealing with temperamental people," Chase responded.

"Bye, Chase," Devyn told her.

After the call ended, she took a long, hot bath, put on her robe, made a cup of tea, then went to sit on the deck. It was a lovely night with a dark sky, full moon, and a gentle breeze. She sipped her tea and closed her eyes. Stop. Inhale. Process. As she began to relax, she thought about how nice it would be if she had someone to share the intimate setting with her. *A charming guy to talk to while I lay my head on his chest, and we stare at the stars, someone to laugh and joke with me.* For a second, she had a flashback to the guy she'd bumped into the other night, the one who'd instantly made her smile. Then her thoughts turned to Ben Maxwell. There was no initial spark when they'd met, unlike all of her exes, but maybe that was a good thing. Maybe he was exactly what she needed to get her feet wet. She was definitely out of practice and needed to start somewhere. *No reason why it shouldn't be Ben,* she thought. She made her decision.

Devyn's anxiety level was on a thousand from the moment she called Ben to accept his invitation, up until he arrived to pick her up. She'd already let him know that although he owned a car service, she preferred not to be chauffeured to their destination. She even offered to drive and meet him, but he insisted on picking her up.

Asha, who'd come over to give her a much-needed pep talk and approve her outfit choice of jeans, white blouse, and colorful pumps, had just pulled out of the driveway minutes before the doorbell rang. *Right on time. Here goes nothing.* Devyn took a deep breath and reminded herself to have fun.

"Wow, you look amazing." Ben stood in the doorway, a smile on his face and a bouquet of roses in his hand. His outfit mirrored hers: jeans, button-down shirt, blazer, and casual shoes. He was just as handsome as she remembered.

"Thank you. You look nice too," Devyn smiled. "I like your shirt."

"These are for you." He held out the bouquet.

"They're gorgeous." She took the flowers from him. "Uh, I'll be right back."

Without thinking, she turned and walked back inside to put them on the kitchen table. As she headed back to the front door, it dawned on her that she should've invited Ben inside instead of having him stand at the front door like a pizza deliveryman waiting on her to get change for a tip. *Pull it together,* she told herself as she set the alarm and rushed to leave.

"You ready?" he asked when she got to the doorway.

"I am. And I'm sorry. I should've invited you in," she explained.

"No need to apologize. I understand." He held out his hand to help her down the front steps and the walkway to where his Acura SUV was parked.

Okay, he's a gentleman. This might not be bad, after all.

"Oh, this is funny," Devyn giggled as he opened the door and waited for her to get into the truck.

"What's that?" he asked.

"You and Asha have the same SUV, exact color and everything," Devyn told him, noticing that even the interior of his vehicle was precisely like her friend's custom model.

"Are you serious?" Ben laughed. "You do know this is a Special Edition, right? They only made—"

"exactly 360 of them." Devyn finished his statement. "Trust me, she's told me enough times before and after she bought it. I am positive."

"Wow, I guess Asha has great taste in cars *and* friends." He raised his eyebrow as he closed her door.

Devyn let Ben do most of the talking while they headed to Culture. He told her that the event they were attending wasn't actually a demo but a cooking class for couples. Devyn almost panicked. Certainly, he wasn't considering them a couple, was he? Then she reminded herself that the word encompassed any two people taking the class together, not necessarily two people in a relationship. At least, that's what she hoped he meant.

Before long, they arrived at the building. This time, there wasn't a large crowd, just those attending the class. She and Ben went straight to the culinary lab.

"Welcome to Culture Culinary. Please sign in here and help yourself to an apron," a beautiful young lady sitting at a table outside the lab greeted them. She reminded Devyn of a young Erykah Badu with her colorful head wrap, Rastafarian printed skirt, and chunky jewelry. Devyn immediately wanted every item for her own wardrobe.

"Thank you." Devyn smiled as she picked up a pen and began filling out one of the class participant forms. "You're outfit is fly, sis."

Ben seemed amused for some reason. "Well, hello to you too, Nadia. Don't we look colorful tonight?"

"Thank you. Some people can't appreciate artistic expression in fashion." The woman glared at Ben playfully. "How quickly they forget how they used to wear BAPE T-shirts and skateboard shoes."

"Wow, it's like that?" Ben's embarrassment was evident.

"You know better than to try to clown me in front of company, Benjamin." She laughed, then looked at Devyn, "Hi, I'm Nadia."

"My bad. Devyn, Nadia, Nadia, Devyn," Ben interjected.

"Nice to meet you." Devyn grinned and handed her the clipboard.

Nadia passed her one of the aprons. "I thought Ben was lying when he said he was coming to the cooking class tonight. Normally, he just calls and asks if we have any leftovers. I never would've thought he had an actual date—and a gorgeous one at that."

"We are holding up the line and need to get inside before the class starts." Ben motioned to the small group of people who were standing behind them, waiting to sign in.

"Nice to meet you again, Devyn. Have fun and enjoy," Nadia smiled.

Devyn followed Ben into the glass-encased studio. They found seats at one of the stations toward the front of the class. Almost all the cooking stations were full, and folks seemed excited about being there. Music was playing as people sipped wine and snacked on grapes and cheese that were at each table. Devyn slipped on her apron and then noticed a small production setup with a couple of cameras.

"Are they filming?" she asked Ben.

"Yeah, it's a trial run. Nigel, the chef who owns Culture with Nadia, his sister, has a decent following on YouTube and IG. Normally, he does his thing at home with a phone and iPad, but now, he's tryin'a step it up a bit," Ben told her.

"Oh, Nadia must be the woman Asha met that she was telling me about," Devyn said.

"Yeah, I introduced them the night we were at dinner," Ben nodded.

"Oh, okay."

This was the first time Devyn heard anything about Asha going to dinner with Ben. Her friend hadn't mentioned *that* at all. Then again, Asha had dinner meetings with clients all the time, so it wasn't out of the ordinary. Suddenly, the soft R&B that was playing stopped and switched to an upbeat hip-hop tempo.

"Welp, here comes Nigel," Ben announced. "Let the fun begin."

"What's up, people? I see we got a full house, and it's only our first time doing this. Y'all ready to burn?" The chef danced as he made his way to his position at the front of the audience. His energy was magnetic. People clapped and danced along in their seats. Everyone except Devyn, that is. She didn't move as she stared at him. His eyes met hers, and he grinned even wider. It was him. The one she couldn't stop thinking about, wondering about, smiling about, since that night. Here they were again. Weeks later, the same place, damn near the same time. The only difference this evening: she was on a date with his friend.

Chapter 12

Asha

The movie was halfway over, and Asha had no clue what was going on. She was too preoccupied with the thought of Devyn's date with Ben to even care about what Samuel L. Jackson was doing on the screen. For the past hour, she'd resisted the urge to take out her phone and send a text asking how things were going. Things had to be going well, Asha was sure. First, because Ben was enjoyable to be around. He'd been quite enthused when Asha gave him Devyn's number and told him she was expecting his call. Another good sign was that Devyn hadn't sent a 9-1-1 text signaling for Asha to call with a fake emergency.

"Whoa!" Sully jumped in his seat, scaring Asha and causing her to scream. He put his arm around her and whispered. "That was crazy, huh?"

Asha nodded as if she knew what he was talking about. "Yes."

Her watch vibrated and lit up at the same time. Asha quickly turned her wrist over to read her caller ID. Seeing that it was Chastity and not Devyn, she hit *ignore*. She's probably checking to see if I heard from Dev. Asha settled back in her seat and tried to focus. A few minutes later, Chase called again, and once more, Asha ignored the call. She sent a quick text through her watch, pretending not to see the annoyed look on Sully's face in the darkness. Then she snuggled next to him for the remainder of the film.

"That was a damn good movie," Sully said as they walked toward the car.

"It really was," Asha agreed, hoping if she did, it would limit any detailed discussion. Sully opened the door, she got in, and immediately took out her phone. There was still no call from Devyn, but in addition to the two missed calls, Chase sent a text asking Asha to call her back as soon as possible. She was about to dial her number when Sully got into the car.

"No phones," he commented. "Devyn is a grown woman. You don't have to check on her."

"I wasn't checking on Devyn. I was actually returning Chase's calls," Asha replied.

"And she was probably calling because she was checking on Devyn, right?" Sully glanced at her from the corner of his eye.

"Maybe." Asha shrugged, hating the fact that he was probably right.

"I think the two of you need to give her some space. She'll fill you in on the details when she gets home. You can wait until then. Now, where would you like to eat dinner?" Sully reached over and held her hand.

"It doesn't matter." Asha put her phone back in her purse.

"Outback, it is," Sully said.

Later, as they sat across from each other in the restaurant sharing a Bloomin' Onion, Asha took the opportunity to ask about Ingrid and her ex finally. As much as she disliked discussing his daughter, if she were going to find out what happened, she would have to ask because he hadn't brought it up at all. And she still owed Devyn the details.

"So, has Ingrid heard anything else about Bear?" Asha made sure to sound as innocent as possible.

"No, thank God. Rumor is he came into some money, and that's why he's back," Sully said. "Ingrid hasn't had any contact with him, though. He's had enough sense to stay away from her."

"That's good. I wouldn't want him to hurt her again like he did before." Asha looked over at him.

"That's an understatement. My baby was messed up for a long time behind him," Sully told her. "She was so scared, she dropped out of school and couldn't work for months. She's still not right."

"How long ago was this?"

"About three years. Bear started out being a nice guy. Everybody loved him. He played semipro ball after college, then moved back home and started working a decent job. He treated Ingrid real good at first. Then he started getting high, missing work," Sully explained.

"Is that when he became abusive?" Asha frowned.

"I guess. All I know is Ingrid called me. He was screaming in the background, saying he was gonna kill her and make her pay. By the time I got to her house, he was gone. Her house was torn up. Looked like a tornado ripped through there. She was curled up in the corner, crying and terrified. That bastard's hand marks were still around her neck." Sully's voice cracked. He cleared his throat. "I wanted to call the police, but she wouldn't let me at first. He skipped town before I could find his ass. She moved back home the next day and stayed until I helped her get a new place. I made sure she had a gun and could protect herself. She healed physically, but emotionally and mentally was another story."

"Wow," Asha exhaled and held his hand tighter. Hearing what Ingrid had gone through with her ex almost made her feel a little sorry for her. Ingrid was manipulative, spoiled, and vexatious, but that didn't mean she deserved to be assaulted. Now that she learned about

Bear, and what he did, Asha was even more perturbed that she'd been in the same room with an abusive, unemployed, dope fiend.

By the time they finished dinner and were back at Sully's, Asha still hadn't heard anything from Devyn, but Chase called again. This time, she answered. Luckily, Sully was in the shower.

"No, I haven't heard anything from Dev. Have you?" She asked without saying hello, making sure to talk low.

"Nope, I haven't either. Which means she must be having a decent time." Chase said. "I have a question."

"What is it and talk fast," Asha told her.

"Oh God, are you sneaking on the phone? Shouldn't your senior citizen be in bed asleep by now?" Chase moaned.

"Chastity, what do you want?" Asha sighed.

"Did you promote the webpage for Pivot?"

"No, why?"

"It's getting mad hits. Something weird is going on," Chase said.

"There's just a landing page. Other than you and me, no one else knows about it. How could it be getting traffic?" Asha frowned.

"Asha, this thing has gotten 3,000 hits tonight. Somebody knows something. You think Devyn maybe has something to do with it?"

"Chase, we can't even get Dev to get business cards."

"True. I don't know. Maybe it's a glitch. That's so strange, though," Chase murmured.

"You think it's been hacked?"

"No, it hasn't been hacked."

Asha heard the bathroom door opening. "I don't have my laptop with me. Call me in the morning, and we can look at it together."

"Okay, will do. Go watch the eleven o'clock news with your boo while I go get ready to hit the club," Chase laughed. "Love you, Ash."

"Love you too, heffa," Asha responded.

"Couldn't resist, huh?" Sully entered the bedroom and asked. "Had to check in with her."

"I wasn't checking in on anyone, Calvin Sullivan. Stop that." Asha shook her head.

Sully got into bed beside her. "So, you didn't just say love you too? I know it was Devyn. Or is there someone else I need to be worried about you saying those words to?"

"Good night, Sully." Asha adjusted her pillow and snuggled under the covers. Arguing was the last thing she felt like doing. She wanted to go to sleep, and that's what she did. A few hours later, she rolled over and opened her eyes. She thought she was dreaming when she saw Sully sitting up in bed, his phone in one hand, while the other was fumbling under the blanket in his lap. *I gotta be tripping. What the hell?* Asha blinked a few times to confirm he was doing just what she thought. Is this nigga watching porn and doing himself while I'm in bed with him?

"Sully, what the hell? Are you beating—?"

Asha's shriek startled him, and he fumbled his phone, dropping it in his lap.

"Asha, what's wrong with you?" he growled.

"Me? *You're* the one having a personal porn viewing party while I'm lying right here beside you." Asha sat up.

"Calm down, Asha. You got the nerve to be talking when you're constantly on your phone: in bed, in the car, and in the movies. Now, since I'm on mine, it's a problem?"

"Uh, I'm not on my phone watching porn, Sully. I'm either working, checking emails, or checking my social media occasionally. That's *way* different," Asha replied.

"And we both know Facebook and Pornhub are two very different sites."

"Whatever, Asha." He got out of bed and went into the bathroom, slamming the door behind him.

Asha jumped up, tossed on her clothes, grabbed her purse, and left. Sully masturbating next to her in bed was terrible, but him having the audacity to deflect and turn it on her was even worse. Had she stayed another moment longer, there was no telling what she would've said to him. It was best that she left. Her mouth could be vicious. Although they'd dated for a while, Sully hadn't felt the wrath of one of her ebonic-filled tirades that undoubtedly would've shocked him. She needed to put some space between them.

As soon as she got home, Asha's initial thought was to call Devyn, who she still hadn't heard from, and tell her what happened. The drive had helped her calm down a bit. The more she thought about it, the more she began to wonder if she'd overreacted. After all, it was just porn. "Isn't that what men do?" But still, it didn't sit right with her for some reason. Why did Sully have to watch it when she was right there next to him? She'd never denied him sex. And it was more of a surprise when they didn't have sex than when they did. *So, why did he feel the need to pleasure himself and not me? Am I tripping? And where the hell is Devyn? I need to talk.*

It was almost two in the morning. She expected her friend would've at least sent a text, but she hadn't. Asha quickly pulled up her contact information in her phone and confirmed that at least Devyn had made it home. Wait, maybe Ben is there with her. Perhaps that's why she hasn't called yet. I can't even say I'd blame her for that. The man is fine as hell. Deciding that no news was good news, Asha decided just to wait it out.

Even in the comfort of her own bed, Asha still couldn't sleep. She pulled out her laptop and pulled up the Pivot website to see what Chase was talking about. Sure enough, the traffic to the site was close to 4,000. Why anyone would be visiting it, she didn't know. Something was driving people to the site. She pulled up the only other place website listed, the Pivot Instagram page she'd created.

"Oh shit." Asha's mouth dropped when she saw the video that was tagged to Pivot's page. Her heart began racing as she watched Devyn walk across the library meeting room. And it wasn't just any walk. D'Morgan had reemerged right before her eyes. She was pure perfection, and so was the video, which had been edited with music and graphics. There was even a slow-motion effect as Devyn turned and posed. Had they needed a promotional video, it would've been ideal. Despite Devyn being a little more comfortable with Pivot's creation, she wasn't ready to be at the forefront. But there she was, front and center, looking fabulous as always.

"It's the walk for me. Our Coach Miss Devyn slays each step. #pivot #pivotpageantcoaching #runwaygoals" the caption read. When she saw the post, which had thousands of likes and comments, was posted by @ Journi2Success, Asha shook her head. This was not good. She slowly breathed as she zoomed in on the number of views, which was over 50,000. To make matters worse, she saw that the video had been shared by thousands of accounts, including those with little blue checks indicating that the owners had been verified.

"Honey, I don't know about Miss Dev or pageant coaching, but I know that walk anywhere. That obviously is the one and only D'Morgan, one of the best. Glad to see she's still got it."

Scorpio, of all people, had made the comment. Had anyone else received that large of a compliment from one of the world's most famous supermodels, they would've been ecstatic. However, Asha knew that Devyn wouldn't see it that way. Scorpio was the last person Devyn would have ever wanted to say anything. The knockdown, drag-out at the wedding was one thing, but Scorpio's appearance later in Tremell's video was the ultimate betrayal. The hurt that Devyn felt from Scorpio's actions was even more profound than Tremell's. She wanted nothing to do with either one of them. And now, not only had her friend been outed, in a sense, but she'd also gone viral. The spotlight that she'd escaped from was headed back in her direction. Asha had to do something fast, but she was going to need backup.

Chapter 13

Devyn

The first thing Devyn noticed when she woke up on Sunday morning was that her face was hurting. She couldn't remember the last time she'd laughed and smiled so long. Couples cooking class at Culture Culinary Lab had been a fun-filled experience and one that she would never forget, thanks to Chef Nigel Brewer, who went above and beyond to keep his pupils entertained, especially Devyn.

"All right, let's get started. Tonight's theme is Southern Charm. We will be preparing Shrimp and Parmesan Grits, Buttermilk Fried Chicken Bites, and for our veggies, we're gonna make an Arugula Salad with homemade dressing. Dessert will be Chocolate Pecan Pie with Bourbon Whipped Cream. It's about to get hot in here, like some of you beautiful ladies." Nigel smiled and looked directly at Devyn, then added, *"Right, fellas?"*

The men clapped, including Ben, who didn't seem to notice Nigel's brief stare at her before he began giving instructions. He was the main chef, but Nadia and another guy walked around to make the cooking experience easy and enjoyable. Everyone worked in four teams, with each person given a different task, but nothing too overwhelming, or so they thought. Soon, the aroma of sizzling bacon, garlic, and onion filled the room.

Devyn tried to focus on the step-by-step directions, but between Nigel's comedic delivery making her laugh, and the fact that every time she looked up, he happened to be looking at her, it was nearly impossible. Before she knew it, the shrimp that she was in charge of sautéing while Ben made the grits were burning.

"Oh, Lawd." Nigel teased when he saw her fanning the burnt pan in front of her. He quickly came over and helped. "I would just like to let everyone know that we do offer remedial classes here at Culture Culinary Lab for those of you who may need it."

"Are you referring to me?" Devyn smirked.

"Not at all, Miss . . ." Nigel moved a little closer to read her name tag. "Devyn."

"Our shrimp is just a little well done, Nigel. That's all." Ben made a feeble attempt to defend her honor.

"No, it's way more *than well done.*" Nigel shook his head. "Maybe if you would've worn your glasses, you could see that."

"It's Cajun shrimp." Devyn shrugged. "And I don't even wear glasses."

"Are you sure about that?" Nigel asked.

Devyn frowned, then thought about the fashion frames she had on the first time they'd seen each other. She was shocked that he remembered them. "Those weren't even prescription."

"I tell you what, how about you come with me so you can see better and get a closer look at what we're doing," Nigel suggested with a grin, then turned to Ben. "You don't mind if I borrow her, do you, Ben? Nadia is supposed to be assisting me, but I don't know where she is."

"Not at all, man. Have at it," Ben laughed.

"*All right, class, give it up for my new assistant, Miss Devyn.*" *Nigel escorted her to the front of the room while everyone applauded. They laughed and joked with one another as she stumbled along beside him while he guided them with the remainder of the recipes. It was such a fun-filled environment, so much so that she forgot all about the cameras. It took about another hour for them to finish the menu. Then everyone ventured back into the lobby area for more wine and socializing for about fifteen minutes while the food was plated and the dishes cleaned up. When they returned to their stations, the music was playing again, and everything was set up for them to dine and enjoy the meal they'd created.*

"*This is scrumptious,*" *Devyn said as she tasted her food.*

"*You are right about that. It's incredible.*" *Ben nodded between bites.*

"*Everything good over here?*" *Nigel walked over and asked.*

"*Everything is amazing,*" *Ben told him. "Man, I gotta tell you, this class is lit. I know I teased you about it when you first told me the idea. But, yo, you're on to something, Nigel.*"

"*He's right, this class is everything,*" *Devyn said. "I can't believe you made fun of him. I would think Chef Nigel is the one with the jokes.*"

"*Ben always clowning. But I ain't say nothing when you told us you wanted to be a bus driver. Now, look at you . . . got a choice of buses you can drive, son,*" *Nigel teased. "Party bus, charter bus, Sunday school bus.*"

Devyn, Ben, and the other couple at the station cracked up.

"*Whatever, Nigel. I'm going to get more wine.*" *Ben picked up his empty glass, then turned to Devyn. "You want a refill?*"

"No, but some water would be great," she told him.

Nigel sat in Ben's empty seat. "Thanks for being a good sport and assisting. I appreciate it."

"It was fun. I had a great time," Devyn smiled. There was something about him that made her feel warm inside. He had good energy, and she was drawn to him.

"I'm glad to hear that. As a matter of fact, here, take this." He reached in his pocket and handed her a business card. "Your next class is on me. Just notate the code in the special request section when you register."

Devyn took the card and looked at it. Seeing him again was something she wanted, and for a second, she considered flirting. You can't do that. You're on a date with someone else. That's disrespectful as hell, Devyn. But she had to do something. So, before she thought about it too long and lost her nerve, she asked him, "Is this for another couple's class or a one-on-one?"

Nigel's entire face lit up. "How about you call me later tonight, and we discuss it?"

"I don't have your number," she told him.

"Yeah, you do. It's the discount code on the back of the card." He winked and stood up. Devyn turned the card over and saw the random numbers written on the back.

After they finished their meal, Devyn was so full that she had her dessert packed up to take home. Nigel thanked everybody for coming and asked that they spread the word. Then it was time for everyone to leave.

"Did you enjoy yourself?" Ben asked as they arrived at her house.

"I had a ball. It was so much fun," Devyn told him.

"I had a great time too. Maybe we can do it again sometime. We didn't get the chance to talk tonight. I'm glad you had fun, though," he told her.

"I did. Thank you for inviting me." Devyn felt a twinge of guilt for not being as attentive to her date as she *probably should have been. He was a nice guy, but she wasn't interested in him. She didn't get a vibe that made her want to go out with him again. At least, not right now.*

He opened her car door, and she gave him a brief hug, then went inside. She put her dessert into the fridge and went to her room. Without even undressing, she flopped back on the bed, grinning from ear to ear. She'd had a great night and was glad that she'd gone out. Kudos to Asha for making it happen. Asha. I gotta call her.

Devyn sat up and took her phone out of her purse. There was a text from an unknown number. At first, she thought it might have been from Ben, whose number she had yet to save. She opened it, smiling as she read the message, then called the number.

"Did you really send me a Groupon for an eye exam?" she laughed.

"Hey, I'm just checking on my prize student, that's all," Nigel told her. "I thought about it and wasn't sure if you were gonna be able to see the numbers clearly on the card. I got your number from the sign-in form. I hope that's okay."

"I'm glad you checked on me, but for the record, I can see just fine," Devyn told him.

"If I recall, you said you bumped into me because you couldn't see," Nigel reminded her.

Devyn cackled at his statement as she lay back on her bed. For the next five hours, they talked on the phone: chatting the entire time he and his team cleaned up the studio, making sure everything was put away, and then locked up the building. Their discussion continued as he drove thirty minutes to his home. She got up and finally ate her dessert while they discussed favorite movies and TV shows. As she put on her pajamas, he listened while she told him about being afraid of the dark until she was well into her teens and still was sometimes. He shared how he was bullied as a kid for being overweight. The conversation between them was natural, easy, and flowed without any awkwardness or dead spots. Nigel was comical, very intelligent, and knowledgeable. Devyn recognized that he was multifaceted. There was more to him than being a chef. Before she knew it, they'd both fallen asleep on the phone. She didn't get to say good night. But she was pleased that when she woke up, he'd sent a cute message and asked her to meet him for brunch. Without hesitation, she accepted. With less than an hour to get to the restaurant, she rushed to get ready.

Cute, comfy, and casual in her joggers, T-shirt, and favorite Nike Air Max, Devyn tossed a baseball cap on her head, grabbed another pair of her fashion frames, and slipped them on her face. Instead of the Prius, she decided to drive the convertible Benz that she hardly used. The light, airy ride would match her mood perfectly. She was backing out of the garage when someone pulled into the driveway and parked behind the Prius. Devyn put the Benz in park and opened the door.

"What the—? Chastity, what are you doing here?" Devyn hopped out, surprised to see her godsister who she'd spoken to less than twenty-four hours earlier. She hadn't mentioned anything about visiting.

"Surprise. I came to see you." Chase walked over and gave her a big hug. "You look cute. Where are you going?"

"A brunch date that I'm gonna be late for if I don't hurry," Devyn told her.

"With Ben? I guess your date went better than you thought. See, you like him." Chastity clapped.

"No, it's not with Ben. It's with someone else. Nigel. I gotta go. I'll tell you about it when I get back." Devyn started backing toward the car. "Go through the garage to get into the house."

"Dev, wait," Chase yelled.

"What is it?" Devyn frowned. She glanced over to see Asha pulling up. "What in the world?"

"Devyn, before you leave, we need to tell you something." Chase walked over.

Devyn's eyebrows furrowed, and she became anxious. Chase and Asha showing up unannounced at the same time couldn't have been a coincidence.

"What's going on?" Devyn turned and asked Chase. When she didn't answer, Devyn directed the question to Asha. "Asha, what's wrong?"

"Dev, let's go inside and talk," Asha replied.

"No, just tell me now. You're scaring me. Did someone die? Is someone sick?" Devyn's heart raced, and her breath became shorter.

"Calm down, Dev. It's nothing like that. Everyone is fine. Jeez." Chase shook her head. "You're about to give yourself a panic attack."

The half smile Chase gave her made Devyn feel slightly better, but she was still uneasy. "Well, whatever it is, can it wait until after I get back?"

"No, it can't," Asha replied.

"Well, it probably can," Chase told her, then after Asha gave her a threatening look, she added, "but maybe we should just spill it."

Devyn looked at Asha. "What up?"

Asha took a deep breath. "Okay, we got a lot of hits on the Pivot website all of a sudden."

"I thought you said the website wasn't up yet. It was still under construction until we decided it was time." Devyn frowned.

"It is, well, it's just a landing page, that's all. But we didn't do anything to promote it yet," Chase explained.

"Which is why we were wondering why it was getting so much traffic."

"Well, what the hell is on the page? My name and picture aren't on there, right?" Devyn gasped.

"No, It's just the name, logo, and services offered. That's it," Chase said.

"Good." Devyn exhaled. "For a second, I thought y'all were about to say people knew I was coaching."

The sudden look Asha and Chase gave each other didn't go unnoticed. Devyn instinctively knew that whatever they were about to tell her, she wouldn't want to hear.

"Dev," Asha's voice softened, "the traffic to the website was because Pivot Coaching was tagged in a video posted on IG, a video of *you*."

Devyn closed her eyes, and her mind flashed back to Journi, holding her phone. "Fuck. I told Journi to delete it."

"I'm sorry, Dev. She didn't." Asha touched her shoulder.

"People don't know that it's me, though, right? The girls don't know that . . . who . . . I . . . We never told them," Devyn stammered.

Chase moved so that they now faced each other. Devyn was almost a foot taller than she was and had to look down.

"People recognized you, Dev, and the video went viral," Chase said.

The video went viral. Viral. Viral. The words echoed in Devyn's head as she jumped into the car and peeled out of the driveway. Life as she knew it was about to change. She wanted to get the hell away from her girls, her house—everything.

Chapter 14

Asha

Asha watched as Devyn pulled off so fast, the tires of the car burned rubber, leaving a cloud of black smoke. Her friend's reaction had been mild compared to what she expected. Asha had prepared herself to be cursed out, insulted, and possibly having something thrown in her direction. The conversation being held outside probably helped the latter not happen.

"That went well," Chase sighed.

"You think?"

"Yeah, she still left the door open for me to get inside and didn't tell me to leave." Chase nodded. "She has been known to kick me out."

"Yes, she has." Asha thought about the times in the past that Devyn and Chase had gotten into a fight that resulted in Chase getting put out until Devyn calmed down a day or so later. Even she'd been on the receiving end of her hot-tempered friend's tirades too many times to count, but she'd never been in a position for Devyn to kick her out. She knew better.

"Where the hell is she going? Should we go after her?" Asha turned around and asked.

"I think we should give her a little time. She might still be headed to her brunch date." Chase shrugged, then walked over to the car that was parked behind Devyn's. After opening the trunk, she took out a large suitcase and another bag.

"Brunch date? With whom?" Asha frowned.

"Don't know exactly, but it's not with Ben. I did ask that." Chase closed the trunk. Asha grabbed one of the bags and followed her inside Devyn's lavish home, compliments of Uncle Julian. The place looked like something out of a design magazine with its spacious layout and natural lighting. If he ever wanted to sell it, undoubtedly, he could get at least a million for it, if not more. It was definitely a dream home, and Devyn was lucky to be able to enjoy living there rent-free.

While Chase took her bags upstairs to the guest room, Asha found her favorite spot in the Moroccan-themed family room: Uncle Julian's recliner. Because of his six-foot, seven-inch height, he searched high and low until he found one that wouldn't make him feel like a grasshopper with his knees to his ears when he sat in it. Asha instantly fell in love with the oversized chair that was more like a mini–love seat.

"Now, what do we do?" Chase asked as she came into the room.

"I don't know," Asha told her. "I mean, we just have to wait and see what Dev wants to do. I thought about telling Journi to take the video down, but that would be pointless, huh?"

"Yep, it actually made The Shade Room this morning." Chase took out her phone and pulled up the popular gossip site for Asha to see. In addition to Devyn's recent video walking, there was an older one of her in a swim-suit show in Miami Fashion Week. Her friend looked phenomenal in both videos, and Asha almost got excited until she saw two other pictures in the brief article. One that captured Devyn and Tremell at the altar in the exact moment that everything happened and another more recent photo of him in the VIP section of some club, surrounded by groupies.

"Shit," Asha sighed. "Dev's gonna flip when she sees this."

"I know. I wish she would stop acting like she did something wrong and has to hide when that's not the case. She's not the bad guy here," Chase pointed out. "The difference between Devyn and Tremell is that he used that moment in the spotlight to his advantage and embraced it. She ran from it."

"She didn't run from it. A whole lot of shit happened at once," Asha said, but in a way, she knew Chase was right. Her friend would never have done to him what he'd done to her.

While Devyn had been hospitalized right after the wedding, Tremell had done interviews with every single media outlet he could find. He made Devyn out to be some erratic, unstable monster who couldn't handle the fact that he wasn't ready to settle down. His newfound fame landed him a deal with a major label, and while Devyn was grieving from the loss of her mom, he released not only a song, but also a video reenacting their wedding, using a model who looked just like Devyn. On top of that, Scorpio, Devyn's mentor and friend, made a cameo appearance in the video. Devyn became a joke. She decided the only way to escape was to retire the professional pseudonym she used as she rose to stardom, and instead, use her legal first name along with her mother's maiden name. This gave her a fresh start and a new life.

"We're gonna figure this out," Chase reassured her.

"How long are you staying?" Asha asked.

"As long as it takes." Chase shrugged. "I probably should've never left."

While Devyn was recovering from her illness, grief, and depression, Chase put her life and education on hold. When Asha couldn't be there, Chase was. They were committed to Devyn and tag teamed to do whatever they needed to do to help her: doctors' appointments, household chores, packing up her things from her old apartment she shared with Tremell. They made sure it was all done, and her life was as stress-free as possible. Slowly, Devyn began getting better. When Uncle Julian, who'd also been a great support, announced he was moving out of the country, they assured him Devyn would be in great hands. After he left, Asha was nervous that Devyn would regress, but she didn't. Soon, she was stable and strong enough to be on her own. That's when Chase went back to finish up her degree. Her showing up for the latest crisis at the drop of a dime came as no surprise.

"Well, I guess we need to get started." Asha pushed down on the chair and stood.

"I guess so," Chase agreed. "We're gonna need some extra guidance ASAP."

They entered the kitchen. Chase went to the cabinet and took out the canister that held Devyn's special brew bags while Asha put water into the kettle and found two mugs. Minutes later, teacups in hand, they went to the deck and settled down into the chairs.

"Aren't we supposed to have music for this?" Asha asked.

"Oh, I forgot about that." Chase reached into her back pocket and took out her phone. "What do we listen to?"

"Something peaceful," Asha suggested. "I know . . . Maxwell."

Chase hit the button, and "Pretty Wings" began playing. Asha felt it was a fitting song. After taking a long sip of tea, she sat back and listened with her eyes closed, then told herself to . . . Stop, Inhale, Process repeatedly in her head the way she'd learned from Devyn's mom when she was little. She was supposed to be focusing on Devyn and her situation, but for some reason, Asha couldn't stop thinking about her own. She'd expected a phone call or at least a text from Sully apologizing for the night before, but she hadn't heard from him at all. He hadn't even reached out to see if she made it home after leaving his place. Certainly, he couldn't have been expecting her to call him after he had been the one in the wrong. This had been the first time since meeting a year ago that they hadn't at least spoken to each other daily. He probably didn't have time before leaving for church this morning. *It's First Sunday, and you know he has to serve communion at both services. He'll call later. Stop tripping.*

"You think she still went on her date?"

"Huh?" Asha snapped back to reality, wondering why she was the only one meditating when they were supposed to be doing it together.

"Devyn. Do you think she went to brunch?" Chase asked.

"I doubt it. She's probably driving around, that's all," Asha answered. "I have her location. Let me check it."

She went inside and grabbed her phone. Curiosity got the best of her, and she checked to make sure Sully hadn't left a voicemail. After seeing that there were no missed calls, she checked to see where Devyn was located.

"Find her?" Chase asked when Asha stepped back out onto the deck.

"I did," Asha said, still surprised at what she discovered. "She's at Sage."

"The restaurant?"

The look on Chase's face let Asha know that she was just as shocked that their friend was at one of the most exclusive restaurants in the city where brunch reservations had to be made months in advance. The only time Asha had ever gone was when one of her clients, who owned one of the largest tax preparer agencies in the country, hosted an anniversary party there.

"Yep." Asha nodded.

"Dressed in sweats? She can't be. Stop lying." Chase reached for the phone and stared at it. "Nah, ain't no way."

"You see it for yourself." Asha sat back down and drank her tea. Her phone rang, and she looked down. Instead of seeing Devyn or Sully's name, she saw Ben's. She glanced over at Chase. "It's Ben. I thought you said she wasn't with him."

"She's not," Chase said.

"Then why is he calling?"

"Answer and see," Chase told her.

Asha paused before saying, "Hey, Ben."

"Hey, Asha, how are you?" His voice was smooth and pleasant.

"I'm great. What about you?" she asked.

"Same here. Did I catch you at a bad time?"

"Not at all." She motioned for Chase to turn down the volume so that Maxwell, who was now singing "Fortunate," was no longer blasting in the background. *He's probably thinking I'm laid up with a man.*

"Well, I was calling for two reasons. One, to let you know how great of a time I had with Devyn last night. It was a lot of fun. Thank you for the introduction," he said.

"I'm so glad," Asha said, wondering if he was about to mention that they were together at the moment.

Instead, he said, "And the second thing is I gave your information to a friend of mine who's planning a vintage car show in a few months. I told him you were the go-to person to get things done."

"Yes, I am," Asha told him. "I appreciate the referral, Ben."

"Speak to you later this week. Enjoy the rest of your weekend," Ben told her before he hung up.

"I take it they weren't together," Chase smirked. "And isn't it weird that he's calling you?"

"No, they weren't," Asha said. "Not really. He was giving me a heads-up on a referral he sent my way. He was also probably using that as a reason to call to see if Devyn said anything to me about their date, which she hasn't because she's out with someone else at Sage."

"Lucky, Dev. Well, anyway, so that you know, I just checked the emails and messages for Pivot, and there are quite a few. Requests for interviews, people asking how to sign up for coaching, or if Pivot will be offering workshops, and, of course, the sleazy requests for nudes and sexual favors. This sudden popularity doesn't have to be a bad thing."

"Yeah, but that's the thing . . . People aren't associating Pivot with Devyn. They're associating it with who she used to be," Asha said, nervously twisting her locs.

"You do know they're the same person, right? It's not like Devyn had sexual reassignment or something."

"I know that. But we both know she's gonna want to shut it down. There's no way we're gonna convince her otherwise," Asha said. "People are always gonna connect her to Tremell."

"Maybe not anymore," Chase murmured and stared at her phone. "I believe he's officially connected to someone else."

"Oh God, please don't tell me that bastard got married," Asha pleaded. The last thing Devyn needed to hear after what they'd told her was that Tremell had a new wife.

"No, not married."

"Thank God," Asha exhaled.

"It's worse than that." Chase passed her cell phone, and as Asha stared at the screen, she realized that Chase was right.

Chapter 15

Devyn

"So, your best friend and li'l cousin are at your house waiting for you, and you're here with me. I feel kind of special." Nigel pretended to pop his collar.

Devyn shook her head. "Best friend and godsister, but, yeah. They're probably debating whether to call the cops right now because I left so fast while they were standing in the driveway."

After leaving the house, she called Nigel to tell him she couldn't make it. He recognized the distress in her voice and convinced her to meet him to talk. They met in the restaurant's parking lot, walked across the street to a small park, and sat on a bench. At first, she tried to give him a vague overview of the situation, explaining that her ex had violated her privacy after their breakup a few years earlier, and she was still dealing with the aftereffects. However, she then found herself doing something she'd never before done . . . telling him everything. Nigel listened. He didn't ask any questions or make comments as he passed her a crumpled Culture napkin from his jacket pocket to wipe the tears she shed. He just let her talk until she finished.

"So, what would make this situation better for you?" he asked.

"If somehow that video disappeared, and no one would've ever seen it," Devyn answered.

"Which video? The one your pageant trainee posted, the one your ex made mocking the wedding, or is there another one?"

"All of them. I want them all to disappear forever as if they never existed," Devyn told him. "And while I'm at it, I want this stupid illness gone too."

"So, in a way, you wish you never existed, huh?" Nigel frowned slightly.

"No, not me. D'Morgan, *that's* who I wish would just disappear forever, and she had—until that stupid video. Now, I have to deal with it all over again. The hurt, shame, and embarrassment. I want to go back to who I was before that damned wedding." Devyn stared at the ground, remembering how great her life was up until the moment Tremell made a mockery of her in front of the world.

"Unfortunately, none of that's possible. And from what I'm looking at here, I wouldn't want D'Morgan to go anywhere."

Devyn glanced over and saw him looking at his phone. "What are you doing?"

"Looking at pictures of D'Morgan. She's a bad chick. Damn." Nigel nodded. "I'm impressed."

"Please don't, Nigel. I'm serious." Devyn immediately became self-conscious and tried to grab his phone, but he pushed her away.

Devyn stood up to leave. "You know what? I don't have to deal with this. I'm out."

Nigel grabbed her hand. "Devyn, stop. Don't leave. Come on, talk this thing through with me."

"There's nothing else to talk about. We've sat here for almost an hour, and I told you everything. That's it. I'm not gonna sit here and be humiliated while you look at memories of a past I'm trying to forget. What's the point?" Devyn glared at him.

"The point is, yeah, you told me the details of what happened and how you're feeling. But what are you gonna do about it?" He stood and towered over her. He was dressed just as casual as she was in jeans, T-shirt, Jordans, and baseball cap. As he took a step closer, she easily recognized the scent of the Bond Number 9 cologne he was wearing.

"What am I supposed to do? I can't make the video disappear, and I can't get my old life back. I have to deal with D'Morgan forever until I die." Devyn shook her head.

"Then stop trying to bury her," Nigel insisted. "Learn to live with her and then outshine her ass."

Devyn looked at him as if he were speaking some foreign language because she had no idea what he was saying. "What?"

"Devyn, stop giving your power and energy away. Every time you try to escape something that's a major part of you, that's what happens. We give away the power to change the narrative and allow people and situations to control us." Nigel's eyes became dark. "You've gotta stop that. You don't want people to remember what happened to D'Morgan back then . . . so, show them how amazing Devyn is now. Take back the power from D'Morgan and your damn ex."

"That's what I was trying to do by moving here and rebuilding my life."

"No. Sounds like you were running away and trying to hide from a whole lot of shit."

Devyn flinched, jolted by his words. Tears began to form in her eyes again. Nigel pulled her back to the bench, and they sat down.

"I get it. I know what it feels like to be judged and ridiculed for some bullshit that was no fault of your own, so you get as far away from it as you can. That's exactly what I did. No matter what, it wouldn't change what had happened. Then I decided to be happy and reminded myself that what went down doesn't define who I am. It didn't take away my dreams or my visions for the life I wanted. And if I really wanted better, I was going to have to make it happen," Nigel shared. "I embraced me—all of me—my past, present, and future. I took my power back. That's what you've gotta do."

"I don't even look like that anymore. I can't be D'Morgan again. The doctors said that I couldn't . . ." Devyn sniffed.

"I didn't say be *her*. I said, be *you,* whoever that is." Nigel stopped her. "But you can't fully be who you are until you acknowledge that D'Morgan is a part of you. Her hiccups are your hiccups, but damn, so are her accomplishments and accolades. Own that shit, Devyn. Build on it. Don't you see that's what your ex did? He built his brand around you. He took your brand and used it to his advantage. Why can't you do the same thing?"

Devyn had never looked at it like that. She'd spent all her efforts and energy trying to forget Tremell and everything that had happened, while he took every opportunity to highlight it. For a while, everywhere she looked, he was there: TV, the radio, magazines. The more Touché shined, the harder she tried to lose herself in the shadow. She always thought he did it to hurt her, and maybe he did. He damn sure used it as leverage to stardom. Perhaps Nigel was right. It was time for her to somehow benefit from who she used to be.

"I need to find a way to use D'Morgan as a stepping-stone." Devyn said the words out loud, more for herself than anyone else. "Make whatever I do next so big that people forget about her."

"Ding. That's correct. Tell her what she's won, Charlie." Nigel's game show host imitation made her smile.

"I hope it's some food because I'm starving," Devyn commented.

"Hell, my stomach has been growling since we walked over here. Why do you think I've been talking so loud? I was tryin'a make sure you didn't hear it."

"You weren't loud enough," Devyn laughed.

"Wow, see, this is what I get for tryin'a play Doctor Iyanla and help you fix your life instead of going to get my grub on down the street," Nigel teased as he stood up. "Come on, let's go eat."

Devyn walked beside him as they exited the park and walked until they arrived at a Hammond's, a small oyster bar in the same shopping center where they'd parked. Devyn had never even seen the place before. Most likely because it was two doors down from Sage, an exclusive restaurant that people raved about.

"Folks go to Sage when they want to look good," Nigel told her after they'd been seated. "Folks come to Hammond's when they wanna eat good."

Nigel was absolutely right. Devyn enjoyed some of the best chicken and red velvet waffles she'd ever had. She also enjoyed the conversation and getting to know Nigel even more.

"We really want Culture to be a vibe venue where people can enjoy unique social experiences. Everyone doesn't like hanging out at the club all the time. Culture is a place you can come, meet people, network, and do something interactive at the same time. The large rooms are big enough to hold sip-and-paint classes, line dancing, wine tastings, mixology demos, and other stuff. We're trying to develop a couple of things for the senior citizens to enjoy twice a week during the day. That's gonna be on Nadia, though. That's her thing. She's the artist in the family. She did most of the artwork in the building and has a studio that she works out of. We're still in the developmental stage, but it's gonna come together."

"I loved the artwork. It's the coolest thing ever." Devyn smiled. She didn't go out much, but if she did, Culture would definitely be an option that she would consider. She used to love doing interactive activities like bowling and arcades. This was right up her alley.

"Wanna hear something crazy?" Nigel asked.

"Crazier than what's going on in my life?" Devyn gave him a knowing glance.

"Yep. My grandmother used to clean that bank for years. When they moved, and the building was sitting there empty, Nadia used to say, 'We should buy it.' I thought she was crazy, until one day, I was like, 'She's right.' We had no idea what we were gonna do with it. We didn't know how we were gonna pay for it. We just knew it was what we were supposed to be doing. It made absolutely no sense at the time, but we prayed and trusted that we were being guided somehow. Sure enough, once we stopped doubting and fully committed to the fact that this was our purpose, it happened." Nigel leaned back in his chair and shrugged.

Devyn thought about the morning she decided to try coaching. She had agreed to do it and started, but the truth was, she wasn't fully committed. Although she didn't want to admit it, she was still filled with fear. That fear was what caused her to insist on all the rules, regulations, and stipulations. But despite all of them, here she was, having to face the one thing she'd been avoiding: her past.

"My mom used to tell me that sometimes you have to do it scared," Devyn murmured.

"Long as you get it done, that's all that matters."

"Thank you, Nigel, for everything. And to think, I didn't even wanna go last night. Who would've thought." She smiled.

"Why not? Ben's a great guy." Nigel looked surprised. "A woman not interested in Ben Maxwell—that's a first."

"I haven't really been in the dating mood. He's a client of my best friend, and I kinda felt obligated. I had fun, though, as you already know," she pointed out.

"See, you did it scared, and look at what happened. You met your new life coach and was treated to the best brunch you've ever had," Nigel pointed out.

"I did," Devyn nodded. "Now, I have to go back home and hang out with my crew, who probably thinks I've harmed myself."

"We definitely don't want you to do that."

"I won't. I actually feel better. You have given me a whole new perspective. I'm kinda excited."

"You should be. Snatch back your power and control your own narrative. Use it whatever way you want to. And for the record, Touché's music is whack as hell, and I'm pretty sure whatever sex tape he has that everyone is talking about, is just as terrible as his lyrics."

Devyn's eyes widened. "What? What are you talking about?"

"Not that it matters, but that's what was on one of the blogs I saw while searching for you. Wait, it's not a sex tape with *you*, is it?" His face was now just as panicked as hers.

"Hell no, it's not with me," she replied.

"Then that ain't your problem. It's his. You got your own brand to build, remember?"

The friendly waitress who'd served them came to clear the table. "Can I get you guys anything else?"

"Just the check, Jodi," Nigel told her.

She stopped what she was doing and shook her head. "Absolutely not. Now, you know your money is no good here, Bear. Don't insult me."

"Bear?" Devyn hoped that she'd misheard the woman.

"Yeah, a nickname from back in the day that I don't use anymore. Kinda like you and D'Morgan," he laughed.

Devyn managed a weak smile, mentally putting two and two together, praying that she could somehow make it five instead of four. God indeed had a sense of humor.

Oddly enough, the revelation of Nigel possibly being Ingrid's ex somehow became more of a concern than her own viral video or the news about the sex tape starring her ex.

Chapter 16

Asha

The sound of the garage door opening caused instant tension, and Asha gasped slightly. Her eyes darted to Chase, who sat upright on the sofa. They'd already decided that they would be accountable, empathetic, and supportive when talking to Devyn, after allowing her to release the cussing out they were sure she was going to unleash. Asha also agreed that Chase could stay with her for the two-day duration that she would have after Devyn kicked her out. They were a united front with a plan, but Asha was still a little uneasy.

"Hey," Devyn said as she strolled into the great room.

"Hey," Asha and Chase spoke at the same time.

Devyn turned and looked at Chase. "How long did you drive to get here? You must've left pretty early, huh?"

Chase looked over at Asha for a second, then answered. "It took about five hours. I left at around six, but I stopped for gas and snacks."

"Okay, cool." Devyn plopped down on the opposite end of the sofa.

Asha and Chase looked at each other again. It was clear that they were both confused by Devyn's demeanor. They'd expected her to be angry, upset, and shedding uncontrollable tears, and that was *before* they broke the news of the latest update on Tremell.

"How was brunch?" Chase asked.

"It was cool. I had a great time." Devyn nodded and pulled her baseball cap off her head, tossing it on one of the large, leather floor poufs. "What have y'all been doing?"

"Uh, talking and waiting for you," Asha told her. "Who did you have brunch with?"

"Oh, I met with a life coach," Devyn said.

"A life coach?" Asha gave her a look that was just as strange as Devyn's response. Hearing her say that she'd met with a life coach was totally unexpected, especially since Asha had the most challenging time convincing her to see a therapist to deal with the grief, depression, and anxiety she suffered from after losing her mother and everything else. She damn sure didn't go willingly.

"Yeah, a life coach." Devyn shrugged. "As I said, it was cool, and the food was awesome."

"I think that's great, Dev." Chase smiled.

"I can't believe they let you in Sage with those sweats on. Usually, they have a strict dress code, especially on Sundays. Your life coach must have pull," Asha commented.

"We didn't go to Sage," Devyn told her. "We went somewhere else."

"Oh," Asha said, expecting Devyn to share where she'd gone and more information about the life coach that she'd never mentioned before, but she didn't.

"Are you okay?" Chase asked.

"I'm a little better. I'm still processing everything, of course. I can't believe this, though," Devyn sighed. "Like, damn."

"We know, and we're sorry. Neither one of us meant for this to happen, right, Chase?" Asha gave the first line of the speech she and Chase had rehearsed.

"That's right, Dev. And we're coming up with a plan to run interference and PR so everything will be handled.

You won't have to worry about any of that. I'm already on it." Chase nodded her head with assurance. "Asha is gonna meet with Dionne and Journi and—"

"No, you don't need to do that." Devyn stopped her. "I'll handle it."

Asha frowned. "Huh?"

"I'll handle it," she repeated and raised an eyebrow.

Devyn's impassive disposition made her uneasy, and Asha wondered if she was devising some kind of vengeful retaliation against the girls for their error in judgment. The last thing her friend needed was something else for people to talk about. Asha wanted all of this to be over and done with so that Devyn could move past it.

"It's no problem, Dev. This whole thing is my fault anyway and wouldn't have happened if I didn't push you to do the coaching thing. This is on me. I'll deal with them," Asha told her in an effort to be as resourceful as possible. This was a mess she'd indirectly caused, so she felt that she should be the one to clean it up.

"Asha, you don't have to do that. I appreciate the offer, though." Devyn turned to look at Chase, "Both of you. But I'll handle it. All of it."

"Devyn, we just want to be here for you to help you deal. Whatever that means, or whatever it looks like. You need it, and you know we're right here." Chase slid closer and touched her arm.

"I know, and I appreciate you both." Devyn nodded. "As I said, I'm still processing it all right now."

Chase raised an eyebrow at Asha, then said, "Listen, there's something else."

"Oh God, now what?" Devyn leaned her head back and groaned.

Asha braced herself for the impact she knew was coming once they answered Devyn's question.

"Well, there's a sex tape," Chase declared with conviction.

Devyn's head slowly rose, and her mouth gaped open as wide as her eyes. "What? You have a sex tape? With WHOM?"

Chase gasped and clutched her chest as if a pearl necklace were around her neck that she could grab. "Bitch, are you crazy?"

The exchange between the two women happened so fast and was so hilariously unexpected that Asha laughed out loud before she could stop herself.

Devyn looked over and said, "What's funny?"

Asha was too tickled to answer, and the innocent look on Devyn's face as she asked the question made her laugh even harder.

"You know damn well that I don't have a sex tape. With whom, Dev? I can't even find a guy I like well enough to hook up with even randomly. What the hell is wrong with you?" Chase shook her head in disbelief.

"Well, I know Sully and Sleeping Beauty over there damn sure ain't make one." Devyn pointed toward Asha.

Asha's humor faded along with her smile. "Whatever, heffa."

"I'm just saying," Devyn said.

"She does have a point," Chase agreed.

"No, I don't have a sex tape either, Devyn," Asha sighed.

"Then who are y'all talking about?" Devyn asked. Neither Asha nor Chase answered, and she said. "Wait, are y'all talking about Tremell?"

It was a moment before anyone spoke. It was as if they were all stuck for a second. Asha just stared at Devyn as she tried to read her face for some kind of emotion, but she couldn't find any.

"Yeah?" Chase sound more like she was asking than stating.

"A mess, ain't it?" Devyn stood. "I need some tea. Y'all want some?"

"Nah, I'm good." Asha frowned. "Devyn, are you sure you're okay with all of this?"

"Yep, I just have to use my stumbling blocks as stepping-stones, that's all." Devyn's words seemed to be more for herself than them as she strolled out of the room.

"Uh, what was that?" Asha hissed when she was gone.

"That was a welcome surprise. Thank God. See, we were worried for nothing," Chase smiled.

"Naw, now, I'm even more worried. You think she had a breakdown and is in denial?" Asha suggested. "I mean, she even said Tremell's name. She *never* says his name."

"She did. And I don't think it's a breakdown. I think she may be in a bit of shock, and that's understandable. But I think she's taking it all in stride. Good for her."

Chase's lack of concern and mild enthusiasm did nothing to ease Asha's uneasiness. "And when the hell did she start seeing a life coach? What was *that* about? And why did she lie about going to Sage when she knows we have her location?"

"I don't know the answer to any of those questions." Chase shrugged. "But based on her reaction, kudos to the damn life coach and the unlimited mimosas at Sage. Wait, maybe that's it. Maybe she's drunk."

"We know she ain't drunk. If that were the case, she'd be blubbering all over the floor. Devyn is a crying drunk," Asha pointed out. Instead of being relieved that her friend didn't have the emotional breakdown they'd prepared for, she was bothered for some reason. Secrets and lies were two things they swore against keeping from one another, and if Devyn wasn't keeping either of those things, she damn sure was acting like it.

After everything that transpired the day before, Asha found it hard to concentrate on work. Instead of tackling her long "to-do" list and work plan for the day, she spent most of Monday morning being anxious about how exactly Devyn planned on "handling" Dionne and Journi. Subconsciously, she was thinking of public relations and marketing ideas that would allow them to use the viral video to their benefit, just in case they continued with the business, which still had yet to be determined. Asha was hopeful that they would continue with Pivot, but she wasn't 100 percent sure. Devyn's nonchalance about the video situation was still concerning. She wondered if it was because her friend was having some kind of psychotic break or in denial. Devyn was always anxious about something. For her to be this unbothered about something so major, intrusive, and public, something had to be wrong.

"Well, someone is obviously special." Libby strolled into Asha's office, carrying a beautiful bouquet and placed them on her desk.

Asha's eyes widened with surprise. "What in the world?"

"Must be nice." Libby stood with her hands on her hips, smiling at the floral arrangement sitting in front of Asha. "What's the occasion? I know it's not your birthday because that's six months from now."

"No, it's not," Asha sighed, reaching for the small card tucked in the flowers. Sure enough, the message enclosed and the scrawny signature confirmed what she already knew: Sully was the sender. "Thanks, Libby."

"No problem," Libby said. After realizing that Asha wasn't going to give her any more information about the delivery, she walked out.

When she was gone, Asha stared at the flowers. She'd been so distracted by what was going on with Devyn that she hadn't thought about what was going on in her own life. Until the flowers, she hadn't even considered the fact that she and Sully hadn't spoken in two days. Not only that, but she also hadn't processed what happened or how she felt.

"I'm sorry, I was wrong. I miss you. Love, Sully."

Asha reread the card. At least he apologized, she thought. But what exactly was he sorry about? *Is he sorry for indulging in a moment of self-pleasure? Because he shouldn't have to apologize for that. Is it because he did it in bed beside me while I was asleep? Then again, if I'd been awake while he was rubbing one out, I doubt if I would feel any better. Or is his apology because he popped off on me when he got caught? Maybe that's it. He's apologizing because I caught him in the act.* Asha was so confused. This was the worst time for all of this to be happening. Despite not being ready to have the conversation, she decided to call him and just get it over with.

"Please don't pick up. Please don't pick up," she whispered with her ear pressed against her work phone, hoping that she'd be lucky enough to leave a voicemail instead.

"Hey," he answered.

"Hey," Asha responded. "I got your flowers. Thank you. They're beautiful."

"I'm glad you like them. I wanted my apology to be an action, not just words."

"Okay." Instead of asking any of the clarifying questions she'd pondered earlier, she decided to allow him the opportunity to speak freely instead.

"Not saying that the flowers are enough of an action, but it is a gesture, if you know what I mean," Sully continued. "I shouldn't have spoken to you in that manner. That was not cool at all. I was caught off guard, and I mean, I didn't know how to respond so I just . . . reacted. I was wrong, and I'm really sorry."

"Okay," Asha said again.

"I wanted to apologize in person yesterday, but when I came by to talk, you weren't home. I figured you probably needed some time and space to kind of think. That's why I didn't reach out via telephone," he explained. "And I guess since you didn't call either, I knew I had to do something. Sending flowers seemed to be the right move."

Asha didn't have the heart to tell him that she'd been so caught up in another situation that she hadn't even thought about the incident. Maybe she did overreact. For sure, she wasn't as angry as she'd been the night it happened. Besides, Sully's apology seemed sincere.

"Were they the right move?" Sully asked when Asha didn't respond to his statement.

"The flowers are nice, Sully. I appreciate them and the apology."

"Whew," he exhaled. "You got quiet on me for a second, so I wasn't sure."

"I think it was just an awkward moment for both of us. I mean, it's . . ." Asha didn't know what else to say. The predicament was both unusual, uncomfortable, and really, she just wanted to move past it at this point. Finally, she said the only word that seemed to fit, "It's resolved."

"I'd still like to see you later and talk, if that's okay," Sully told her. "Maybe we can go to dinner, or I can cook dinner."

"I have a meeting this evening," she replied, opting not to mention that it involved Devyn and the girls. They were barely back on speaking terms, and she didn't want to risk him pissing her off with one of his comments. "I'll call you later tonight, though."

"Sounds good to me. Enjoy the rest of your day, sweetheart," he said before hanging up.

The conversation had gone much better than she'd expected. She was still a little uneasy but decided that the incident didn't seem worth dwelling over. There were more important things that needed her attention. Sully and his midnight self-pleasuring moment was a thing of the past . . . or so she hoped.

Chapter 17

Devyn

Devyn's day at work had gone better than she'd expected. There were plenty of looks, whispers, and comments from the students and staff members who'd seen the video. Thankfully, no one had been disrespectful or disruptive. Most people were more impressed with her former status of being D'Morgan, the runway model, than the tumultuous public humiliation and fight with her now-famous rapper ex-fiancé. Devyn was sure that the incident had also been discussed, but the students and her peers were kind enough not to mention it in her presence. Finding out that she would be substituting for the still-absent Mrs. Hughes was more irritating than anything.

"I thought you said she'd be back after Spring Break," Devyn reminded the principal, Mrs. Warren, who delivered the news after school, conveniently right after excitedly discussing Devyn's former modeling career. "School has been back in session for a week."

"I know, and we expected her to return, but she hasn't. I think she's a little embarrassed about what happened with her husband. I'm sure you've heard the rumors that have been circulating. It's a little hard for her." Mrs. Warren shrugged. "Hopefully, she'll be back soon. Miss Douglass, you're doing a wonderful job covering her class. The students adore you, and so do I."

In the almost four months that Devyn had been a substitute teacher at the school, Mrs. Warren had barely held a conversation with her. Now, Devyn wondered if her sudden niceness was because she knew of Devyn's apprehension about having to teach a subject she knew nothing about or because of the revelation that Devyn and D'Morgan were the same. Either way, it didn't matter because she was still going to be stuck in that class.

"Mrs. Hughes is gonna have to get over it," Devyn murmured when Mrs. Warren walked out of the still-hot-as-hell classroom. She grabbed her lukewarm bottle of Voss and took a long swig. Her school day was over, but she still had to deal with some other students.

"What's up, superstar? We need to chat." Jeffrey strolled into the room. From the look he gave and his animated demeanor, Devyn knew what he wanted to talk about before he even said it.

"Can this wait until tomorrow?" she sighed. "I've talked about this enough today."

"I'm just saying, if I would've known you was gonna be hanging out at Culture last weekend, I woulda slid through."

"What? How do you know I was at Culture?" Devyn frowned.

"Somebody posted some pics of the cooking class, and I saw you. You looked good with your li'l makeup and cute outfit on," Jeff grinned.

"Social media. I should've known," Devyn commented. "People stay posting shit without my permission. Damn."

"Don't be like that. The chick that posted the pics is cool. I don't think she meant any harm."

"That never seems to be the case these days." Devyn plopped down in her seat and took another swig of water. "That's not the point."

"From what I heard, it was lit, and you were quite funny, the life of the party, I mean, cooking class. And here I thought you were a homebody, and you were hanging at the newest hot spot entertaining folks. See how you do?" He shook his head in mock disbelief. "A brother couldn't even get an invitation."

"That's not what I was doing at all, Jeff. I couldn't invite you because I was a guest myself." Devyn smiled, a little pleased at the thought of someone saying she was entertaining. "And I wasn't the funny one. The instructor was."

"Yeah, my boy is funny as hell." Jeff nodded.

"You know Nigel?" Devyn gasped, slightly.

"Yeah, we go way back; grew up together. Remember I invited you to come hang out at the card party because my boy was cooking and I wanted you to meet him?" Jeffrey explained.

"Vaguely," Devyn murmured.

"Well, that's Nigel. He's good people."

"Yeah, he is." Devyn nodded. "Culture is such a unique spot."

"A dope spot, for some dope people, such as yourself. I'm glad to see you getting out and enjoying yourself. You needed it." Jeff's voice was endearing, and it felt like there was something more telling in what he said. Devyn didn't realize she was staring at him until he asked her, "Why are you looking at me like that?"

"Huh? Oh, I just thought when you said you needed to talk to me about something, you were gonna mention something else," she told him.

"Like what?" He frowned.

"Come on, Jeff, you know what I'm talking about. It's been the topic of conversation around here all day." She made her eyes small and peered at him.

"Uh, what? The D'Morgan stuff? What about it? That's old news." He shrugged.

"Old news?" Devyn blinked.

"I been knew who you were since day one."

"How? And why didn't you ever bring it up?" Devyn was shocked to hear this and wondered if he was being truthful or joking.

"I mean, you never mentioned it, so I figured it was something you didn't wanna talk about," Jeff explained. "And come on, D'Morgan is one of those badass chicks guys like me drooled over in college. How could I not know? Remember that silver bikini you wore in *Shape* magazine that time? Boy, the fantasies I have had about—"

"Okay, I get it." Devyn held her hand up to prevent him from saying anything else.

"Aye, I'm a kept man right now, but if I wasn't—"

"I said I get it," Devyn yelled. They laughed until they were both in tears. A moment later, Devyn said, "Thanks, Jeff."

"For what?"

"Just being you, that's all." Devyn nodded.

"Well, I can't be anyone else, right?" Jeff told her. "Ain't no need."

Devyn was certain that he had no idea how powerful of a statement he'd made without even trying. It was as if he'd confirmed what she'd been questioning for the past twenty-four hours. She'd come to terms with having to face her past, but what did that mean for who she was now, and how did it fit in with her future? That was the question.

"Furthermore, what you ladies did was a violation of privacy. Your actions resulted in my having to deal with attention I wasn't seeking. Actions like this are harmful and, in some cases, illegal. You used my image without permission." Devyn's tone was so stern that Journi and

Dionne began to cry. When the girls arrived at the library, they were excited about their viral post and instant fame—until instead of being met with praise, they were instructed to have a seat. Asha, along with Chase, stood in the back of the room and watched as Devyn lectured them.

"W-we're s-sorry," Dionne sniffed. "W-we d-didn't mean t-to hurt y-you."

"She's right, Miss Devyn. We just wanted to brag, that's all. You're the best, and, I mean, we . . ." Journi couldn't even finish her sentence.

"I understand, and I know you had no malicious intent. But there was a reason I said no pictures or videos without permission. You're never supposed to post anyone, not just me, without their consent. Imagine if someone had put a horrible picture of you on their social media without your knowledge. How would *you* feel?" Devyn asked.

"Angry and upset," Journi whimpered.

"Embarrassed," Dionne added.

"Right, and that's exactly how I felt," Devyn told them. "The only reason I even agreed to coach you was because you asked, and I felt like you needed me. Now, I don't know."

Devyn knew it was heartbreaking, but she had to teach them a lesson. Each time she felt the urge to soften, she reminded herself that they needed to understand the severity of what they'd done. She also didn't want to give them any false hope that she would continue being their pageant coach. She still hadn't decided. Asha had asked her right before the girls walked in, but Devyn told her she was still processing, which she was still in the middle of doing even as she spoke.

A knock on the door caused Devyn and the girls to turn around. Asha, who was the closest one to the entrance, opened it and was surprised to see Dionne's parents, whom she'd met during one of the first coaching sessions. They were very friendly and excited about the training she and Devyn were providing the girls. And just as Dionne said, not only did they pay for their daughter's tuition, but also Journi's as well. There was also another woman along with them.

"Good afternoon," Asha greeted them as they entered. The cautionary look the woman with Dionne's parents gave Chase didn't go unnoticed. Devyn knew it was probably due to her half-bald head and chic bohemian attire that most people weren't accustomed to.

"Daddy, Mom." Dionne looked just as surprised as everyone else to see them.

"Hi, Mr. and Mrs. Phillips, how are you?" Devyn nodded toward them.

"Hello, Miss Douglass. Sorry to interrupt, but we need to speak with you," Mr. Phillips said.

"About?" Devyn raised an eyebrow.

"Well, we received a call, and we have some concerns," he said.

The way he said it and the smug look on the other lady's face were a clear indication that whatever it was, it was about to be some bullshit. Devyn glanced over at Asha, who wasted no time and quickly tried to intervene.

"Miss Douglass is actually in the middle of an important discussion with the girls right now. Why don't we go into another one of the conference rooms and talk?" Asha suggested in her most professional voice.

"Considering that this matter involves Miss Douglass, I believe *she's* the one we need to talk to," the woman answered, and the fake smile on her face was just as irritating as the condescending tone of her voice.

"It's fine, Asha," Devyn stated. "I have no problem addressing any issues you may have."

"Dev . . ." Asha went to speak, but Chase touched her shoulder.

"No, Ash. Hold on," Chase whispered.

"Uh, maybe we should discuss this in private." Mrs. Phillips looked nervous.

"What's wrong, Mom?" Dionne jumped up and asked.

"We just need to talk to Miss Douglass, that's all, honey." Mr. Phillips put his hands on Dionne's shoulders. "Someone shared some information with us, and we just have some questions."

Devyn immediately knew what this impromptu visit was concerning.

"I'm sure the information shared was quite eye-opening, am I correct?" Devyn asked. "If so, I would be concerned as well. Whatever questions you all have, feel free to ask them here."

"I don't know if that's a good idea," the woman said.

"I think it's a great idea, and honestly, it really isn't up to you. Who are you again?" Devyn asked of the other woman, well aware of who she was because they researched everything about her and the pageant.

"I'm Marcia Thompkins, director of Miss Teen Elite. It was brought to my attention that you are providing some kind of coaching services to these young ladies," she stated.

"That's correct," Devyn replied. "I am their pageant coach."

"Miss Douglass, do you even have any formal pageant experience?" The arrogant woman stepped toward Devyn. "Because prior to this weekend, I've never heard of you. And to be honest, what I did find after researching you was disturbing."

"Excuse me, Mrs.—" Asha went to speak again, but Devyn interrupted her.

"No, I don't have any formal pageant experience," Devyn answered. "But neither do most of the male coaches in your arena, right? I do, however, have plenty of other modeling experience that I'm sure you discovered. I desire to help these young ladies achieve their dreams, unlike any of the other coaches."

"I hardly think that's the cause for their concern," Mrs. Thompkins huffed. "I have recommended several reputable area coaches for the young ladies' choosing."

"Then to what are you alluding? Could it possibly be the horrible moment in my life that happened to be caught on video, and instead of it remaining private as other people would have it, it was put out for the world to view, judge, and ridicule?" Devyn turned to the Phillips. "I'm sure you all saw the video, and I'd bet that she was the one who showed it to you. Yes, it happened. No, I wasn't on drugs, and I did not have a nervous breakdown. Was I wrong? Absolutely. Worst decision of my life—the relationship, more so than the wedding. Do I have what it takes to coach these beautiful Black queens on grace, dignity, and empower them to win a pageant and be successful in whatever they pursue? Yes, I do. Now, is there anything else you're concerned about?"

Silence filled the room. Everyone stared at Devyn, who looked from one person to the other. Asha was stunned. Never had she heard Devyn speak about what happened to her with such conviction. It was damn near endearing.

"Uh, no. I think you've cleared everything up," Mrs. Phillips grinned.

"I agree," Mr. Phillips nodded.

"Good, now, I have a concern for you, Mrs. Thompkins," Devyn said. "Since you denied Dionne the opportunity to participate in the pageant, why was it necessary for you to contact her parents? Journi is the contestant. Wait. You didn't get the Black girls mixed up, did you?"

"I, well, of course, not." Mrs. Thompkin's face reddened, and she looked around nervously.

"Great, now, if you all would excuse us, we only have the room for another hour. There's still lots of work to do," Devyn announced with a clap of her hands.

The Phillips hugged the girls, then shook Devyn's hand before leaving. Mrs. Thompkins walked out without another word. Asha excused the girls for a water and bathroom break, and they rushed out as well. When the room cleared, Devyn let out a long sigh of relief. Asha and Chase went to her side.

"Devyn, what the hell? That was awesome." Chase threw her arms around Devyn's neck.

"Hell yeah, it was," Asha told her. "You know I wanted to slap that blond witch so hard that them blue contacts woulda popped out of her eyes."

"She was about to go off. I had to stop her. Normally, Asha's the cool, calm, collected one. You handled her ass, though," Chase grinned. "You didn't even need Asha to put on her white-girl voice. You used your own. Now, I wish we had *that* on video."

"No, no more videos, please," Devyn moaned.

"For a moment, I thought you were about to tell the girls you were done," Asha pointed out.

"I was." Devyn looked at her. "That's *exactly* what I was about to tell them."

"What stopped you?" Asha frowned.

"A knock at the door and a wake-up call to finally stop letting people try to use my past as a weapon against me," Devyn told them.

"Damn right." Chase gave her a high five.

"About time," Asha beamed with pride.

Standing up to Mrs. Thompkins reminded her of how fiery she used to be. For the first time in years, she allowed a glimpse of D'Morgan to emerge . . . and it felt good.

Chapter 18

Asha

"Well, I think that's all we need for now," Gail said as she took the papers that Asha and Ben had just signed and placed them in a folder.

"That's it?" Ben frowned.

Asha nodded. "We still have a lot more to do, sir. Right now, all you have is a venue, date, and time."

"And a theme," Ben told her.

"Oh, what is it?" Gail asked.

"We don't have one." Asha shook her head at the thought of all the horrible ideas that Ben had suggested.

"I was thinking maybe 'Turn Up for the Ta-Tas,'" Ben said with a prideful smile. His eyes went from Gail, who was so tickled that she was cackling, to Asha, who hung her head. He gave a quick shrug and asked, "What?"

"That's actually kinda cute," Gail told him.

"No, it's not," Asha laughed. "I refuse to allow you to turn the amazing event you have entrusted me to plan into a 'Boobs and Balloons' party. No way, no how."

"Now that, I love. Boobs and Balloons. Big thing popping. Yes, sir. Do you know how many guys would show up for something like that?" Ben turned toward her.

"Probably a lot, considering it sounds like a stripper convention rather than a fund-raiser for breast cancer," Asha laughed.

"Maybe you can consider it as an after-party idea," Gail added. "You could raise even more money for the cause."

"This meeting is officially over," Asha stood and announced. "Gail, as usual, it's been great seeing you. Email a copy of the contracts over to me, and I'll get them to Ben."

"No problem. Ben, it was a pleasure meeting you. I'll check on those dates for the other convention you mentioned as well. I think this event is gonna be fun, no matter what theme you all decide," Gail said as she walked them out of her office.

"Turn Up for the Ta-Tas." Ben shook Gail's hand.

"Hey, I'm all for it," she told him.

"And I told both of you, it's *not* happening." Asha playfully tugged at Ben's sleeve and told him. "Let's go."

Their meeting with Gail had been successful. Asha was able to negotiate a fantastic cost that fit Ben's budget, and they had a little wiggle room to spare. Based on his reaction when he saw the amount on the contract they'd just signed, Asha knew he was pleased.

"I have to admit, I'm officially excited, Ms. Bailey." Ben grinned as they exited the building. The afternoon was warm and sunny, mimicking exactly how she felt.

"That's great, Mr. Maxwell. I told you not to worry and that everything would be fine. Now, you got the chance to see for yourself," Asha said. "I can also assure you that the car show in November will be amazing as well. I got this. Thanks again for the referral. I'm meeting with Mr. Haven to sign the contract next week."

"Congratulations, and you're right. You definitely know what you're doing. I didn't mention this, but it's crazy. I reached out to the Convention Center before contacting you. They told me the entire month of October was booked. They didn't have anything available until after the new year. I don't know what you did, but I'm glad you did it."

"What can I say . . . I have magical powers," she told him.

"Indeed, you do," he said. "You're better than Frosted Lucky Charms."

Again, Asha hung her head and giggled. "I swear, Ben, you are . . ."

"What?"

Asha was tempted to say the word "corny," but remembered that although she felt quite comfortable around him, he was still a client. She needed to remain professional. Instead, she said, "Unique."

"Is that a good or a bad thing?" he asked, stopping when they got to the edge of the parking lot.

Asha turned toward him, then forced herself not to stare at his handsome face too long. *Lawd, this man is beyond fine,* she thought before quickly glancing away and reminding herself that she was trying to set him up with her best friend.

"It's just an observation," she finally answered, then proceeded into the parking lot.

"Hey, Devyn was right. We have the exact same truck. That's crazy," Ben said when they got to her car.

"This truck? It's a Limited Edition. Are you sure?" Asha frowned.

"Absolutely." Ben took out his phone and showed her a photo of himself standing in front of a truck that was exactly like hers: color, make, model, even the rims.

"Well, damn, and here I thought I was special, and you have the same one," Asha smiled.

"Aw, that means you're as unique as I am, huh?" Ben smirked.

"I guess so," Asha agreed as she unlocked her door.

"Hey, Asha, listen. If you're not busy, how about we head over to Sage for happy hour."

As much as she wanted to take him up on his invitation, Asha had to decline. "Unfortunately, I have a prior engagement. I've been dying to go there too, though."

"We'll have to check it out soon. How is Devyn, by the way? I reached out a couple of times, but she hasn't responded," Ben commented.

"She's actually good. Um, the past couple of days have been kind of busy because Pivot has kind of taken off. She's been working hard on that," Asha explained. Although it sounded like she was making an excuse for her friend's unavailability, she wasn't. Devyn had done a complete turnaround when it came to her attitude toward their latest venture. Not only did she have Chase do a mini shoot of her and uploaded the gorgeous pictures to the website and Instagram page, but she'd also filmed a mini, two-minute video introducing herself: *Devyn Douglass, Professional Modeling and Pageant Coach.* All of this had been done without Asha's knowledge. Although she was elated, she felt a little left out.

"I'm glad things are going well for her." Ben nodded.

"I'm sure she'll reach out soon," Asha reassuringly told him. "I promise, once you get to know her, you won't be disappointed. Don't give up too quickly. Dev sometimes needs to be nudged."

"Noted," Ben said. "I'll also keep trying to come up with an event concept you'll like."

"Please, don't," Asha laughed as she climbed into her truck. They said their goodbyes, and Asha watched him walk away in the rearview mirror. He got into a shiny pickup truck with his company logo on the side, parked a few spaces down, and waved as he drove past. Asha took out her phone and dialed Devyn's number. She was going to have to do a little nudging of her own.

***

"Devyn Douglass!" Asha yelled as she walked into Devyn's house a little while later.

"Why the hell are you coming in here yelling like the damn police?" Chase walked out of the kitchen, eating a bowl of cereal.

Although it had only been four days since they'd seen each other, something was noticeably different about Chase. Asha mentally counted the colorful tattoos and multiple ear piercings, but nothing looked new. Her head was still half-shaved; the shoulder-length hair that remained was now braided and pulled into a bun. And it was no longer purple but a deep auburn.

"The hair," Asha murmured.

"What about it?" Chase asked. "You like it?"

"It's red, not purple. And when did you get braids?"

"Last night. I was bored. You should let me color your locs. They would be fabulous. Give you a little flair," Chase suggested, walking over to the sofa and curling her legs under her after sitting.

"I'm good," Asha told her, then turned toward the steps and yelled, "Devyn, why didn't you answer your damn phone?"

"Stop yelling. She ain't even here," Chase said between slurps of milk.

Asha frowned, both from the agitation of the sound and from what Chase said. "What do you mean? I checked her location before I drove over here."

"She must've left her phone. Dev is definitely not in this house. She came home, changed clothes, and dipped out."

"Where did she go? You didn't tell her about that blog story suggesting that she's the woman in Tremell's stupid sex tape, did you?" Asha remembered the dumb post that they'd read the day before that they'd kept from Devyn.

"Of course, I didn't. I don't know where she went. She didn't say, and I didn't ask. I think if she left her phone, she won't be gone long. She's probably with her life coach. She never takes her phone when she has a session with Iyanla, Dr. Phil, or whoever is fixing her life these days." Chase shrugged, then turned the bowl up into her mouth like a sippy cup.

"Why wouldn't you ask where she was going, Chastity? What if something happens to her or she gets sick? How will we know where she is? And who the hell is this life coach? I swear, I told you to come here to help out, and you're just chilling." Asha gave a frustrated sigh. Devyn was God knows where with God knows who, and instead of worrying, Chase was munching on Honey Nut Cheerios like a toddler.

"First of all, I have been helping a lot. Who do you think has been managing the social media accounts, updating the website, and fielding emails this week? I took those bomb-ass pictures of Dev, shot the video, and I'm scouting locations for the shoot with the girls. Lastly, Devyn is a grown-ass woman. What I look like asking her where she's going? You know better than that, Asha." Chase set the empty bowl on the floor and looked Asha up and down. "I'm not Devyn's babysitter, and she don't need one. As far as the mysterious life coach, I don't care about that either. This week, she's been the happiest I've seen her in a long time, so whoever it is, kudos to them. Why are you tripping?"

Asha realized that she might have seemed overzealous with her questioning. It wasn't her intention. Devyn being somewhere without her phone and unable to be located bothered her. But Chase was right. Devyn seemed happier, but she'd also been distant. Although they still talked and texted daily, there was a lot that hadn't been shared. This was the first time she'd heard anything about a photo shoot with the girls.

"I'm not asking you to babysit her, Chase. That's not what I meant at all. I'm glad Devyn is handling all this better than we expected. I appreciate you. Hell, at this point, you're just as much a part of Pivot as Dev and I. We should probably discuss your being a full partner. It's just that I don't want her to be somewhere and fall out. What if she needs us?" Asha explained.

"She's fine, Asha. Chill out. You want some cereal? Wait, how about some wine?" Chase smiled.

"Nah, I'm good. I need to get out of here. I'm meeting Sully for dinner."

"Oh, damn, I was about to offer some weed to help mellow you out, but you don't need it. I'm sure y'all talking about Sully's Social Security check while y'all enjoy the Senior Special at Denny's will be relaxing enough for you," Chase teased. "Did you need Devyn to give you one of her special tea brews to keep you awake? She told me how you always fall asleep with him."

"Shut the hell up, Chase. Ain't nobody going to no damn Denny's, and you know it. I came to talk to Devyn about Ben. We had a meeting today, and he mentioned her. She needs to hop on that, or he's gonna be snatched up by someone else," Asha told her, hoping that Chase would see the importance of Devyn not letting this opportunity pass her by and give their friend a push as well.

"I don't know, Ash. I think she don't wanna hop on him. She ain't feeling him."

"Why not? He's perfect for her. Lord, I know Dev's all into building the Pivot brand right now, but she's gonna have to make time for this to happen. She's just gonna have to balance," Asha said matter-of-factly.

"I don't think that's gonna happen, but whatever. If he's such a great catch, then why—" Chase stopped midsentence.

"Why what?"

"Nothin'. Never mind. I'll tell Dev you stopped by." Chase picked up the bowl and walked toward the kitchen. "Set the alarm before you leave."

As she left Devyn's house, Asha's mind was all over the place. She tried to put her thoughts about what was going on with Devyn out of her head and hoped that dinner with Sully would give her something else to think about. She was too distracted, and he noticed.

"Do you think you can make it?" he asked.

"Huh, make what?" Asha blinked, realizing that she had no idea what he was talking about.

"The Jazz Brunch next month. I just said I wanted to get us tickets, but I don't know how your schedule looks." He frowned.

"I'm sorry, Sully. I didn't hear you." She apologized, feeling guilty because she knew he'd gone out of his way to make their evening special. When they arrived at her favorite steakhouse, flowers were waiting for her at the table and a bottle of wine. He was still on a mission to make up for the argument the week before. She had been looking forward to enjoying their night out, but her focus was elsewhere.

"More like you weren't listening. Jesus, woman, your body's here with me, but your mind is on the other side of town," he smirked.

"Huh?" Asha shrugged. "The other side of town? What do you mean?"

"Never mind. It's a song by The O'Jays, sweetie. What's going on?" He reached across the table and grabbed her hand.

Asha sighed, thinking that maybe talking to Sully would give her another perspective on how to handle getting Devyn to be more open to dating Ben. "Well, remember my client, Ben Maxwell? He owns the transportation company and sent the limo to pick us up that night?"

"I'd rather forget about that night." The smile faded from Sully's face.

"This isn't about that night. It's about Ben and Devyn," Asha stressed.

"Okay, what about them?"

"Well, Ben likes her, but Devyn isn't even giving him a chance. She's been talking about meeting a nice guy, and now that she has one in front of her face, she's acting like he's invisible. Guys like Ben Maxwell don't come around every day," Asha told him.

Ben released her hand and used his fork to pick up a piece of the fried calamari in the middle of the table. After chewing it, he said, "Maybe she's not interested."

"You sound like Chastity. Dev hasn't been around him enough to know whether she's interested in him, that's the problem. There's nothing about him for her not to like, believe me." Asha took a sip of her wine.

"I see. Well, if she's not responding, then it's safe to say that she's not interested. Devyn doesn't seem like the type to not know what she wants." Sully took another bite.

"True. But there's gotta be something else, and I don't know what it is."

"So, you think he's that great of a guy?" Sully looked at her.

"Yes," Asha nodded. She could see the wheels turning in Sully's head. He was thinking hard. Asha began nibbling at their appetizer while she waited for him to speak.

"Well, here's a thought," he told her. "Seeing that Devyn doesn't want him, why not introduce him to Ingrid. He sounds like he's her type."

Suddenly, the wine Asha was in the middle of sipping became lodged in her throat along with the calamari, and she began coughing uncontrollably. The glass slipped from her hand, and the shattering sound it made as it hit the floor echoed through the restaurant. Sully jumped from his seat to help. Other diners at nearby tables and the waitstaff stared in disbelief. Tears formed in her eyes as Asha struggled to breathe. Sully pulled her from her chair, wrapped his arms around her, and squeezed into her diaphragm with enough force to dislodge the mass in her throat. She gasped.

"Oh my God, baby, are you okay?" Sully panted.

Asha, still unable to talk, nodded, and sat down again. Someone rushed over and handed her a glass of water. She took small sips as people began to applaud Sully for his heroic act. He kneeled beside her, rubbing her back.

"We called 9-1-1," one of the waiters informed them.

"I think she's okay," Sully told him. "But maybe we do need to go and get her checked out."

"Wow, you saved her life," a woman sitting at a table beside theirs said to Sully.

Asha closed her eyes and concentrated on her breathing. Yes, Sully had saved her life. But the only thing Asha could think about was the thought that had entered her head as soon as Sully made the horrific suggestion . . . *Over my dead body.*

Chapter 19

Devyn

Smitten. That was the only word Devyn could think of that described how she'd been feeling for the past week. Someone had disrupted her cocoon of a sedate, protected life. She found herself exposed and vulnerable. In a matter of days, she'd faced her past, conquered her fears, and created a plan for her future. Best of all, she'd laughed and smiled, thanks to Nigel Brewer, who, ironically, wasn't what Devyn would ordinarily consider being her type. Granted, he was tall, like most of the guys she dated, but Nigel wasn't overwhelmingly handsome. He was cute, in his own way, with attractive eyes, a strong jawline, and a dominating presence because of his size. But Nigel's magnetism went beyond his physical appearance. Her newfound ally proved himself to not only be supportive and motivating, but also quite entertaining. His quick wit, off-the-wall humor, and subtle intelligence kept her engrossed. Each morning, he sent a text with a motivational quote or funny meme.

Devyn quickly began looking forward to their nightly phone conversations that would last for hours. Simply put, Nigel had good energy, and Devyn liked him. She also knew that he liked her. But she couldn't really tell precisely in what way. He was flirtatious, but that was part of his charm. Devyn didn't know whether he was joking or serious. *Why does it matter? I mean, I've only known this man for what? A week? Chill out.* There was also the small detail about his past with Ingrid that she hadn't mentioned. She thought about bringing it up, but each time, she decided not to, for some reason. Just have fun and play it cool.

Just as she was leaving work, Nigel called and invited her to keep him company while he set up the lab for his next class. Not having any Friday night plans, Devyn quickly accepted and made a beeline to change into something a little more flattering than the drab black pants and gray cardigan she had on. She paused long enough to have a five-minute conversation with Chase, then headed to Culture.

"That looks good. What is it?" Devyn asked when she walked into the lab.

"Honey garlic glazed salmon." Nigel looked up from the pan of fish that he was garnishing. The smile he gave her was bright and instantly let her know that he was as happy to see her as she was him. The warmth of his aura was seductive. Even in his jeans, Culture apron, and matching baseball cap, there was no denying to her that he looked good.

"Why are you cooking it now? Are you testing out the recipe?" She gave him a quick hug before hopping on one of the stools.

"No, I got a last-minute call from a client who needed me to whip up dinner," Nigel explained. "Normally, I would go to their kitchen, but I still have to prep for tomorrow's class, so I'm kinda killing two birds with one stone. Hook everything up, pack it, and he'll swing by and pick it up. All he has to do is pop the pan in the oven and bake for twenty-five minutes, heat the glaze, and pour on top. Then sauté the veggies which have already been seasoned, open a bottle of wine, and voilà."

"Wait, so I'm gonna assume whoever he's serving has no idea you cooked it and not him, huh?" Devyn shook her head. "Guys are so shiesty. Here you are, helping them lie to these poor, unassuming women."

"Whoa whoa whoa. Technically, he *is* cooking it, not me. I'm just giving him a hand, that's all. Ain't nobody being dishonest." Nigel tossed one of the carrots he was chopping at her. Devyn caught it and threw it back at him.

"I must admit, this is kind of a cool idea. You should market it. 'Date night boxes' or something like that. Create a menu for folks to choose from. People could order them ahead of time for special occasions and stuff. Kinda like they have those meal prep boxes," Devyn suggested. "Imagine if someone could pick up Sunday dinner in a box: chicken ready to be fried, greens seasoned and ready for the stove, oh, and macaroni and cheese."

"Don't forget sweet, hot water corn bread mix that you can either pour to make muffins or bake in a skillet," Nigel laughed.

"Exactly. It can be a meal kit service for Black people. Genius." Devyn began clapping. "Just don't forget about me when you make your first million."

"Never. I should be the one telling you not to forget about me. I saw your little Pivot video with you looking all cute. I liked it." Nigel sprinkled some seasoning on the vegetables he'd finished chopping, then put them into a plastic container.

"Did you really, or are you just saying that? Be honest."

The video had been Chase's idea after they finished the impromptu photo shoot. Devyn had been so nervous while filming that it took nearly twenty takes until she was semisatisfied. After a little editing magic from Chase, the final result was almost decent. In her opinion, even though she looked fat, she did sound way more confident than she was.

"I really did, and the pictures are excellent too. It was a great marketing move."

"The jury's still out on that," she sighed.

"How so?" Nigel frowned.

"People are saying that my sudden reappearance is because D'Morgan is the girl in Tremell's upcoming sex tape. They're accusing me of doing damage control so that my image won't be tarnished. As if that's even possible," Devyn explained. Despite Chase's efforts to hide the ridiculous blog posts insinuating that Devyn was Tremell's costar, Devyn read them. "I'm hoping I'm doing the right thing, especially since the girls and I are doing this photo shoot next week. I'm more worried about their reputation than mine."

"Considering the fact that you aren't in this alleged sex tape that no one has even seen, I think you'll be fine. Devyn Douglass and Pivot are definitely gonna be a force. I'd holla at her before I would check for D'Morgan's ass, for sure." Nigel raised an eyebrow, once again, causing Devyn to wonder if he was flirting to show genuine interest or to be funny.

"Would you really?" Devyn smirked at his enticing vote of confidence.

"Well, maybe . . . It depends," he shrugged. "I mean, she's beautiful, smart, and all, but . . ."

"But what?" Devyn put her hands on her hips and waited for his answer.

"I mean, I'm a big guy. I need a woman who can cook, and we all know one thing Devyn Douglass can't do is prepare a meal," Nigel teased. "The woman burned shrimp—the easiest thing in the world to cook."

"I did not," Devyn replied.

"He's right. I was there, remember?" Nadia walked in and added.

"Look at this. The two of you double-teaming me." Devyn shook her head.

"Nope, we're just honest with you. That's what friends do," Nigel said.

Friends. Devyn's heart sank a little. She'd gotten the answer she'd been looking for. He just wanted to be friends. At least, she knew now, before she played herself by thinking anything else. *Be relieved. Being friends means there's no pressure. The last thing you need in your life is the pressure of being in a relationship.*

"Don't let him get to you, Devyn. He doesn't think anyone can cook, including me. And I *know* I can burn," Nadia told her.

"Yeah, burn some cinnamon rolls," Nigel responded.

"That was one time, jerk. I was 12, and that was only because I fell asleep. If you're gonna tell the story, tell it all." Nadia walked over and punched him in the arm. "Where's Hakeem's order? He's on his way to pick it up."

Nigel boxed up the food and handed it off to his sister.

"Nice seeing you again, Devyn," Nadia said.

"You too," Devyn replied.

When she was gone, Nigel looked at her. "You hungry?"

"I mean, I can eat," Devyn told him.

"Cool, how about I give you the chance to redeem yourself?"

Devyn gave him a suspicious look. "What do you mean?"

"You cook us dinner while I finish setting up for tomorrow night," Nigel offered. "I mean, I have some leftover salmon here, and all you have to do is chop the vegetables. But if that's too hard . . ."

Devyn stood up. "No, it's *not* too hard, jerk. Give me an apron."

For the next two hours, they laughed, talked, and listened to music while he guided her as she prepared the meal, which turned out amazing. After eating, she washed the dishes while he packed up the leftovers for her to take home.

"This was a lot of fun. Thanks for the invite," she said as he walked her out the back entrance to her car. "And dinner."

Nigel pulled her in for a hug. Devyn closed her eyes and enjoyed the warmth of his body against hers. He put his chin on her head while her head rested on his chest. It was the perfect ending to a great night. The only thing that would've possibly made it better would've been a kiss.

Friends, she reminded herself, and friends don't kiss.

"Don't forget to call me and let me know you made it home. As a matter of fact, call me before then," Nigel smiled when he released her from his arms. "You can keep me awake while I drive home. A brother is tired."

"Oh, so, now, I'm your entertainment while driving?" Devyn asked.

"Don't act like you don't wanna call, Devyn. We both know you do." He playfully patted her on the shoulder.

"How about I call you now before I even get in the car?" Devyn reached into her back pocket, expecting to take out her phone, but it wasn't there. It dawned on her that her phone hadn't made a sound all night. "Shit, my phone."

"Where is it?" Nigel asked. "Did you leave it inside?"

"No, I don't think I brought it with me." The image of her tossing her phone on her bed when she was changing clothes flashed in her mind. She'd been in such a rush that she'd forgotten to pick it up on the way out. She could only imagine the number of texts and calls she's probably missed.

"I guess you won't be calling me, huh?" Nigel smiled.

"I'll text you when I get home." Devyn gave him another hug, this one much shorter than the last. After tossing the bag of leftovers onto the passenger seat, she hopped into the car and headed home.

"Chastity, I'm back," Devyn yelled when she walked into the house. "And guess what? I got dinner."

Devyn expected to hear some sort of response. When she didn't, she put the food in the kitchen and went into the spare bedroom that Chase had claimed as her own. Chase wasn't there. Devyn headed to her room and grabbed her phone, still on the bed where she left it. She had a couple of missed calls from Asha, and a few from a number she didn't recognize. After sending Nigel a quick text letting him know she made it home safely, she called Chase.

"Devyn, where the hell are you?" Chase answered.

"I'm home. Now, where the hell are *you* because you *aren't* here," Devyn answered as she sat on the side of her massive bed that she inherited from Uncle Julian.

"I'm at the hospital with Asha. We're in the ER."

Devyn's heart began beating so fast that she could hear it. Her fingers trembled, and her phone nearly slipped from her hand. "Hospital?"

"I'm fine, Devyn. I choked on some damn calamari, that's all," Asha yelled in the background. "Chase, I told you not to say anything. You know she's probably about to freak out. Gimme the damn phone."

"Hold on," Chase said.

A few seconds later, Asha's voice was loud and clear. "Devyn, girl, nothing's wrong. Food went down my windpipe the wrong way."

"Asha?" Devyn's voice cracked, and she blinked away the tears.

"Dev, breathe. I'm fine and literally getting ready to walk out of here." The relaxed, calmness of Asha's voice gave Devyn a slight bit of relief, but her anxiety was still at full throttle. She hated hospitals for so many reasons, and to know that Asha was at one was frightening. In Devyn's mind, Asha being there meant that she had to be sick or hurt, and if she was either, there was a possibility that she might die. Death, especially that of a loved one, had become her biggest fear.

"I'm on my way. I can come right now," Devyn softly told her in an effort to be supportive to her best friend.

"I won't be here when you arrive. Hold on," Asha told her. A few seconds later, the phone chimed with an incoming FaceTime call. Devyn hit the answer button and stared at Asha's smiling face on the screen. "See, I'm fine. I'm just exhausted."

"She is." Chase's head popped over Asha's shoulder, and Devyn could see they were walking. "I'm taking her home now."

"What happened?" Devyn asked.

"I told you, I choked," Asha said.

"Sully, the Senior, gave her the Heimlich and saved her. He's her hero." Chase leaned into the screen and announced.

"Shut up, Chase. You talk too much." Asha began running her hand through her dreads. "I really need to get these retwisted."

"I told you I could do them and add some color to give you some flavor." Chase smiled.

"No, thanks, I'm good." Asha shook her head. "Dev, I'll call you when I get home. Love you."

"Love you too." The panic attack Devyn was on the brink of having minutes earlier disappeared, and she laughed at the two people who meant the world to her. Asha and Chase had always been in her corner no matter what, especially Asha, which was why Devyn decided not to mention anything to her about Nigel. Besides, she and Nigel were just friends, nothing more. But even a simple friendship with him had the potential to cause major complications, considering the circumstances. Unless something between Nigel and her changed, the less Asha knew, the better.

Chapter 20

Asha

"You're leaving?" Sully rushed to Asha's side as soon as she walked into the waiting room of the ER. She'd insisted he go home and get rest as soon as Chase arrived, but he refused.

"I'll go get the car," Chase told her. "Be right back."

"No, you don't have to do that. I'll take her home," Sully offered, then clarified. "She's staying at my house."

Chase looked at Asha, waiting for confirmation of some sort.

"No, Sully, I'm going home, to *my* house," Asha told him. "I'll call you in the morning. Chastity will make sure I'm good."

Chase gave Asha a nod, then headed toward the exit.

"Asha, you don't need to be by yourself. I'll come to your house and stay with you." Sully put his arm around her as she started walking toward the same door Chase had gone out of.

"Goodness, Sully, there's nothing wrong with me. There really wasn't a reason for me to even be brought here, especially by ambulance." Asha shook her head. Seeing the disappointment in his face, she said, "I am grateful for your help. But even the doctors said it was just a scare."

"Then I should be with you in case you have another one and need me," he told her.

Asha was exhausted and didn't have the energy to argue. All she wanted to do was go home, take a shower, and get into her bed. Had it not been for Sully, she could've been checked into the morgue instead of being checked out at the hospital. The least she could do was let him take her home.

"Fine," she relented.

He gleefully slipped his arm through hers and escorted her outside, just as Chase was pulling up to the door. "I'll go get my car. Wait right here."

Asha motioned for Chase to roll down the window. "He'll take me home. Thanks."

"You sure?" Chase asked with a look of uncertainty.

"I'm sure." Asha nodded. "Thanks, Chase. You had my back tonight. I take back every bad thing I said to Devyn about you. I appreciate you."

Chase smiled. "It's all good. No one pays attention to anything you say about me anyway. I love you, Ash."

"Love you too," Asha told her. Chase waited until Asha got into Sully's car, and they all drove off.

"Are you sure you don't want to come to my house?" Sully asked again.

"Yes, Sully, I'm sure."

"It's just that I don't have any pajamas or anything to sleep in or even a toothbrush. You have all the essentials at my place that I don't have at yours," he pointed out.

"I didn't think about that. But you can always—" Asha's sentence was cut off by a pair of headlights pulling into the driveway.

"Who's that?" Sully frowned.

Asha turned around to get a better look at the car that was now parked behind hers. The driver opened the door, and Asha smiled at the long legs that stepped out. "Devyn. Who else would it be?"

*****

Knock, knock, knock.

"Ash, you asleep?" Devyn asked softly.

Unfortunately not, Asha thought as her eyes fluttered open. Between Sully's calls and texts every thirty minutes to check on her, and Devyn's frequent check-ins throughout the night, sleep was damn near impossible. They both meant well, though. She really couldn't be upset.

"Nope," Asha said as she sat up.

"Asha, your eye!" Devyn gasped.

Asha picked up a small mirror from her nightstand and stared at her reflection. The corner of her eye that was usually white was bright red. "Oh, yeah, it's a hemorrhage from when I was coughing so hard. The doctor said it should go away in a week or two."

"Does it hurt?"

"No, it looks worse than it is. I don't feel it at all."

"Oh, well, I brought you some tea." Devyn handed her one of the two mugs she was holding.

"Thanks, Dev." The potent herbal scent filled her nostrils. Whatever was in the cup wasn't the standard Earl Grey that she kept in the cabinet. It had to be one of Devyn's blends. "Hold up, what's in this?"

"Green tea, lemon verbena, ashwagandha, and, uh, honey with a little cinnamon," Devyn told her. "Taste it; it's good."

Asha took a sip, and it tasted like magic. Within seconds, she was alert, and the sluggish feeling was gone. She glanced at Devyn, who waited for her reaction. "It is good, perfect. But how did you make it?"

"I brought the blend with me last night. Grabbed it from the cabinet as I was leaving the house. I figured you would need something strong." Devyn sat on the foot of the bed, drinking from her mug.

Asha took another taste. "There better not be anything 'extra special' in here, Dev."

Devyn laughed. "God, Asha, there's not. The only person I give the 'extra special' blend to is Chase, by request. Now, if you would like me to make you some of *that,* I can."

"Definitely not." Asha shook her head.

"Don't act like that. I remember a time when you used to get down with the 'special' herbs quite frequently," Devyn teased.

"Heffa, I wasn't the only one. We both indulged in herbal enjoyment. I wasn't smoking by myself," Asha reminded her.

"Chase is such a negative influence on us," Devyn laughed.

"Yes, she is. But I have to admit that she wasted no time getting to the hospital when Sully called and told her what happened. He tried calling you first, but . . ." Asha took another sip of tea.

"I didn't recognize his number." Devyn sighed. "He didn't leave a message or a text. I just saw the missed call from an unknown number. I don't have Sully's number saved in my phone. Why would I?"

"Chase said you weren't home when he called," Asha told her. "You weren't home when I came by to talk to you earlier, either. We didn't know where you were."

"Oh." Devyn shrugged.

Asha waited for her to give some kind of explanation. When she didn't offer one, she asked, "So, where were you?"

"I had an appointment."

"With your life coach?"

"Uh-huh." Devyn nodded and took another sip.

"Until after nine o'clock?" Asha continued questioning.

"Oh no, I went and got something to eat too," Devyn told her.

"By yourself?"

Devyn turned around and looked at Asha. "What did you come by to talk to me about?"

Asha had almost forgotten about the reason she'd stopped by Devyn's house in the first place. She paused for a moment, then said, "Oh, because Ben asked about you. He said he'd been trying to reach you but couldn't."

"Ben?" Devyn looked confused for a second. "Oh, Ben."

"Yeah. Tall, handsome, sexy, single Ben," Asha reminded her.

"He has? Oh, I probably don't have his number saved in my phone either. Dang." Devyn nodded.

It was a horrible excuse, but considering the fact that one of Devyn's bad habits was not saving phone numbers, it was valid. Asha was glad to hear the reason, which was better than Chase's suggestion that Devyn wasn't interested in him. There was hope for a romantic future, after all.

"Devyn! Oh my God, what's wrong with you? How many times do I have to tell you to save people's contact information? I'm really gonna need for you to please add Ben to your contacts ASAP, please." Asha chastised her.

"Okay," Devyn said.

"And Sully's," Asha added.

Devyn turned her nose up. "Now, that's a stretch."

"Only in case something happens like last night. What's the point of having your ass as 'ICE' on my phone if you don't even answer unknown numbers? You are supposed to be the first person people call IN CASE of EMERGENCY," Asha sighed. "It's imperative because, God forbid, I have to give that role to Chastity. I really don't wanna have to do that, Devyn."

Devyn laughed. "Lesson learned. I'll save Sully too. Damn."

The doorbell and Devyn's phone began ringing at the same time. Asha checked the security app on her phone and saw that Sully was standing at the front entrance.

Devyn looked down at her watch and said, "It's Journi."

"I'm surprised you have *her* number saved. I'll get the door. You get your phone." Asha stood. She grabbed her robe, hanging on the back of her bedroom door, and slipped her feet into her slides.

"Good morning. How did you sleep?" Sully asked when she let him in.

"Okay," she answered as he leaned in to kiss her.

"That's good. I brought you breakfast." He held up a Panera bag. "And I figured I'd make some coffee."

"Thanks, Sully. Actually, Dev made me some amazing tea, but I *am* hungry." Asha took the bag from him. He followed her into the kitchen. Inside the bag were her favorite bagels and flavored cream cheese. She found a large platter in the cabinet and arranged them while Sully sat at the table. "Would you like some tea? It's delicious; one of Devyn's special blends."

"No, I'm good." Sully shook his head. "I'm surprised she stayed the night. Especially after not showing up at the hospital when I called. I wasn't gonna say anything, but that really bothered me, Asha."

Asha turned around and frowned. "It's no big deal. She didn't recognize your number. Don't worry. I already told her she needs to save it on her phone. There may come a time where I'm with her, and something happens, and she needs to know how to reach you as well."

"Well, that's good, I guess. I'm just saying, I would've expected—" Sully stopped midsentence, his attention now on the doorway of the kitchen.

"Hey, Sully," Devyn greeted him.

"Oh, hey, Devyn. Good morning. Uh, thank you for taking care of my baby last night. I told her I woulda stayed, but she said she was in good hands with you," he smiled nervously.

Asha wasn't sure if Devyn overheard their conversation. If Devyn did hear Sully, she didn't show it as she strolled into the kitchen nonchalantly and rinsed her mug in the sink.

"Of course. No thanks needed. I didn't do anything that she wouldn't do for me," Devyn said.

"Are you leaving, Dev?" Asha noticed Devyn changed from pajamas a few minutes earlier to jeans and a T-shirt.

"Yeah, Journi is going to look for her pageant dress today and asked if I would come along." Devyn shrugged.

"Oh, okay, that should be fun," Asha told her, excited at the thought of a little purposeful shopping and girl time. It had been a minute since she'd hit the mall.

"Yeah, and Chase is gonna come too and see if she can get a couple of shots for the website. It shouldn't take too long, though. I'll come back later and check on you," Devyn said.

"Girl, you don't have to do that. I'm fine." The spark of joy Asha felt earlier fizzled.

"And I'll be right here with her all day," Sully beamed. "I'm not going anywhere."

"Well, if you need anything, just call me." Devyn gave her a quick hug.

"She won't," Sully said matter-of-factly.

"Have fun and send pics." Asha waved as Devyn walked past.

The sound of the front door closing signaled that she was gone. Sully didn't waste any time resuming his dissatisfaction with Asha's best friend.

"Okay, now, she's dead-ass wrong, and you know it," he jumped up and said.

"What are you talking about?" Asha picked up one of the Cinnamon Crunch bagels and opened it.

"The way she just up and left. It's like she couldn't wait to get outta here. What kinda shit is that? First, she doesn't show up at the hospital. Now, she just abandons you this morning." He leaned against the counter and folded his arms, waiting for Asha's response.

"You're reaching, Sully. She was here all night, and she left because she had something important to do, for a business that I'm a part of, remember? She has to meet with our client." Asha spread the cream cheese on her bagel.

"You're her best friend—the hell with the business and that client. None of that is more important than making sure you're good. You almost died last night and look at your eye. You busted a blood vessel, *that's* how serious it was. I know she's your girl, but if you ask me, her priorities are messed up, Asha." Sully put his hands on her shoulders and stared into her eyes. "When life comes hard at Devyn, you're right there for whatever she needs. Last night *and* today, she should be here for you. Where is she?"

Asha tried to think of an appropriate answer for him but couldn't. Instead, she looked away and took a bite, hoping the effort it took to chew the thick, sweet dough would be enough of a distraction from the fact that maybe he was right.

Chapter 21

Devyn

"You're such a liar."

Devyn smiled at Chase and nodded emphatically. "I'm not lying. It's the truth."

"I don't believe you. First of all, this tastes like something from a restaurant—a good one at that. Plus, I've been here for a damn week and a half, and the only thing that stove in there has been used for is heating a tea kettle. Now, where did you get it, Devyn?" Chase gave her a side-eyed look.

"I'm not saying where I cooked it, but I honest to God did." Devyn shrugged and turned back around to the computer screen. They'd spent most of Sunday afternoon going through and editing the pictures Chase had taken the day before during their dress-hunting adventure. Although they hadn't found a dress suitable for Journi's pageant debut, they'd had a lot of fun. Chase not only took plenty of great shots of Devyn and Journi, but she'd also got some of Dionne who tried on dresses as well.

"Whatever." Chase returned to her seat beside the one Devyn was sitting in.

"I'm telling the truth, and who gave you permission to eat my leftovers anyway?" Devyn asked.

"Do you know how excited I was when I saw there was actual food in the fridge when I got back from holding Asha's hand after her near-death experience since your ass was in the wind?" Chase asked.

"That was a long-ass question, and your shade did not go unnoticed." Devyn shook her head.

"Subtlety has never been one of my strengths. You do realize that, right?" Chase shrugged as she clicked the mouse. A picture taken at one of the three boutiques they'd visited popped on the screen. The moment captured was Devyn, arms folded and staring at both girls as they emerged from the dressing room, each wearing a beaded gown. Dionne looked coy yet captivating in ivory, while Journi exuded boldness and emotion in red. The intensity in Devyn's face as she stared at the two beautiful girls was intense, as if she were an artist studying a masterpiece she was trying to perfect.

"Whoa." Devyn gasped at the image.

"I know. *That* is a dope pic, huh?" Chase enlarged photo.

Devyn didn't realize Chase caught the moment on film, but she was glad she had. Chase was right. It was a fantastic picture. In fact, so were all the others.

"Asha is gonna love this one. I wish she were here to help us go through them," Devyn commented. "I called her, but she didn't answer. She's probably laid up with Sully. I sent a text and told her to call me if she needed anything."

"Her boo got her. Speaking of, do you need any of these single shots for your personal use?" Chase asked, then clicked on a picture of Devyn posing alone in a mirror. "This one is really cute."

"I told you I'm not gonna have any online activity. These are for business use only. That's it," Devyn answered.

"I'm not talking about social media."

Devyn frowned. "Chase, I'm not joining any dating sites. And you'd better not create any profiles for me either."

"I don't think I need to do that." Chase raised an eyebrow at her. "Someone has already caught your eye, haven't they?"

"What? No." Devyn shook her head. "Why would you even ask that?"

"What day is it again?" Chase swiveled around in her chair and peered at her.

"Sunday," Devyn shot back at her.

"Oh, I was just making sure because you chock-full of untruths today, sis," Chase laughed.

"What are you talking about, Chastity? I hope you ain't talking about Ben."

"Nope, I know it's not him. Someone else has been making you laugh late at night and sing in the morning. I'm just waiting for you to tell me who it is." Chase sat back in her chair.

"You're tripping," Devyn tried, but ultimately failed at hiding her smile at the mere thought of Nigel. She couldn't help it. She wanted and needed to tell someone, especially since this wasn't something she could share with Asha. "I do have, like, someone I'm getting to know."

Chase turned around so fast that she nearly knocked Devyn out of the chair. "I *knew* it. Who? When? Where? I need details—*now*."

"First of all, calm down. We're just cool. His name is Nigel, and he's a chef," Devyn told her.

"I knew you didn't cook that damn salmon." Chase pointed her finger accusingly.

"I *did* cook it." Devyn continued to tell her about how she and Nigel met, how easy he was to talk to, and how supportive he'd been. She purposely kept out the detail regarding his being Ingrid's ex. "He's really given me a new perspective about everything that happened since the wedding and how limitless the possibilities are with Pivot."

"And here I was thinking Asha and I were motivating you to be great when it was this dude the entire time. Ain't this a bitch?" Chase threw her hands up in defeat.

"You both inspire me to do my best, Chase. I appreciate the love and support y'all constantly give. I'm determined to make Pivot a success, for all of us," Devyn smiled. "Nigel helps me see a different view of the big picture that you all show me."

"He sounds cool, Dev. But why the secrecy? Wait, does Asha know about this? She doesn't, does she?"

"No, and I'm just not ready to tell her yet," Devyn sighed. "Not that I'm trying to hide him or anything. It's just, complicated . . ."

"Listen, I get it. Asha can be a bit much, especially when it comes to you. I agree. Don't mention this fella until you're ready. Lord knows she's gonna give him the third degree, run a background check, credit check, ask for his medical history, birth certificate, and copies of his tax returns for the last three years to make sure he's good enough for you, honey." Chase laughed. "Enjoy it while you can."

Devyn was relieved. Chase's optimism about her growing friendship with Nigel, along with her understanding of the reason for her confidentiality, confirmed that she was doing the right thing.

"Thanks, Chase." Devyn gave her godsister a big hug. "I'm glad you're here with me, even if I had no idea you were coming or how long you'll be staying."

"I mean, I can always leave right now. I still have a whole basement apartment in my mama's house. You know she tries to convince me to come home daily," Chase warned.

"You're not leaving me. Besides, if you did, how would you be able to work for Pivot? We don't allow our employees to telecommute. You have to be here in the office daily," Devyn said, gesturing around them.

"Oh, really? Then I suggest we come up with a plan for Pivot to generate a hell of a lot more income. Ain't no way y'all are gonna be able to afford my salary with just two clients. Folks have been in-boxing and emailing all day about how to sign up for classes. Don't you think we need to say something other than 'more information coming soon'?" Chase asked, grabbing her cell phone off the desk. "I'm calling Asha. We need a staff meeting."

"I told you I tried calling her a little while ago, and she didn't answer," Devyn reminded her as the phone dialed. "She's probably asleep."

"Yes, Chastity? How can I help you?" Asha's voice was alert when she answered.

"Hey, Asha, so, I'm here with Devyn, and we're going over the pictures from yesterday and kinda talking about how we wanna move forward with Pivot," Chase told her.

"Okay?" The bland confusion in Asha's voice caught Devyn by surprise. For a second, she wondered if she were tripping.

"We are ready to pop out and get paid. What about you?" Chase responded with an emphatic tilt of her head.

"Oh, I was waiting on Dev. I know you guys have been working on some stuff, but she hadn't said anything about what she wanted to do," Asha said. "I assumed that she still wanted to take things kinda slow since she hadn't mentioned anything different . . . to me."

"It's not my sole decision, Ash. We are a team." Devyn frowned slightly. The vibe was off, and she didn't understand why. *Wait, does she know about me hanging out with Nigel? Maybe she found out. How? I'm tripping. She's probably just relaxing.* Devyn was about to tell Chase to mute her phone and ask if Asha sounded odd, but Chase began talking before she could.

"And that's why *we* are calling you, chick. You're the PR guru. Remember, all of this was your idea, and a very good one," Chase said. "The three of us are ready. Let's go. It's time to give the people what they want."

"Let's make it happen. You know I'm down for whatever." Asha's tone was more positive now, which put Devyn at ease. "Let's make it happen."

"That's what's up. It's time to show the world what Pivot is all about." Chase smiled.

"I'm on my way. Be there in twenty minutes," Asha blurted out. "I have so many ideas. Devyn, have some of that tea ready for me to sip when I get there."

"I'm on it," Devyn yelled, hopping up, excited about the brainstorming session that was about to take place. *Okay, maybe I was tripping. Everything is fine. But sooner or later, I'm gonna have to say something. Nigel isn't a bad guy, at least I don't think he is.*

Forty-eight hours later, they damn near broke the internet with an event announcement and invitation created by Chase. The visual masterpiece opened with a black-and-white silhouette of Devyn, sitting on a throne and wearing a crown. Female lyricist Chika's inspirational hit "Crown" played in the background. Video footage of Devyn coaching Dionne and Journi as they walked in various random locations, including a grocery store aisle, a parking lot, and the hallway of Devyn's school faded in and out, while others featured Asha adjusting their posture and listening while they spoke. There were also shots of Chase capturing footage. The entire production was crisp, clean, and ingenious. Within an hour of its release, they'd maxed out the RSVP list for the "Pivot Preview and Launch Experience" to be held in two weeks. Devyn, Asha, and Chase were shocked at the overwhelming response. They didn't have a moment to process because there was so much to do in so little time.

Chase suggested that even though they couldn't accept any more guests to the event, they should keep the momentum going and continue to post and promote daily on social media. Asha reserved the library auditorium, sent out a press release to the media outlets, and ordered cute shirts for them all to wear, including the girls who would be part of the demo events. Devyn was responsible for creating the schedule and itinerary for the four-hour event.

Despite having a full plate with all she had going on, Devyn made time for Nigel, who'd become her sounding board, the voice of reason and comic relief, when needed. They hadn't seen each other because his schedule was just as hectic. Nigel was traveling on business, but they spoke daily.

"Tomorrow's the big day, huh?" he called as she was picking up some last-minute items before heading to meet everyone at the library to set up.

"It is. I'm so anxious. Pray that I don't faint," Devyn said, putting the armload of bags she was carrying into the trunk of the car. "My nerves have been shot, and they'll probably be worse tomorrow."

"You'll be fine. I have a surprise for you. Can you meet me so I can give it to you?"

"You're here? I thought you weren't coming back to town until tomorrow afternoon?" Devyn said excitedly.

"My meeting with my client finished a little early. I'm heading to Culture. Pull around back."

Devyn got into the car, thrilled to see Nigel, even though her unexpected pit stop would cause her to be delayed. *Asha will not be pleased. I'm only gonna stay a few minutes. Long enough to get the surprise and a quick hug, that's it.*

Nigel must've been just as short on time as she was because instead of being inside the building, he was sitting in his Suburban waiting for her. Devyn took notice of his outfit. It wasn't the first time she'd seen him in jeans, but the blazer he wore over a fitted black shirt and the leather Chukkas on his feet were a welcome surprise. His neatly trimmed beard, freshly lined edge up, and designer sunglasses gave him even more swag than usual. Nigel had never mentioned any other women, but Devyn wondered. Especially since his attire would be exactly what she'd want him to wear if he took her out on a Friday night. He was sexy as hell.

"Pop your trunk," he told her after she parked beside him.

"I have bags in the trunk," Devyn answered as she stepped out of her car, trying not to stare. Nigel walked over and gave her the hug she'd been looking forward to receiving. There was something about the way his strong arms encircled her that made her feel warm and tingly inside. The anxiety that had been building over the past week lessened, and she exhaled, enjoying the moment. For a second, he seemed just as reluctant to end their embrace as she was. *It's a friendly hug, Dev, that's all.*

"I guess we're gonna have to put them in the backseat." He shrugged when he finally released her.

"What is it?" Devyn asked. Her initial thought was maybe he'd gotten her some flowers in honor of the event, but obviously, she was wrong. She walked with him to the back of his truck, and he opened it. Inside were several boxes, labeled with "Pivot."

"Nigel, what the hell?"

He grabbed one of the boxes and reached in, taking out a smaller white box. "Edible merchandise. My contribution to building your brand."

A wide smile spread across Devyn's face as she stared at the white chocolate-covered candy apple in the box, emblazoned with the Pivot logo. "Oh my God, Nigel, you did *not*."

"I did," he nodded. He handed her the apple, then reached into another box and took out a cellophane-wrapped cookie, with the Pivot logo. In addition to the apple and cookies, he also had an assortment of cupcakes.

Devyn was elated and threw her arms around his neck. "You are the absolute best. I can't believe you did all of this. How? This is too much. You have to let me pay you something, Nigel."

"Nah, I can't take your money. It's all good. I've been Team Pivot since day one. Besides, I'm working on something of my own inspired by you. So, I owe you. It's the least I can do," he told her as he began putting the boxes into the backseat of her car.

"Really? What is it?" she said, now curious about what he was talking about.

"Hopefully, you'll find out soon enough," he smiled.

Devyn's watch vibrated with a text from Asha. Without reading it, she said. "I gotta get going. We're setting up for tomorrow. Thank you so much, Nigel."

"Yeah, I got somewhere to be myself. And you're welcome. You know I got you. That's what friends are for, right?" He hugged her again, but this time, Devyn's heart sank a little. She knew they were just friends, but he didn't have to keep reminding her.

"Yep," she agreed.

After somehow managing to make it to the library in record time, Devyn hoped that her tardiness would be excused, especially since she'd arrived with the goodies Nigel had gifted them. She pulled into the parking space beside Asha, and as soon as she stepped out of the car, she heard her name being called.

"Miss Douglass."

Devyn turned around to see Dionne's mom walking toward her. "Hey, Mrs. Phillips, how are you?"

"I've been better, unfortunately," she said. The worried look on her usually pleasant face made Devyn uneasy.

"Uh-oh, what's wrong?" she asked. "Where are the girls?"

"They're on their way. I wanted to talk to you and Asha before they got here." Mrs. Phillips sighed.

"You wanna tell me now, or should we go inside to find Asha?" Devyn became nervous.

"Well, I received a letter today, and Journi is no longer a contestant in the pageant." Mrs. Phillips took a certified letter from her purse and handed it to Devyn.

"What? Why?" Devyn slowly inhaled as she slid the letter out of the envelope and read it.

"Something about a 'morality clause' in the regulations being violated, and her going against standards." Mrs. Phillips verbally confirmed the words that stared back at Devyn. "I don't understand. It doesn't make any sense. What could Journi have possibly done that they would consider immoral and against pageant guidelines? The girl is a straight-A student, vice president of the SGA, and president of the Black History Club.

"There has to be some mistake, Mrs. Phillips." Devyn shook her head. She then noticed Asha and Chase walking out of the library, pushing a cart full of decorations they were using for the event. "Asha, we were just heading inside."

"Don't bother." Asha pushed the cart to the back of her truck, opened the liftgate, and grabbed items, tossing them inside.

"What's going on?" Devyn walked over with Mrs. Phillips by her side.

"Oh, hey, Mrs. Phillips, I didn't notice you," Asha spoke. "I was about to call the girls and tell them they don't have to come to help set up."

"Why not?" Devyn asked.

"Well, apparently, we no longer have usage of the library," Chase replied.

"But we reserved the auditorium weeks ago. They can't cancel our reservation the day before," Devyn said.

"Well, they did just that. And not just tomorrow either. Permanently, per the director of Library Services for the city. It's a wrap." Asha shook her head.

"Wait, huh? Why, Asha?" Devyn shook her head in disbelief. Too much was happening at once, and none of it made sense. Asha's silence and the odd look she gave Devyn indicated that she knew the answer, but didn't want to say anything. "Ash, what's up?"

"Tell her," Chase said, shrugging.

Asha took a deep breath before speaking. "Apparently someone called and made a complaint about our coaching sessions, or rather, the coach. It's stupid, and even my friend who works here tried to explain it to the director, but it was useless. Whoever filed the grievance said that we shouldn't be allowed to use the library because of your 'illicit behavior.'"

"I should've known this would happen. It's those stupid blogs talking about Tremell and that damn sex tape." Devyn held her breath, fighting tears as she processed her thoughts. Once again, someone was attempting to portray her as something she wasn't. It was as if she would never be able to escape a reputation that had been tarnished through no fault of her own. Devyn felt like someone had punched her in the stomach and knocked her down. There would be no point in getting up. The old familiar feeling of hopelessness and doubt slowly started creeping into her mind once more.

"You gotta stop allowing people to steal shit that doesn't belong to them: your joy, peace, happiness, and your character. Every time you allow others to cause you to doubt yourself and your purpose, you give away your power. They can't take what you don't give them."

Chase touched her arm. "But we all know you're not the one in the tape, Devyn."

"Why would someone be doing this to you?" Asha shook her head. "What's the point? How would blocking the library matter?"

The only person Devyn thought would be vindictive and ruin her new business was Tremell, but this was too petty, even for him. It had to be someone else. Devyn turned and stared at Mrs. Phillips, who hadn't said anything. "Well, I'll be damned. That low-down cow. *She* did this."

"Devyn!" Asha shrieked. "I'm sorry, Mrs. Phillips, we know you didn't—"

"Oh my God, you're probably right." Mrs. Phillips's eyes met Devyn's, and they nodded at each other. "She had to."

"I'm missing something. Who are y'all talking about?" Asha asked.

"Mrs. Thompkins. That's also why she kicked Journi out of the pageant. She's blaming you," Mrs. Phillips explained.

"Journi got kicked out of the pageant?" Chase's mouth hung open. "Now, *that's* messed up."

"It is. But don't worry. By the time my husband finishes with her ass, we'll *own* the entire pageant. Believe that," Mrs. Phillips announced.

"Wow. How is Journi? I'm sure she's upset," Asha commented.

"I didn't even mention anything to her about it yet," Mrs. Phillips said. "Which is ridiculous because, once again, the correspondence was sent to us, and we aren't her parents. It's like you said, all Black girls must look alike to her."

"Mrs. Phillips, can you do me a favor and not mention anything to the girls about Journi being removed? I don't need anything negative to distract them from the event tomorrow. They should be focused and on their A-game," Devyn told her. "I mean if you'll still allow them to participate, of course. With all of the rumors and everything going on, I'd understand if you'd—"

"Don't be absurd, Miss Douglass. You've worked wonders with those girls, and I wouldn't think of them not having you as a coach. I'm excited that more young ladies are gonna have the opportunity to learn from you." Mrs. Phillips touched Devyn's arm. "I won't say a word."

"Thank you." Devyn smiled.

"Wait, Devyn, how do you expect us still to have the event? I just told you we couldn't use the auditorium, and there's no way I'll be able to find a venue to host us this last minute, even with my connections. We're gonna have to cancel," Asha said. "Even if we had the budget."

"We're not canceling anything. Don't worry. I know a venue we can use. And it's within budget," Devyn assured her. "All we have to do is send out an email blast to the RSVP guests with the new location, right, Chase?"

Chase shrugged. "Pretty much."

"Cool. I gotta go make this happen," Devyn said, then hugged Mrs. Phillips. "Thank you."

"Devyn, wait," Asha called after her as she ran toward the car.

"Ash, I got this. Trust me," Devyn yelled. As soon as she got into her car, she made a call and prayed that she was right.

Chapter 22

Asha

Asha wasn't an alcoholic by any means, but she knew exactly how they felt. It wasn't even eight o'clock in the morning, and she needed a drink. For the past two weeks, she'd put everything into the launch event for Pivot. At this moment, she had no idea what the hell was going on. Not only that, but also, the person who had just as much to lose, if not more, if things didn't go perfect, wasn't acting as if she had a reason to panic. Maybe if she'd known the business calls and strings that had been pulled to ensure the success of their first event, Devyn would've shown a little more distress. In an effort not to worry her best friend and take some of the pressure off, Asha kept her mouth closed. The only thing she could do at this point was the same thing she'd been doing since Devyn drove out of the parking lot of the library: pray.

"Devyn, what the hell?" Asha asked when she saw the updated flyer.

"What's wrong? I told you I had a venue. The only thing is we can't set up until morning," Devyn told her when she called later that night. "We'll still have plenty of time to pull it together."

"Culture?" Asha sighed. "I don't know, Dev. I mean, it's a cool spot for a girls' night or something, but this? Besides, you know how people are gonna act when they see it's on the West."

"It's perfect for what we're doing. And we'll be supporting another Black-owned business. And it's not on the West," Devyn told her.

"It ain't on the East," Asha countered.

"It's dead ass in the center. The people will come. Honestly, Culture gives us more space, which allows us to expand our guest list. Relax, Asha. It's going to be fine," Devyn reassured her. "We got this. Get some rest. We've got a long day ahead. See you in the morning, Ash," Devyn said before hanging up.

"I mean, I don't have a choice, now, do I?" Asha sighed.

How Devyn expected her to relax was beyond reason. After tossing and turning most of the night, Asha finally got up, took a shower, and threw on a pair of leggings, a T-shirt, and sneakers. She then packed up the outfit she'd be wearing for the event.

"Are you sure you don't have another slot for Ingrid? She said she tried to reserve a ticket, but it was full," Sully asked during his morning call.

"Positive." Asha tried her best to sound as disappointed as he did. "The space is limited, and tickets went fast."

"It sounds like it's gonna be nice. I guess I thought since you're one of the owners of Pivot, you would be able to let her come as your personal guest. Then again, I don't wanna get you in trouble with any of your business partners," he said with sarcasm.

Asha almost giggled at the thought of how Devyn would react if she told her Ingrid wanted to come. Undoubtedly, they probably would've gotten a good laugh, followed by the same outcome: her presence would not be welcome.

"What can I say, Sully? It was first come, first serve, and there was nothing anyone could do. None of us anticipated this big turnout. She's not the only one who wanted to attend but can't. Besides, Pivot is for aspiring models and pageant contestants. Ingrid isn't either one of those. This really isn't something she'd be interested in," Asha explained as she turned into the parking lot of Culture, which was empty.

"I understand, but—"

"Listen, I've gotta go. I'll call you later tonight," Asha told him, alarmed that she was the only one on time.

"Good luck," Sully told her.

"Thanks." Asha parked near the front of the building and was about to call Devyn when Chase appeared in the doorway, waving.

"Good morning, sunshine."

"I didn't think anyone had arrived yet," Asha said as she stepped out. "Are you the only one here?"

"No, everyone else is inside. We parked in the back," Chase told her.

"Well, sorry. No one informed me on where to park," she commented and gathered her things.

Asha stepped into the building and was even more impressed than the first time she'd been there. A beautiful abstract mural was painted on the far wall, and a gorgeous chandelier, reminiscent of falling teardrops, hung from the ceiling. Someone had already set up the backdrops, "step and repeats," signage they'd ordered for the event, and the registration table was covered with a signature tablecloth. So far, everything looked amazing.

"Ash, you're here." Devyn ran over and hugged her. Clearly, she had the same idea as Asha because she also had on leggings and sneakers. Instead of a T-shirt, she wore a hoodie, and her hair was pulled on top of her head.

"I am. I see y'all already got started." Asha pointed to the setup.

"We got here a little earlier and did a bit of work. But you know we have plenty more to do. I'm thinking since we have so much space and the use of the other rooms, we can rotate people out. You can talk about PR and media in one room, and I can do the whole runway and pageant stuff in another room. Chase is gonna do mini photo shoots in the corner back there." Devyn put her arm around her neck. "I mean if you think all that'll work, of course. It's nice, though, huh?"

"Yeah, it is, but when you said Culture, I thought you meant using one of the rooms, not the entire building, Devyn. How did you even manage this?" Asha wondered.

"I made a call to a friend. They were happy to help out." Devyn shrugged.

"Hey, Devyn, where do you want the goodie table set up?" a deep voice asked. Asha looked up and recognized Nadia, who walked into the entrance hall along with a man so huge, he towered over her.

"Nadia, nice to see you again." Asha smiled, now understanding how Culture had become available. *Of course, it all makes sense. Obviously, Devyn had called Ben, and he made it happen for us. Thank God.*

"You too." Nadia hugged her.

"What do you think, Asha?" Devyn asked.

"Huh?" Asha blinked.

"The goodie table. Where do you want it?" Nadia repeated.

Even though she had no idea what goodies they were talking about, she looked around the room for a moment, then finally said, "How about we put it on the opposite side of the room over there, but line it up with the Registration Table? Oh, but we only have one Pivot tablecloth, though."

"No worries. I have a plain white one we can use, and I'll add some flowers and crystals I have in the back to glam it up. I'll get it," Nadia told her, then said to the big guy. "You heard the woman, Nigel. Put the table over there."

"Hold up, now. Ain't gonna be too much more of this ordering me around," he warned.

"Over there," Devyn laughed as she pointed to where the table needed to go.

"Whatever. Bossing me around like I ain't the owner," Nigel grumbled as he followed the instructions he'd been given.

"Why the extra table?" Asha turned her attention to Devyn.

"Oh, we have some sweet takeaways for our guests," Devyn told her.

"I thought we were only doing light hors d'oeuvres and water. You didn't say anything about buying or serving anything else." Asha recalled Devyn's debate because she was afraid serving food would be associated with her noticeable weight gain. They tried telling her how ridiculous she sounded but agreed to a happy medium. Her friend's sudden delight over desserts was surprising.

"I didn't buy them. Someone donated them. Wait 'til you see them. You're gonna love them," Devyn told her, her eyes still on Nigel, who was setting up the table. When he finished, she grinned and told him, "Perfect. Thank you. Now, come and meet my bestie."

"You must be the infamous Asha." He smiled and held out his hand out. "I'm Nigel."

He was so tall that Asha had to lift her head slightly to look at him. She figured that he had to weigh at least 350 pounds. Asha wondered if he was the security guard. Even though he was big, there was something kind in his eyes and smile.

"Nice to meet you," Asha nodded.

"Nigel is Nadia's brother. He's also my lifesaver and not the sweet kind either," Devyn said with a mischievous grin Asha couldn't remember the last time she'd seen. If she didn't know any better, she would've thought Devyn was flirting. Her friend never went for big guys, though. Tall was one thing, but Devyn liked them slim or naturally athletic and cute. Nigel wasn't any of those. His arms, shoulders, and chest were massive. He was nice looking, but cute wasn't a word she could imagine anyone using to describe him. Clearly, Devyn was just being amiable because of the manual labor he was providing. That had to be it.

"I'm actually sweeter than the candy." Nigel tapped Devyn's shoulder playfully.

"Okay, enough small talk. Let's get to work." Devyn pulled her along. Asha was now excited about the day ahead. She went into the event-coordinator mode, arranging chairs, tables, décor, and giving instructions between answering calls and emails. When they completed the setup and everything was in order, Asha was beyond pleased. They were ahead of schedule, something she never even thought was possible. Even the surprise gift she had for Devyn arrived at the perfect time.

"This place is amazing," Qianna, affectionately known as "YaYa," yelled when she walked in, along with her assistant, Camille.

"YaYa!" Asha rushed over and grabbed her. "Thank you so much for doing this. My God, it's good to see you. You look amazing."

Yaya, their friend and celebrity makeup artist, was the owner of "After Effex," one of the city's hottest beauty bars. The last time they'd seen her was when she'd done Devyn's makeup for the wedding. Since then, like many of Devyn's other friends in the industry, they'd lost touch. But when Asha reached out to her and asked if she'd bring her talents to the launch party, Yaya didn't hesitate to say yes. Asha couldn't wait for Devyn to see her.

"Thanks, Ash. You're still fly, rockin' with the locs." YaYa playfully grabbed Asha's hair. "Where's Dev?"

"In the back with Chase getting her students glammed up. Everyone is excited. She's gonna freak out when she sees you," Asha told her.

"At first, I thought I was at the wrong place when I saw the protestors outside," YaYa said.

"Me too," Camille nodded.

"Protestors?" Nadia, who'd been helping Asha put the final touches on the carpet that they decided would be used as a runway in the middle of the venue's main area, jumped up and asked.

"What? As in marching and chanting? Are they down the street?" Asha knew there was a Women's Clinic in the nearby shopping center but thought they'd be closed on Saturdays. "Pro-Lifers, probably."

"No, *here*. There are some chicks right out front of this building with signs, yelling at people as they drive by," YaYa explained.

"I'll take care of this, Asha. You go ahead and take them back so that y'all can get ready," Nadia told them and headed toward the front entrance.

"Come on." Asha tried to remain calm, but the thought of someone holding some kind of demonstration outside was disturbing. She quickly led YaYa and Camille to the back room where Devyn, Chase, Journi, and Dionne were getting dressed.

"Don't you need to be back here changing?" Devyn asked when Asha walked in. "We're almost ready, and you haven't even started."

"You're not ready yet. You can't be. I just got here." YaYa declared, pushing past Asha and jumping into the room.

"Oh my God, Yaya!" Devyn's eyes widened, she screamed, and the two women began dancing in a circle. Seconds later, Chase joined them, along with Camille, and soon, Journi and Dionne. After enjoying the reunion for a few moments, Asha slipped out the door and rushed to see what was going on outside.

This had to be the actions of Marcia Thompkins. It was as if the woman were on a warpath and wasn't going to stop. *Hell no, she must not realize who she's messing with. I got something for her pale, white ass. She will not destroy our event. She's gone too far.*

"I'm telling you, leave now before I call the police and have you removed." As soon as she opened the door, she heard Nadia's yelling.

Asha looked at the bottom of the entrance steps, expecting to see Mrs. Thompkins and her cronies. But she came to a halt before taking another step. She was too shocked to move. Instead, she just stared. It wasn't who she thought. Nadia was yelling at someone much worse—Ingrid.

"Call them! I don't give a damn. We have every right to be out here letting everyone know exactly who is up in this place," Ingrid yelled and held up a flimsy poster board. Asha tried to read the sloppily written words, but couldn't make out what they said.

"Don't be stupid. She's crazy, and so are y'all for going along with this stupid shit." Nadia addressed the two women standing on each side of Ingrid holding their own posters.

"No, you're crazy, and so is anyone else who steps foot in that building, especially women. We are gonna tell every person who comes here today that an abusive man runs Culture. You know it, I know it, and now everyone else will too," Ingrid screamed. "Culture is for vultures. Beware of Bear."

Ingrid's companions began chanting along with her, waving their signs, looking more like sex workers than protestors in their booty shorts and fitted white T-shirts with *"No Bears Allowed"* printed across the front.

Asha finally regained control of her motor skills and marched over to them. "Ladies, she asked you all nicely to leave."

"Fuck you, Asha." Ingrid stopped yelling and looked Asha up and down. "You're the biggest vulture of them all. How the fuck you're gonna hold your whack-ass party here, of all places? You're fake as hell, and I can't wait to tell my father."

"I don't know what you're even talking about. There's nothing to tell him. You can't speak about a party you're not invited to, nor are attending. Now, get the hell away from here." Asha stepped toward her.

"Beware of Bear! Beware of Bear!" Ingrid began screaming again and moved past Asha. Nadia went to grab her, but Asha pulled her back.

"Nadia, don't. Just stop," Asha pleaded.

"She's got an ass whooping coming, and today, she's about to collect." Nadia was breathing so hard that Asha could see the rise and fall of her chest.

"What the hell are y'all doing?" Ben's voice seemed to come from nowhere. Within seconds, he'd walked past Asha and Nadia and was in front of Ingrid and her friends.

"Minding our fucking business," Ingrid snapped. "Now, move out of the way, Ben. This ain't got shit to do with you."

"Really, Ingrid? Haven't you had enough of tryin'a be the center of attention?" Ben was clearly annoyed at her.

"Fuck you, Ben." One of Ingrid's fellow protestors stepped forward.

"You tried that a few years back. I turned you down then, and I still don't want it," Ben said with a repulsed look, then turned around toward Asha. "You ladies go ahead inside. I'll handle this bullshit."

"You want me to get—" Nadia volunteered.

"No. Don't get anybody," Ben said forcefully. "I got this. Ingrid may be crazy, but she ain't stupid. She don't want this smoke. Go."

The way he said it let Asha know it was best that they leave now, rather than later. She and Nadia quickly returned to the building. They had less than an hour before the start time, and she was nervous. Guests would be arriving at any moment. Everything they'd worked hard for was happening. This was something they shouldn't have to deal with. *Maybe I should call Sully and have him come get his tacky-ass daughter.*

"I hate that bitch, I swear." Nadia looked like she wanted to cry. "I'm so sorry, Asha. She's been a pain in our ass for a while, but I never thought she would pull a stunt like this. I'm glad Ben showed up when he did. He'll make sure she's gone in a few."

"It's not your fault, Nadia. I already know she's a hot-ass mess. But what the hell does her ex, Bear, have to do with Culture? I'm so confused." Asha shook her head in disgust.

"Bear is my brother Nigel's nickname," Nadia said. "Unfortunately, he's Ingrid's ex-boyfriend."

Chapter 23

Devyn

If Devyn needed a sign from God or some sort of divine confirmation that Pivot was part of his plan for her life, then the overwhelming success of the Premiere and Preview Launch was definitely it. Every moment of the event was absolutely perfect. The guests were blown away with everything: the venue, the décor, the mini seminars given by Asha and her, the runway and pageant demos by the girls, and the mock photo shoots by Chase. Even the light menu and the custom confectionery delights were a big hit with everyone. In addition to the RSVP guests, they also had a few VIP attendees that Devyn had no idea would be there. YaYa wasn't the only surprise Asha had. Several other beauty influencers and bloggers were there to enjoy and support Devyn's latest endeavor. Devyn faced her fears and gave interviews to the media and press members that promised to spread the news of their positive experience and Pivot's services. To her relief, no one mentioned the extra pounds she now carried, Tremell, or his sex tape. She posed for pictures and smiled brightly. After a little coaxing from Asha, Devyn treated their guests to a walking demo of her own, hitting her signature strut. The day exceeded her expectations.

"Well, you did it," Chase announced and flopped into one of the chairs behind the registration table that had been manned all afternoon by Nadia and Mrs. Phillips, both of whom stepped up to help without even being asked.

"*We* did it," Devyn corrected her. "Right, Asha?"

"Definitely. I can't believe it. I mean, I knew it was gonna be phenomenal, but I can't lie. I didn't expect the magic that happened here today." Asha was ecstatic. "Holy crap."

"Now, we get to clean up," Devyn moaned, looking at the aftermath of their success. Asha had always said that the setup was hard work, but the cleanup was the *real* work. They began putting Culture back the way they found it, thankfully, with the help of everyone, minus Nigel, who had to run an errand. While Nadia and the girls put the chairs away in the rooms, Chase took down the backdrops, other signs, and her photography equipment and began loading them into Devyn's car.

"I can't believe YaYa came. You kept that one real hidden." Devyn nudged Asha as she folded up the tablecloth.

"I knew you were gonna be excited, and she beat the hell out of your face," Asha responded. "And mine."

"Yes, she did." Devyn picked up the end of the carpet and began rolling it up. "I can't wait to see how the pictures turned out, not just ours, but everyone else's. I even saw Chase taking a few of Nadia. I love her so much."

"She is really cool," Asha said. "And so is her brother, Bear."

Devyn stopped rolling and stood, taking a deep breath before turning to face Asha. "Yeah, they're both good people."

"Why the hell didn't you say something?" Asha hissed.

"I didn't think it was a big deal. There was so much going on that I didn't have a free moment to tell you. We've been going nonstop all day. What was I supposed to do? Stop you in the middle of the party and say, 'Oh,

Ash, Nigel is Ingrid's ex-boyfriend, Bear, but don't trip.'"

"Well, that might've been better than being pretty much blindsided by Ingrid and her thottish-ass friends who decided to post up outside earlier and hold a damn protest." Asha tossed up her hands.

"Wait. What?" Devyn looked at her as if she were crazy.

"Yeah, they showed up with signs, shirts, and everything." Asha continued telling about what took place while a clueless Devyn was being glammed up by YaYa. "There's no telling what would've happened if Ben hadn't shown up."

Devyn recalled seeing and speaking to Ben, but she thought Asha had invited him as a part of her matchmaking efforts. "I thought Ben was here as *your* guest."

"No, I mean, he came to support both of us, but he really saved the event. Who knows what kind of damage Ingrid would've caused. Can you imagine if people would've rolled up and seen that, especially the bloggers? Devyn, that kind of stuff can't happen. We can't risk it," Asha warned, pulling Devyn toward the hallway that led to the back of the building.

"You act like Nigel knew Ingrid was gonna pull a stunt. I'm sure he was just as surprised to hear what happened as I am—if anyone has even told him yet," Devyn sighed. Ben certainly hadn't mentioned anything about the incident, and neither did Nadia or Nigel, which made her wonder if Asha was making a bigger deal out of whatever happened. "Do you think I don't realize how much today meant? He knew that too. That's why he allowed us to hold the event here. Nigel is also the one who donated all those Pivot goodies people were fighting over."

"I get that. And I'm grateful. But the fact remains, psycho or not, something bad went down between him and Ingrid. He seems cool, but hell, so did Ted Bundy."

Devyn flinched slightly at Asha's words. She knew the only reason she felt that way was because she didn't know Nigel yet. "Asha, you're ridiculous. He's not a damn serial killer."

"Who's not a serial killer?" Chase walked up behind them.

"Nigel, otherwise known as Bear."

Devyn shook her head at Asha's sarcastic tone, which, in her opinion, was unwarranted. Nigel hadn't been anything but pleasant and helpful to all of them. It was as if Asha were blatantly disregarding everything he'd done to help out and make the day go smooth.

"Oh, not him. He is most definitely a sweetheart, and he's funny," Chase commented.

"Thank you," Devyn said with pride, glad that she wasn't the only one who noticed Nigel's sense of humor.

"Using Culture as the new location for class is a good look too, for them and us. I told Nadia I'd create some graphics from a few of the images I shot today. They can use them on their social media pages. I'm also gonna do headshots of her and Nigel next week," Chase said.

"Hold up, what do you mean by a new location?" Asha folded her arms and looked at Devyn.

"They offered. I was gonna talk to you about it later. It's a good idea, considering we don't have anywhere else right now," Devyn told her.

"Am I missing something here?" Asha asked.

"Like what?" Devyn raised an eyebrow, confused by her question.

"Like what's up with this dude? Why is he so generous? What is he tryin'a gain?" Asha's line of questioning continued before Devyn could even respond. "Helping us out today is one thing, but now he seems to be doing the most. Why?"

"Maybe he's like plenty of other guys who have a thing for Devyn. He did seem to keep his eye on her today," Chase teased. "And that brother even made sure he had a bottle of Voss right there whenever she needed it. I was impressed."

"Okay, you're trying to be funny." Devyn shook her head and tried not to blush at the thought of Nigel watching her and being so attentive.

"Clearly, that's a joke. He can watch all he wants, but he definitely won't be touching. Can you even imagine Devyn with him?" Asha smirked. "He ain't even on her level, which is exactly my point. Today, we put Pivot not just on the map, but we will be on the radar of a lot of key players. Just watch and see what happens. We can't afford to be attached to anyone or anything that puts our potential in jeopardy."

"Asha, that's not fair," Chase told her.

"No, it's not." The elation Devyn felt moments earlier about the launch diminished. The last thing she felt like doing was using what little energy she had left defending a man who had done nothing but help. The entire conversation was pointless and unnecessary. As far as Devyn was concerned, it was over. "No one is being used, Asha. Nigel and I are friends, that's it. And as for Pivot or me being associated with him or Culture, relax. It's business, not personal. There's nothing for you to even trip about."

"Good," Asha smiled. "Now, let's finish cleaning up so we can get outta here and go celebrate."

By the time they finished, it was almost nine. The girls were long gone. Nadia had agreed to join them for dinner and drinks. Devyn noticed Nigel walking past the hallway toward the lab.

"Nigel, wait," she called out, but he didn't stop, so she followed him inside. "Hey."

"Yeah?"

"You know what I just thought about?" She smiled at him.

"What?" he said with a blank stare.

"We didn't get a picture together." Devyn held up her cell as she walked up to him. "Now, you know we have to fix that, right?"

"I didn't realize it was broken."

Devyn was taken aback by his nonchalance. If she didn't know any better, she would've thought he was upset or angry at her. But there was nothing she did that could've caused him to have an attitude, so that couldn't be the case. *Maybe he's tired. It's been a long day for all of us.*

"Uh, yeah, it's broken, so let's fix it. You're acting like you don't wanna take a pic with me," she said, putting her arm around him as she tried to angle the phone so that both of them fit into the screen. It was difficult because he was much taller than she was. When he didn't try to assist, she said, "A little help here, please."

He took the phone and held it perfectly. She leaned her head against his shoulder and smiled, but his face was stoic. He took several shots but didn't smile in any of them. "Here."

"Okay, Mr. Serious, well, we're gonna go and have a couple of drinks and get some dinner. You wanna come?" Devyn asked, feeling awkward from the unusual tension instead of the positive energy they usually shared. "After all, today's success wouldn't have happened if it weren't for you."

"Nah, I'm good," Nigel shrugged.

"Is everything okay? You good?" she asked softly.

"Nothing at all. I'm fine." He pulled out a pan from the shelf he stood in front of. "I got work to do."

"Are you sure? If you need me to stay and talk, I will. I don't have to go," Devyn offered.

"Nope, I don't need you. I'm good," he said.

"Nigel, something's wrong. I can feel it. Talk to me, please. Is this about that little stunt Ingrid pulled earlier? Asha told me what happened and—"

"Ready when you are, Dev." Chase stuck her head in the door. "Nigel, you're coming right?"

"Nah, I've got some stuff to catch up on that I should've got done today. Thanks for the invite, though." The half smile he gave Chase was better than the emotionless response he'd given Devyn, solidifying that whatever was bothering him had to do with her.

"Well, thanks again for everything, and we'll get those headshots done later this week," Chase said. "Dev, we'll wait for you in the car."

"I'll be there in a few." Devyn nodded. When Chase was gone, she turned her attention back to Nigel. Her hand touched his shoulder. "Nigel, tell me—"

"Devyn, there's nothing to say. Can you please just leave?" His icy glare was startling.

"Fine." Devyn removed her hand and stepped back. "Thank you again for all of your help today. I appreciate it."

Nigel exhaled and said, "No thanks needed. No need to trip; it's business, not personal. Goodbye, Devyn."

It became clear why he was so cold and distant toward her. *He heard me. He heard what I said to Asha and Chase.* The thought of how callous and shallow she probably sounded caused her to cringe. *I only said that to satisfy Asha so she would shut up.*

"Nigel, I think you misunderstood—"

His cell phone ringing interrupted her. Nigel turned his back and answered. "Hey, there, beautiful. I was just about to whip us up something good."

Devyn's heart sank. She slowly turned and walked out, fighting tears as she exited the building into the back parking lot. *He heard what I said.* In a matter of minutes, her perfectly good day ended in heartbreak, and all she wanted to do was go home and cry. That was going to have to wait, though. Her friends had put in too much work, and they deserved to celebrate, even if she didn't want to.

"Pull it together, Dev," she told herself as she wiped her tears before reaching her car.

"Are you okay?" Chase asked when she got in.

"I'm great," Devyn lied. "I need a drink. As a matter of fact, I need several."

Chapter 24

Asha

Ding. Dong. Ding.

The chiming of the church bells got louder and louder. Asha glanced down at her watch and saw that the wedding was now over two hours late. She turned around in her pew, stared down the aisle, and wondered what was going on. Seeing that she was the only guest in the church, she began to panic. The bells continued to ring until her head started pounding, and she couldn't take it anymore.

"Stop it," she groaned, opening her eyes to awake from the torture of her dream. The ringing continued, however. She sat up, recognizing it as the sound of her doorbell. Without even checking the security camera, she got up and dragged herself to the door. There was only one person who would show up unannounced and uninvited on a Sunday. For a second, she thought about not answering the door, but her desire to get the constant ringing to stop was motivating enough to put a little more pep in her step.

"Good morning, Sully," she grumbled as she let him in.

"Morning? It's after three, Asha," he said.

"Oh." Asha took notice of his suit as he walked past her, indicating that he'd gone to church. They went into her living room and she half-sat, half-leaned on the edge of the sofa while he sat on the chair. Her head throbbed, and there was a horrible taste in her mouth. She closed her eyes and tried to recall what she ate for dinner. There was a vague memory of some kind of chicken, crab dip, and lots of drinks. Her hangover was well earned, thanks to not only Devyn and Chase, but also Nadia, YaYa, and Camille, who also joined the fun.

"You look like hell," Sully frowned. "Did you sleep in your clothes?"

Asha looked down at the same "Pivot" T-shirt and black, wide-leg pants she wore the day before, now noticeably wrinkled, that served as her pajamas. Another sign that she'd had a hell of a night.

"I guess I did," she told him. "I need some water and coffee."

"You also need a shower. I'll get the drinks for you." Sully stood and took off his jacket, laying it across the back of the chair before going into her kitchen.

Asha closed her eyes, listening to the sound of her Keurig brewing and her refrigerator opening. Sully was soon back with a bottle of water, a cup of coffee, and a disgruntled look as he handed them both to her.

"Thank you." She drank nearly the entire bottle of water first, then sipped the coffee. She would've liked to have a little more sugar, but she was grateful for what she had. The room was quiet, and neither one said anything for a while. Asha was sure that although Sully was nice, he was probably pissed about what happened at Culture with Ingrid. There were also the back-to-back calls and texts from him that she ignored. *I'm in the middle of an event. I do not have time to argue about Ingrid and her ex right now,* she thought as she blocked his number. She would've turned her phone off completely but couldn't in case VIP guests or anyone needed to reach her regarding the event. Blocking Sully and the drama with his daughter seemed to be the best option.

"Asha, Ingrid called and told me about what happened at Culture yesterday." He finally spoke. "I gotta say, I was upset and disappointed."

Asha took another sip of the slightly bitter coffee, then said, "Did she tell you she and her little friends showed up at my event half-dressed and trying to cause a scene?"

"That wasn't quite the story I got from her," he sighed.

"I'm sure it wasn't," Asha murmured. "Look, Sully, before you start, I didn't even know Nigel was Bear, or that he was connected to Culture. We needed a venue at the last minute, and that's what we found."

"When you did find out who he was, did you care? Did the fact that you held an event for women at a business owned by a violent man even *disturb* you? A man who you know I don't care for." Sully leaned forward and waited for her answer.

"Honestly, Sully, I didn't have a chance to think about any of that because while Ingrid was screaming and cussing, I was trying to hold someone else back from beating her up. That's all I was concerned with at the moment," Asha replied.

"Wow, another owner of the venue demonstrating violence. Do you see a pattern here? Can you understand why Ingrid and I are upset?" Sully asked. "It's like you took their side. You defended them, not her."

Ingrid's feelings were of no concern to Asha, but she didn't want Sully to think she didn't care about his. "I didn't side with anyone. The only thing I was trying to do was get Ingrid to leave and diffuse the situation, Sully. What did you expect me to do? My event was about to start, and they were all out front being loud, ghetto, and causing drama. That's the last thing Devyn needs to be associated with her new business."

"Devyn? I don't give a damn about her, Asha. I'm worried about my daughter, and if you gave a damn about me, you would understand that," he yelled.

"You need to calm down," Asha warned. "I get that you're upset, and even more so because you weren't there to actually see what happened. Why did Ingrid pick yesterday, of all days, to show up with her protest?

Did you ever think about *that,* Sully? From what I was told, her ass ain't never showed up before. But all of a sudden, when she finds out I'm holding an event there, she arrives."

Sully didn't respond. Instead, he stared at the floor. Asha finished the rest of her coffee, then went into the kitchen and made another cup, this one with plenty of sugar and cream. She popped two Aleve at the same time, then returned to the living room where Sully was still sitting and staring at the same spot.

"Sully," Asha said.

"Yeah?" He looked at her.

"I didn't do anything intentionally to hurt you or your daughter, and neither did Devyn. I don't have anything to do with what happened with her and Bear. You have to know that I don't condone any type of violence or disrespect against women. Not comparing the two but for God's sake, look at what my best friend went through with her ex. I wouldn't wish that on anyone. Our choice to do business with Culture wasn't personal. It was just business, that's all." Asha relented and said to him the same thing Devyn told her. "No need to trip."

"I hear you." He nodded. "I was gonna see if you would offer Ingrid an apology, but I guess it's not necessary."

Apology? It'll be a cold day in hell before I ever speak to her ass again. She *should be apologizing to* me.

"No, it's not." Asha inhaled deeply.

"Well, we have another service this afternoon at church. I gotta get back. I guess I'll let you get some rest." He stood and picked up his jacket.

"Thanks for checking on me, Sully. I appreciate you." Asha reached for him. He hugged and kissed her softly.

"Call me if you need anything," he told her.

"I will. Oh, and Sully." Asha stopped him before he walked away. "Just so that you know, Pivot classes will be held at Culture temporarily until we find another location. Again, business, not personal. I'm hoping you will let Ingrid know so there won't be any other confusion."

"That's up to Ingrid." Sully shrugged. "But we can always hope, right?"

As he walked out the door, a thought crossed Asha's mind that took her by surprise. *I'm tired of dealing with this. If that's the last conversation I have with him, I wouldn't be sad. Something's been off with Sully and me for a while. It may be time to end it sooner than later.*

Asha spent the remainder of Sunday and most of Monday recuperating from the eventful weekend. She didn't leave her house until it was time to meet at Culture for the class that evening. Devyn and Chase were already there when she arrived. Based on the feedback they'd gotten via email and social media, Pivot definitely made its mark. Asha walked in, set a smile on her face, and put away all thoughts of Sully and Ingrid. Her focus was on how proud she was of the hard work they all had done.

"You ladies don't understand the impression you made on Saturday," Devyn told Journi and Dionne at the start of class. "People could not believe you've only been coached for a few weeks. You were poised, engaging, and, most of all, professional. I am so proud of you."

"We've been practicing, Miss Devyn. We wanted people to see how good we are because of you and Miss Asha," Dionne spoke out.

"You were phenomenal, Dionne." Asha beamed. "I peeped that interview you gave to the blogger from *Black Women Today*. I can't wait to read it."

"Really? I was so nervous." Dionne grinned.

"You didn't show it, D." Journi hugged her.

"That's because of Miss Asha's media training. See how it all comes together? You look good and sound good," Chase added her two cents, surprising Asha with her compliment.

"Now, before we continue, I want to apologize to you, Journi," Devyn said.

"Me?" Journi gave her a confused look.

"I know about your being ejected from the pageant, and it's unfair."

"Oh, that." Journi's eyes widened, and she looked down.

"The pageant organizers have no right to hold you accountable for my actions. I've scheduled a meeting with Mrs. Thompkins. I'm going to ask if she would allow you to reenter if I'm no longer your coach." Devyn swallowed hard.

"Dev," Asha whispered, seeing the hurt in her eyes.

"No, Miss Devyn, you can't do that," Journi exclaimed.

"There have been some rumors on the internet . . . uh, about a video—" Devyn started.

"False rumors," Asha pointed out.

"Wait. What? Miss Devyn, Miss Asha, I think y'all got it twisted." Dionne shook her head. "Journi, you need to tell them what happened."

Asha frowned. "What's she talking about?"

"I cussed Mrs. Thompkins out," Journi sighed.

"You what?" Asha and Devyn said simultaneously, looking at each other, then back at Journi.

"Lord," Chase giggled, and Asha nudged her.

"I cussed her out." Journi repeated the statement as if it were no big deal. "She called me last week telling me she'd talked to a friend of hers who agreed to coach me. I'd be provided a more 'professional environment' to improve my skills. All of a sudden, she saw potential in me." Journi rolled her eyes as she continued. "I told her I wasn't interested. Then she went on to threaten me, running her mouth about building bridges and not turning down help from people in high places who don't usually consider young ladies of my 'demographic.' I immediately informed her that I didn't need her kind of help, and she could take her whack, lily-white, racist pageant and kiss my black—"

"Journi!" Again, Asha and Devyn yelled at the same time.

Chase was laughing so hard that her entire body was shaking, and tears were streaming down her face. Devyn hung her head and closed her eyes.

Asha suppressed her own urge to laugh as she stared at Journi, determined to stay as professional as possible. "Well, Devyn, if it's all right with you, I think we should focus on conversation etiquette today."

"Sounds like a good idea," Devyn managed to say just before she erupted into uncontrollable laughter.

"I think we all need to take five," Dionne snickered.

"I agree. As a matter of fact, take ten." Asha pointed toward the door. Dionne snatched Journi by the arm, and they rushed out.

"What the . . .?" Asha finally released the laughter she'd been holding in. "Can you believe that?"

"That girl is going to go far in life," Chase said. "I love it. She makes no apologies for who she is or what she does. Reminds me of you, Asha. I gotta say, they did a great job on Saturday, but this proves that what the two of you are doing is so much deeper than teaching them how to win some beauty contest."

Asha looked over at Devyn, who'd become quiet. "She's right, Dev. You taught them to know their worth. It's not about what anyone else says or thinks. They're valuable, and they won't be diminished or discounted."

"And will cuss folks out who try it." Chase snapped her fingers.

"Okay, we gotta work on that part," Asha said.

"True," Devyn sighed. "I'll be back."

"Dev, you all right?" Asha questioned. Devyn walked out the door without answering. Asha looked at Chase, "What's that about?"

"I don't know. She's definitely still processing everything that's happened. You know how Dev can get," Chase told her.

"I know the feeling. It's a lot." Asha sat in one of the empty chairs.

"Did you and Sulky talk about his spawn popping up with her friends?" Chase plopped into the chair directly beside Asha, despite there being at least ten other empty chairs in the room.

"Yes, Sully and I did," Asha corrected her. "You know her version of what happened differed from the truth. But I handled it. I'm not really concerned about either of them. I have more important stuff to deal with."

"Facts. Ain't nobody got time for Salty or his kid," Chase declared, then became serious. "I'm glad Journi stood up for herself, but it sucks that they put in all this work, and she won't compete. It would've been cool to see the fruits of her labor. Know what I mean? That also might be why Dev is a little upset. Imagine how impactful it would've been to see her get a crown."

Asha looked over at Chase with her legs folded under her and her auburn braids hanging from one side of the colorful scarf tied on her head. She always reminded Asha of Denise Huxtable from *The Cosby Show*. Beautiful, artistic, often clueless, but she would have brief moments of brilliance now and then.

"You are absolutely right," Asha said. Devyn and the girls deserved a big finish. Now, all she had to do was figure out how to make it happen.

Chapter 25

Devyn

It had been two weeks since the launch, and Devyn still hadn't seen or talked to Nigel. Her calls and texts went unanswered and showed "delivered." She tried to find comfort in the fact that he hadn't blocked her. On Monday evenings, she tried arriving early and staying late, hoping to run into him, but it didn't happen. The thought of showing up when he would be hosting one of his culinary classes crossed her mind more than a few times. She also considered asking Nadia, who was always in the building, about his whereabouts. But her pride wouldn't allow her to do any of those things. *Girl, why are you even sweating him? He's probably boo'd up with that chickenhead tramp he was "whipping something up" for. You around here worried about him. Meanwhile, he ain't thinking about you or your friendship. Let it go.* She tried convincing herself in an effort to feel better, but it didn't work. Instead, she sulked, which was precisely what she was doing when Uncle Julian called.

"How's my favorite niece, the world's greatest pageant and runway coach?" Uncle Julian greeted her.

"I'm your only niece and the only pageant and runway coach you know, Uncle Julian," Devyn sighed. "How are you?"

"I'm great, sweetie. Sitting here poolside watching my husband make margaritas," Uncle Julian bragged. "It's a gorgeous morning here."

"It's nighttime here." Devyn rolled on her back and stared at the ceiling.

"Wait, were you sleeping? It's too early for you to be in bed. You're not sick, are you?" Uncle Julian asked.

Does heartache count? Devyn wondered, "No, I'm not sick. I'm lying across the bed, that's all."

"Oh, well, I just wanted to tell you that picture posted on the Pivot page today was jaw-dropping. Absolutely beautiful. And the caption . . . my goodness, girl. I know you've probably got more business than you can handle right now," he said proudly.

Devyn smiled. The picture he was referring to featured her on the day of the launch, posed in front of what used to be the bank's vault. Devyn stood with her hands on her hips, legs spread apart, and eyes looking straight at the camera. She was dressed in a white Pivot T-shirt which had been cut to expose one shoulder, a red sequin mini-skirt, and black, thigh-high boots with six-inch heels. Her bob layers framed the fiercest makeup created by YaYa, a look worthy of a British *Vogue* editorial. The caption of the photo read: "*Unlock the Possibilities Within.*" The post had been shared endlessly. Uncle Julian was right. Business was booming. Starting the following month, Journi and Dionne would be joined by eight new class-mates, and the first runway workshop was being planned. Chase's photography clients had picked up as well.

"Thanks, Uncle Julian. We have a lot going on," Devyn told him.

"I see. Classes, workshops, interviews. Pretty soon, you're gonna have to start paying rent," he teased.

"And I have no problem doing that, Uncle Julian. Just let me know how much."

"Stop it. You know I would never take money from you, Devyn. I'm proud of you. It's nice to see that passion and fire from you again. I missed it. This new beginning is great. It's gonna take you farther than you ever imagined."

Hearing him say he was proud brought tears to her eyes.

"I can see your mother now, looking down, saying, 'That's my beautiful baby, doing her thing. I just wish her skirt was longer,'" Uncle Julian laughed.

"That's exactly what she's probably saying," Devyn giggled, remembering how her mother would love seeing her modeling on the runway, but cringed at the tiny bikinis she'd wear, or even worse, the sexy lingerie.

"Speaking of your mother, I sent you a congratulatory gift that you should be getting any day now. I can't wait for you to try what's inside. You have to let me know what you do with them," he said.

"You didn't have to do that. The money you deposited to help out with the launch was congratulations enough." Devyn referred to the $5,000 that showed up in her bank account on the day of the event.

"That was seed money to help grow your vision, not a gift. You've managed to pivot. Now, I expect you to blossom. Not just in business either, young lady, but also in everything your heart desires. Full speed ahead, Devyn. I love you," Uncle Julian told her.

"I love you too, Uncle Julian." Devyn swallowed the lump in her throat as the call ended. She sat up, now angry at herself. All of these amazing things were happening. And instead of being grateful, she was moping. Asha and Chase had ventured to Pablo's for Taco Tuesday. They invited her, but she declined. Now, she'd changed her mind and wanted to enjoy the company of her amazing friends. She jumped up, put on something cute, and headed out.

Devyn thought her mind was playing tricks on her when the silver Suburban pulled up to the front of the restaurant just as she was about to walk in the door. Her heart raced. She froze and locked her eyes on the driver and the silhouette of the woman beside him. Holding her breath as the passenger door opened, she waited for the occupant to emerge.

"Hey, Devyn." Nadia waved at her.

"Nadia," Devyn said with a sigh of relief, gazing past her to Nigel, who quickly glanced away when their eyes met. "Hey, Nigel."

"What's good?" he murmured.

"Big Head is dropping me off since my car is being serviced. Chase promised to give me a ride home, if she's in any condition to drive," Nadia smiled. Since the event, Chase and Nadia had become fast friends, and Devyn could see why. They were both young, artistic, free spirits.

"If she isn't, I'll get both of you home. No problem," Devyn assured her.

"Cool, Dev, and thanks for the ride, Big Head," Nadia said before walking toward the entrance.

"Nadia, the door," Nigel called out.

"My bad. Get that for me, Devyn, please?" She gave Devyn a wink as she walked past.

Welp, it's now or never. Here's your chance. Devyn hesitated for a second. Her hand touched the door, but she didn't close it until after she'd climbed inside. Nigel looked at her as if she were crazy.

"What the hell are you doing?" he grimaced.

"Calm down, Nigel. This ain't a carjacking. I just wanna talk to you for a few minutes. I mean, unless you don't have time," Devyn added for good measure.

"I got a minute. What's up?" he said, his eyes still forward.

"You tell me. I've been calling and texting, and you haven't responded. You used to be at Culture all the time. You said it was your favorite place in the world. Now, you're never there, especially when I am," Devyn told him.

"I got some stuff I'm handling and can't be there like I used to. You ain't the only one taking care of business, Devyn." His tone was contemptuous.

"I know you're busy," Devyn sighed, ignoring the way he said the word "business," "but you used to make time for me."

"What's your point?" Nigel shrugged.

"My point is I miss you. And I need you to hear me out, please." Devyn touched his tattoo-covered arm. Nigel finally looked at her, but he still didn't say anything, so she continued. "I know you heard what Asha said that night in the hallway, and you heard my response. But it's not what you think. Asha was being all extra because of what happened with Ingrid and making assumptions about you. She means well but can sometimes be over-protective. So, I just said what I knew she wanted to hear to shut her up, for lack of a better term. I wanted her to drop the subject. My words hurt you, and that's very personal. I'm sorry."

"Cool. Now, I gotta go," he told her.

"That's all you have to say? Really?" Devyn's voice was an octave higher.

"Were you expecting something more?" he frowned.

"Yes, I was. I, at least, thought you would accept my apology." She threw her hands up in frustration.

"Okay, apology accepted." He glanced at the door as if to remind her it was time to go.

"Unbelievable." Devyn shook her head. After all of that, Nigel was still dismissive.

"I don't know why you're upset. I heard you out and accepted your apology. What more do you want?" he said with annoyance.

"I want us to be friends again." Devyn was now on the verge of tears, and her voice cracked. "I want you to tell me how the hell you feel."

"Fine, Devyn. I'm disappointed in how I watched you finally embrace who you truly are: the good, bad, and indifferent. Not only did you discover an opportunity for yourself, but you also created a space to help others reach their dreams. You realized how strong you could be and took control of your life. But then, you turned around and gave that power away without anyone even reaching for it. You just handed it over to your girl," he told her.

Devyn tried to process what he was saying, but it didn't make sense. "How can you even think that? I haven't looked back, except to see how far I've come. You're wrong. Pivot has changed my life, and I'm not giving it to anyone."

"This isn't about Pivot. This is about you. As soon as Asha commented about Culture being associated with me and my negative past, what was the first thing you did?" Nigel didn't wait for an answer. "You folded instead of standing up for our friendship. It was easier for you to allow her to think she was right. Real talk, we can be cool, Devyn, but I don't need those types of friends in my life. I'm good." Nigel stared at her. "So, that's how I feel."

Devyn didn't bother to wipe away the tear that slid down her cheek. Her fingers wrapped around and pulled the door handle. She hopped out of the truck and closed the door. Neither one of them said goodbye.

"Hey, you okay?" Nadia stepped out the door and put her arm around Devyn,

"Oh yeah, I'm fine." Devyn quickly dabbed at her tears with the corner of her fingers. "I thought you went inside."

"Nah, I know my brother, so I decided to stick around." Nadia reached into her purse and handed Devyn a crumpled napkin.

"He's something else, I tell you that," Devyn sniffled.

"I'm glad y'all finally talked because he's been moping since the event. He told me not to say anything to you about it, but whatever," Nadia sighed. "I take it the talk didn't go very well?"

"It did. We cleared the air, and he pretty much put me in my place. He let me know he wanted me to leave him alone and doesn't want to be friends anymore." Devyn almost choked on her words.

"Devyn, girl, that's just fear. He's afraid to be your friend again because he'd been so guarded until you came along. His feelings are hurt, and he's having a hard time with it. He doesn't want to disappoint you. Nigel may be a big guy, but he ain't as hard as he portrays." Nadia rolled her eyes. "Hell, his *real* nickname is Teddy Bear."

"But that's it, Nadia, I would never hurt Nigel, not intentionally. The crazy thing is, before the launch, being friends is all he *ever* talked about. What's there to be afraid of?" Devyn whined. "I don't get it."

"The fact that he wants to be more than friends, maybe? And the off chance that if he were honest and told you that he was in love with you, you wouldn't want to be his friend anymore. Then there's also the possibility of his past being bad for the brand you're building." Nadia shrugged. "I told you, he's more afraid of hurting you than he is of being hurt."

Devyn's heart swelled. Nigel wants to be *more* than friends? *We want the same thing. Why didn't he say anything? Wait, why didn't I?*

"At the end of the day, when all is said and done, you're still D'Morgan the Supermodel. You were Nigel's dream girl for years off of the pictures alone. Then he got to know you, and you wanted to be his friend? Mind blown. You falling for him probably never even registered," Nadia smiled.

"Nadia, your brother has had my heart since the night he made me burn the shrimp," Devyn confessed. "I guess it's too late now. He's met someone else."

"If you think that, you're crazier than he is," Nadia laughed.

"What should I do?" Devyn asked aloud without realizing it.

"How about you go tell him how you feel?" Nadia put her hands on Devyn's shoulders and playfully shook her. "He's probably gone home to cry. I'll even text you his address."

It took Devyn ten minutes to gather enough nerve to drive to Nigel's place. Even after arriving at his town house, she remained in her car another ten minutes trying to figure out if this was a good idea. Was it worth even taking a chance? There was a strong possibility that he wouldn't even open the door, let alone invite her inside. Unable to conquer her fear of rejection and humiliation, Devyn changed her mind. She was just about to start her car when Nigel's door opened, and he stepped out, carrying a garbage bag. God, please, don't let him see me, she prayed, knowing it was useless, especially since she'd parked in the driveway right beside his truck.

"Dev?" He frowned as he stepped closer.

Devyn opened her door and got out. "Oh, uh, hey, Nigel."

"What in the world are you doing here?" he asked.

"I was hoping maybe we could talk some more," she said nervously.

"Wha—? How?" He shook his head, then said, "Yeah, lemme throw this out."

Devyn waited while he disappeared on the side of the house, then returned empty-handed a few moments later. He waved for her, and she followed him inside.

"Have a seat," he murmured when they entered the living room.

Devyn looked around the well decorated space, which was contemporary and modern with a large leather sofa and matching recliner, both with geometric-patterned pillows. Mounted on the wall were a massive, curved television and a game system on a table underneath. There was a framed poster of the Culture logo and family photos displayed as well. His place was warm and comfortable, just like Nigel and exactly what Devyn expected.

"Nice place," she commented as she sat on the sofa.

"Thanks," he politely replied. "I'll get you something to drink."

A few moments later, he returned with a large bottle of Voss water and held it toward her. She smiled at him, having the so-called uppity bottled water in his refrigerator that he always teased her about. "Thank you."

"I guess you had more to say?" Nigel muted the television and sat in the recliner.

"Yes," Devyn nodded, wondering if the long basketball shorts and white T-shirt he had on was what he typically wore to bed.

"Well, talk."

She put the bottle of water on the floor without even opening it. Her mind went blank for a second. She tried to think of where to start. *Just tell him the truth. Be honest about how you feel.* Devyn took a deep breath and uttered the words before she lost her nerve.

"I like you, Nigel. No—I more than like you. You are the person in my life I didn't realize I needed, no—I wanted until I met you. I've known that from the start, and I should've told you, but I was afraid," she confessed.

Nigel's face was a mixture of confusion and surprise. He leaned forward. "Why would you be afraid to tell me how you felt?"

"Because I was scared that you wouldn't feel the same way about me." Devyn shifted in her seat and picked up one of the throw pillows. She needed something to occupy her hands that were shaking. "You kept stressing that we were friends. So, I thought that's all you wanted."

"You never said you wanted more, Devyn," he sighed.

"Neither did you, Nigel," Devyn pointed out. "Maybe if you wouldn't have been ignoring me for the past two weeks, I might have mentioned it. Hell, I apologized and opened up to you, and the best response you give me is that you don't wanna be my friend. You know what? This is a mistake. Goodbye, Nigel."

Devyn dropped the pillow and jumped up to leave. Nigel grabbed her by the arm. They stared at each other longer than either one of them wanted. The anger in his eyes she saw earlier was gone and replaced by longing.

"Wait. What do you want, Devyn? Tell me." Nigel was breathing so hard that she saw the rise and fall of his chest.

"You, Nigel. I want you," Devyn said with boldness in her voice so that there would be no more confusion.

Nigel pulled her to him, and she willingly accepted the kiss that she'd desired for weeks. His mouth was warm and inviting, their tongues intentional as they explored each other. Devyn playfully sucked on his bottom lip and tugged at his T-shirt as he slipped the cardigan she wore off her shoulders and slid his hand under her tank top. Her nipples hardened through the lace of her bra as his fingertips brushed across them. Devyn took off her shoes and quickly stepped out of her pants, kicking them across the floor.

"Damn, Dev, you're so beautiful." Nigel's sexy growl and the lust in his eyes made Devyn even wetter. She bit her bottom lip as she gazed at his shirtless torso, amazed at the size of his broad, muscular chest and arms, covered with tribal tattoos. Her gaze lowered to his groin and the noticeable protrusion under his shorts.

"Oh damn," she gasped at the thought of what was underneath.

"Don't get scared now, Dev. You said you wanted me."
Nigel picked her up.

Devyn squealed as she wrapped her long legs around
him while being carried into his bedroom. He placed her
into the center of his king-size bed, then used his teeth
to take off her panties. The only light came from the
moon streaming through the windows. She didn't even
have the chance to be self-conscious about her fuller
figure because she was too busy enjoying the sensation of
Nigel's tongue tasting every inch of her body. He kissed
and licked her from her forehead to the bottom of her
pedicured feet. Then he devoured the sticky, sweet center
between her legs as if it were a secret recipe he'd carefully
prepared and couldn't wait to taste. When she erupted,
his fingers replaced his mouth, which was now sucking
her breasts one at a time, restarting the fire that she
thought was extinguished by her climax moments earlier.

"Oh shit, Nigel," she moaned and arched her back.
Her hands reached for the shorts that were no longer
there, and instead, were met by his hardened, massive
manhood.

"You ready?" he whispered.

Devyn nodded, eager with anticipation of what was
about to take place. Nigel paused long enough to remove
a condom from the nightstand. Devyn happily assisted
him in opening the gold, foil wrapper, and slid it on.

"Lie back," she told him.

"You sure?" Nigel raised an eyebrow.

"I wanna enjoy this ride," Devyn grinned and straddled
on top of him, carefully guiding him into her moistness.
She teased herself by rubbing his swollen tip against her
clit, intensifying the anticipation before finally accepting
the gift she'd been looking forward to receiving. The
slight pain as it entered took a split second to wear off,
soon replaced by a level of pleasure she'd never before

experienced. She rhythmically maneuvered herself up and down, forward and backward, gyrating her hips slowly, then faster. Nigel's hands alternated between holding on to her waist and smacking her ass as she rode him.

"Shit, Dev," he moaned.

Devyn was in total control and enjoyed every moment until they both arrived at the point of satisfaction. Then she collapsed on his sweat-covered chest, breathless and happy that they both finally knew exactly what they wanted.

Chapter 26

Asha

"Are you coming back after your two o'clock?" Libby poked her head into Asha's office and asked.

Asha looked up from her computer screen. "Let me double-check."

There were now three different schedules she had to keep up with: work, personal, and Pivot. She already knew the only thing she had on her work schedule was a two o'clock appointment at the Chamber of Commerce. Her personal schedule was quite empty these days, especially with her now-strained relationship with Sully. The biggest adjustment was her schedule for Pivot that became busier and busier each week.

"I can," Asha told her, seeing that the rest of her day was empty in all three categories. "I don't have to if I don't need to, put it that way."

"Understood. It's just that the guy from the Iron Workers Union is coming to meet with Greg. I peeped at the contract and noticed a transportation request for buses to take members from the hotel to the convention site, and since your client . . ." Libby lowered her voice and gave her a knowing look.

"Good looking out, Lib. What time is he coming?" Asha asked.

Libby turned toward the sound of approaching voices in the hallway, then held up four fingers.

"I'll be back before then," Asha whispered, picking up the phone and dialing Ben's number. He didn't answer, so she sent a text asking him to call her back as soon as possible. They hadn't spoken since the day of the launch. She'd meant to reach out but never got around to it. Now, she had a reason. The Iron Union Workers were one of the company's biggest clients, and they hosted several large events throughout the region each year. Connecting Ben with them would be major. When he hadn't responded to her message by the time she walked out of the Commerce Building at three o'clock, Asha decided to visit him.

"Can I help you?" a nice, older woman dressed in one of the same company polo shirts that Ben often wore greeted her when she walked into the offices of Maxwell Transportation.

"Hi, is Mr. Maxwell available? I'm Asha Bailey with Great Expectation," Asha introduced herself.

"Oh, the party coordinator. I've heard so much about you. I'm Deloris, his aunt. I help run things around here and try to keep him in line." The woman shook Asha's hand.

"Nice to meet you. I tried reaching Ben on his cell, but I couldn't, so I just popped in, hoping to see him if he's not too busy," Asha explained. "It's kind of important."

"He's been working in the garage. They got that music blasting back there, and he probably didn't hear the phone. Come on." Deloris stood and led Devyn down a long hallway lined with photos of various vehicles with the Maxwell logo on them.

"Wow, that's a lot of cars," Asha commented.

"Honey, that ain't the half of them. And his fool self done went and bought a doggone camper, of all things.

It's always something. My nephew is obsessed with anything on wheels. Been that way since he was little. All he
wanted to do was play with cars. He used to get in trouble
in school because instead of paying attention and doing
his work, he'd draw cars and trucks all day." Deloris
laughed and pointed to a large oil canvas of a beautiful
woman that hung in the center of the wall. "Used to drive
my sister Beverly crazy. He loved his mama, though.
Took care of her until the very end. That's why this party
is so important to all of us."

"I understand. We are gonna have a beautiful time,"
Asha said.

"Gives me a reason to get fancy," Deloris laughed.
She pushed a door open, and the sound of rap music
came blasting from the other side. Asha's eyes widened.
Deloris leaned over and yelled. "Told you."

"I see." Asha nodded as she looked at the rows of buses
and vans lined up in the garage. A couple of guys in
grease-covered coveralls were working, but she didn't see
Ben anywhere.

"Mickey, where's Ben? Ben!" When no one responded,
Deloris hit a button on the wall, and the music stopped.

"What the . . .?" One of the guys turned around to see
what happened.

"Hey, who touched the music?" Ben came sliding from
under the RV that Asha now noticed at the back of the
garage. It must've been the latest four-wheel purchase
his aunt was referring to. *Wow, he really bought an RV.*

"I did. Can you get from under your new toy? You've got
a visitor," Deloris told him.

"Asha, hey there." He smiled and stood up. "It's good to
see you. What brings you to the grease pit?"

"Well, I called and sent you a text about a potential
opportunity, and when you didn't respond, I decided
to come by," she explained, noticing the specks of what
must've been oil on his face.

"Aw, man, my bad." Ben shook his head. "I can't hear nothing back here."

"You could if you turn that loud, thumpity-thump mess down," Deloris snapped at him.

"Come on inside, and we can chat." Ben's eyes remained on Asha for a moment. They followed Deloris back into the building. Instead of going to the entrance area, though, Ben led her into his office.

"This is nice," Asha commented as she looked around the large, comfortable room. A large leather sofa with a matching chair stood to the side, a nice mahogany desk was centered, and shelves of model cars lined the walls.

"Thanks, it's chill." Ben sat on the sofa and motioned for her. "Come, sit."

"Oh, okay." Asha was caught off guard, expecting him to sit behind his desk. She placed her purse on the chair, then sat on the opposite end of the sofa, angling her body to face him the same way he'd done his.

"So, what's this opportunity you've got for a brother?" Ben asked.

Just as Asha was about to tell him, her phone rang. She checked the caller ID of her Apple Watch and saw that it was Libby. "Excuse me, it's work."

"Take your time. Hey, you thirsty? I have water, juice, and soda," Ben offered.

"Water would be great," Asha told him.

"Be right back." He jumped up and walked out.

"What's up, Lib?" Asha said after retrieving her phone from her purse.

"Hey, nix the four o'clock. They just called to reschedule for next week. You don't have to come back. I'll lock up your office," Libby told her.

"Oh, well, thanks for letting me know. Keep me posted on the rescheduled date. See you in the morning," Asha said and put her phone away.

"Here you are." Ben returned with two bottles of water and handed her one.

"Thank you. Now, I feel bad for bothering you because the meeting I came to tell you about just got canceled. That's why they were calling me," Asha informed Ben.

"Mm-hmmm. Just admit you wanted to see me. And it's no bother at all. Besides, I know you've been dying to hear my latest ideas," Ben teased.

"That is definitely *not* why I'm here. Please, spare me." She opened her water and took a sip.

"I see Pivot is blowing up on the Gram. Y'all know if you need security, I'm always available," he nodded.

"God, I'm hoping that was just one isolated incident. I appreciate your saving the day, literally. That was crazy," Asha told him.

"And I heard Dev and Nigel are happy. That's great. They both deserve it." Ben said it in a way that let Asha know he was sincere.

"Yeah, that took me by surprise. I must admit I'm not too thrilled. But it's her choice, not mine, so I guess there's not much I can do," Asha exhaled. She thought Devyn was joking when she told her she was in love with Nigel.

"Girl, you play too much." Asha smirked and shook her head as they sat in Devyn's backyard, talking and enjoying a "sip" of tea that Uncle Julian sent.

"I'm serious, Asha. I am. He makes me happy," Devyn said with a dreamy look in her eyes.

"Devyn, You hardly know him or anything about—"

"I know him well enough, Asha," Devyn replied. *"Once you get to know him, which I'm asking you to do as my sister and best friend, you will understand why I love him. And you will too."*

"*What's wrong with you? Why do you insist on build-ing relationships with guys who aren't good enough?*" *Asha demanded.* "*You're D'Morgan, for God's sake. You're in the middle of making a huge comeback. He's a nobody with a history of putting his hands on women.*"

"*Asha, you got it twisted. First of all, I'm Devyn, and there's nothing wrong with me. Again, once you learn who Nigel is, you'll see that I'm the lucky one. As far as his past accusation, he has no problem telling you about it.*" *Devyn was downright pleasant, which led Asha to understand what was really happening.*

"*Did you fuck him?*" *Asha took another approach.*

"*Well, duh.*" *Chase, who'd been silently observing, interjected,* "*You don't fall in love with bad dick, Asha. It's unlovable.*"

"*That's not true,*" *Devyn countered.*

"*Devyn, you won't even date a guy that's a bad kisser, so shut up.*" *Chase raised an eyebrow.*

"*Well, Asha loves Sully.*" *Devyn pointed toward Asha.*

"*That is true. Point made.*" *Chase nodded, then shud-dered.* "*Ewwww.*"

"*This ain't about me,*" *Asha shouted, now irritated and ready to go.* "*You know what, Devyn? You wanna be with Nigel—fine. But, don't expect me to have anything to do with it.*"

"*That's your choice, Asha. Nigel is mine,*" *Devyn said.*

From that moment, there was an unwritten rule, much like the one they had for Tremell, but this time, it applied to Nigel. Devyn didn't talk about him, and neither did Asha. At least, not to each other. Now, here she was discussing him with Ben, of all people.

"Why wouldn't you be thrilled? Nigel is one of the good ones," Ben told her.

He's not you. You're the great guy she needs to be with—that's why.

"I want Devyn to be safe, and let's be real. From what I've been told, Nigel has a history of being hands-on. I don't want to kill him, but if he ever—" Asha stated.

"Whoa whoa whoa. Ain't nobody gonna catch a case. You wildin', for real." Ben shook his head.

"Ben, I know what he did to Ingrid. Even though she was showing her ass, literally, while protesting, she kinda had good reason," Asha told him.

"Nah, Asha, she didn't. And don't get me wrong, I don't condone putting hands on women, but if anybody had a cause to do so, Nigel did," Ben told her.

"There's never an excuse." Asha shook her head.

"You think so, huh? Well, let me tell you what happened, and I'm sure you'll see it differently." Ben sipped his water, then told the story. "What Bear saw in Ingrid, I'll never know. But somehow, they started dating. Bear was working for me as a driver, going to culinary school, and working at an Oyster bar part time. He did this to pay all the bills: his and Ingrid's. He was working so hard that he began sleeping a lot. It got to the point where he was oversleeping and running late to everything. Some days, he'd come in and be out of it. That's my boy, so I ain't really say nothing. One morning, though, he's driving one of the vans and, *bam,* he drifts off the road and hits a tree."

"Oh, wow," Asha whispered. "Was he okay?"

"Yeah, or so we thought. They take him to the hospital to get checked out: a few bruises here and there, no broken bones. Of course, he's a Black man, so they run a tox screen. Lo and behold, he pops positive."

"He was on drugs? Oh my God." Asha began to panic. Instead of Ben's story helping, she was even more worried.

"No. But there were drugs in his system—a lot," Ben explained. "Nigel never messed with anything, not even weed. This dude had prescription drugs in his system, and he hadn't been to the doctor. Enough drugs were in him to the point where he really could've died. It was crazy. Well, he went to Ingrid's crib, opened the medicine cabinet, and *bam*. There they were. Bottles of sleeping pills—all kinds."

"Wait, Ingrid was drugging him?" Asha gasped.

"Yep. And when he confronted her, she tried to flip it on him, and he lost it. He choked the shit out of her. It was wild." Ben exhaled loudly. "He was facing some serious charges, but eventually everything got dropped. It still messed him up. Folks talked about him for a while. So, he left. I'm glad he came back, though. Culture is gonna be big for him. He's a smart guy with a great future."

"Damn." Asha was stunned. She'd misjudged Nigel and hadn't even given him a chance.

"So, your girl is gonna be fine," Ben assured her.

"I still feel kinda bad," Asha told him. "I thought you and Dev would've hit it off. You were into her."

Ben shook his head. "Nah, not really."

"What? Yes, you were." Asha shook her head in disbelief. "You told me she was beautiful and stuff."

"She is. That doesn't mean anything," Ben said softly and moved closer. "Asha, you wanted me to be with Devyn. I wanted to be with you."

In one swift motion, he leaned in and kissed her, gently at first, just enough to make sure she understood his action. It took a split second for the initial shock to wear off. Then as her lips responded to him, the intensity grew. Her mouth opened and welcomed his tongue as her arms caressed his neck. Time seemed to stand still as their mouths explored, tasted, and enjoyed each other. Asha became lost in the moment as Ben's fingers traced along her neck as he nibbled her collarbone and triggered the warm sensation between her legs. Her hands moved down his back, and a soft moan slipped from her lips.

"Ben," she managed to call his name.

"Oh, my bad." He finally sat up and smiled. "I've wanted to do that from the moment I walked into your office."

Asha adjusted her blouse that was now half open and exposing more than her cleavage. Ben had to do some adjusting of his own. Asha smiled at the noticeable bulge of his crotch. *He definitely ain't on blood pressure meds. And I ain't gotta take a nap before he's ready.*

"Wow." Asha picked up her water bottle that had slipped from her hand and drank every remaining drop.

"Are you okay?" Ben asked, his voice now nervous.

"I'm great," Asha replied. "I . . . I didn't know."

"And now that you do?" Ben took her hand in his.

"I damn sure ain't mad," Asha laughed, still shocked by his confession.

"Does that mean you'll go to dinner with me? We can go someplace nice, get a good meal, share a bottle of wine." He brought her hand to his lips. "Then maybe you can come back to my place and talk."

Asha's eyes went back to his crotch. A myriad of scenarios flooded her mind. Suddenly, she snatched her hand away and sat back.

"Asha, what's wrong?" Ben noticed the sudden change in her demeanor.

Her eyes met his. "Why was Ingrid drugging Nigel?"

"Huh?" Ben gave her a confused look.

"Why was Ingrid giving Nigel the sleeping pills?" she asked again.

"No one ever figured it out. Some said it was so she could sneak out of the house to see other dudes. Others thought she was stealing money from his wallet. I know this is gonna sound weird, but Nigel thought it had something to do with sex. She got off on him being asleep. There were times that he woke up, and there would be signs that they'd had sex, but he wouldn't remember or thought he'd only dreamed it. He'd go to sleep with his shorts on and wake up naked. Little stuff like that."

Asha jumped up and grabbed her purse. She had to get the hell out. "I gotta go."

"Wait. Hold up." Ben stood and reached for her.

"I-I-I'll call you later." Asha was so distraught. She rushed out the door and into the hallway, unsure of where to go. She panicked.

"Asha, what's going on?" Ben steadied her.

"I gotta get out of here. Please, help me get out of here," Asha pleaded.

Ben grabbed her hand and led her out of a side door to the parking lot. Asha was shaking so badly that she kept fumbling her keys and couldn't even hit the unlock button.

"Give me those." Ben took the keys and hit the button. He walked her to the passenger side and opened the door.

"What are you doing?" she whispered.

"Taking you wherever the hell it is you're trying to go. Get in and put your seat belt on," he said. After they both were seated inside, he looked over at her. "Now, where to?"

Asha was still trembling as she pulled up the GPS and said, "Sully's house."

Chapter 27

Devyn

"What the hell is that? I didn't even hear the delivery driver ring the bell," Chase asked when Devyn walked into the house with the large cardboard box. "Did Uncle Julian send another package? Is there something in there for me?"

"No, this isn't from Uncle Julian," Devyn answered. She continued into the kitchen and put the box on the marble island.

"Ooohhhh, is it another gift from an influencer?" Chase, being her usual nosy self, strolled into the kitchen. One of the perks of Pivot's recent success was the frequent arrival of items from fashion sites and beauty brands, hoping to get a shout-out on social media accounts. They'd discussed the possibility of doing paid endorsements as another stream of income for the company, but Devyn wasn't too thrilled with the idea. However, she wasn't opposed to the freebies they'd been receiving.

"No, it's from Nigel. I honestly don't know what it is. He asked me to pick it up and told me not to open it until I got home." Devyn stood back and stared at the package.

"Oh God, shouldn't this be in your bedroom? It's probably something kinky. Nigel looks like he got some freak in him."

In an effort not to confirm or deny the insinuation, Devyn ignored the knowing glance Chase gave her. Unfortunately, the slight smile she tried to suppress was a dead giveaway.

"You're unscrupulous, you know that?" Devyn shook her head.

"I knew it. You can try to play it off if you want, Dev, but I know better. Chef Nigel looks like he can flip more than pans. I must say, I'm impressed with you, though. Lawd knows that's a big tree to climb. Kudos, sis. Them arms, that chest, those tats. I don't blame you for saying the hell wit' what Asha thought," Chase teased.

"Chastity Domonique, please," Devyn exclaimed.

"Please, what? I'm happy for you. Hell, at this point, I'm Googling to find a life coach so I can get my life fixed and my own back blown out." Chase reached for the box. "Now, let's see what Nigel 'Vanzant' sent you."

"Move. I'll open it." Devyn pushed her away and pulled the box open. Sitting on top was a piece of paper with the Culture logo, and a sticky note addressed to Devyn.

Hey, Beautiful,

Inspiration comes from many places. My latest venture came from you. This is the first official box for Culture Cuisine Meal Kits. So simple even you can make it. Test it out and call me when dinner's ready. Watching you Pivot your life motivated me to do the same. I've already secured my first investor. We launch in six months.

Love, Nigel

"Oh my God," Devyn exclaimed, reading over the instructions before looking inside. Everything was proportioned and prepped for an entire Sunday dinner: chicken that could either be baked or fried, collard greens, yams, macaroni and cheese, dressing, corn bread, and a peach cobbler. All she had to do was follow the simple directions. In addition, there was a link to a video featuring Nigel, who gave step-by-step details, if desired. It was like having a personal cooking demo in her home. Devyn was flabbergasted. A comedic moment shared between them resulted in something that could propel Nigel's culinary success.

"Dev, this is crazy. You know neither one of us can boil water, right?" Chase stared at the paper and sifted through the items in the box as Devyn removed them.

"You were the one who raved about the fish I cooked. This is the same thing. Everything we need is right here. We can do this." Devyn nodded. "We just need pans and the stove."

While Chase opened the cabinets and began taking out pots and pans, Devyn grabbed the cooking utensils. They washed their hands, turned on some music, and went to work. Within an hour, Devyn's kitchen smelled like Thanksgiving dinner at her grandmother's house back in the day.

"Holy shit, I think it worked." Chase peeked into the oven at the browning marshmallows on top of the yams, and golden corn bread baking beside it.

"I told you." Devyn plated the perfectly baked chicken on a serving dish, then set it beside the pan of macaroni and cheese that looked like it had come straight from a soul food restaurant.

"Nigel is a damn genius, for real. Do you know how many dudes I'm about to catfish with this service? I'm finna be somebody's wifey. I'ma have a ring on it," Chase cackled.

"You know how cheap guys are already. I can hear them now. 'Nah, boo, I don't wanna go out to eat. Let me cook you a homemade meal,'" Devyn mimicked in a deep voice. "Okay, I'm gonna text Nigel, then take a quick shower. You got this?"

"Yep." Chase went and grabbed her iPad.

"Chase, please don't let anything burn. You said it yourself . . . Any dummy can do this," Devyn reminded her. "Remember, when you take the yams out, put the cobbler in."

"I got it," Chase nodded.

Devyn went upstairs and was deciding on the perfect outfit when the doorbell rang. She hadn't texted Nigel and wasn't expecting anyone. *It's probably just a delivery from UPS.*

"Dev, get down here, quick," Chase yelled.

"Please don't tell me you don't know how to take something out the oven, Chase, I asked if you—" Devyn stopped midsentence when she got to the bottom of the steps and saw Nigel standing in the great room. "Nigel, what are you doing here? Dinner isn't ready yet."

"Hey, Dev." Nigel gave her a half smile. "It smells good too. But dinner's gonna have to wait."

"What's going on? What's wrong?" she asked, noticing the solemn look on his face.

"I just got a call from Ben. He's been arrested," Nigel told her.

"Devyn's Ben?" Chase asked. Devyn shot her a startled glance, and she quickly regrouped. "I mean, uh, Asha's client, Ben?"

"Yeah, that one." Nigel raised an eyebrow.

"Arrested, for what?" Devyn asked.

"Assault and breaking and entering. Asha's with him," Nigel answered.

"Who did he beat up? Where? And why is Asha with him? She should be at work." Devyn was bewildered as she looked around for her cell phone while waiting for Nigel to answer her.

"Sully, at his house." Nigel stunned her. "I told him we were on the way."

"Shit, let me turn off the stove and grab my shoes." Chase rushed toward the kitchen. "Don't leave me."

Devyn stood and stared at Nigel. "Why would Ben assault Sully?"

Nigel took a deep breath, then said, "I don't know. Ben's not the violent type. I guarantee whatever Sully did to make him do this, it was bad."

Devyn spotted Asha as soon as they entered the police station. She was sitting on a bench in the lobby area, crying. Devyn didn't hesitate to rush to her side.

"Asha, girl, are you okay?" Devyn put her arm around her best friend, anxious to hear what caused her to be there.

"Oh, Dev, this is all fucked-up. I can't believe him. I can't believe he would even do something like this." Asha sobbed into Devyn's shoulder. Chase made her way to Asha's other side while Nigel watched from a safe distance.

"It's okay, Ash. We're here. You're safe now." Devyn rubbed her back. "Calm down."

"It's just . . . I just . . . How can someone hurt people like this? He's crazy." Asha wept. "He's sick."

"I know, Asha. Don't worry, though. He's been arrested," Devyn assured her. "He's not gonna get away with this."

"He has?" Asha finally raised her head. Devyn used her fingers to wipe Asha's tearstained face. "They said they took him to the hospital. The ambulance came. They put him on a stretcher. I saw them."

"No, he's in jail, boo. He called Nigel and told him." Chase rubbed Asha's back. "That's how we found out."

"Wait—what? Why would he call Nigel?" Asha asked.

"I don't know. Because that's his friend. The important question is why was he at Sully's house in the first place? Did he attack you too?" Devyn asked.

"Attack me? No, Ben was there to help me. He drove me to Sully's house, and we were inside going through the medicine cabinets when Sully showed up. He started screaming and grabbed me, and that's when Ben hit him," Asha explained.

"Well, damn." Chase said the words that Devyn was thinking.

"What were you looking for?" Devyn asked.

Asha reached into her purse and took out a handful of prescription pill bottles. "These."

Nigel stepped closer to where they were sitting. "Nah, it can't be."

"What are all of these, Asha?" Devyn frowned, looking at the bottles, most with names of other people. "Ambien, Lunesta, Halcion."

"Trazodone," Chase exclaimed. "That's some powerful stuff."

"That bastard," Nigel snapped.

"Asha, why would he have all of these?" Devyn prayed that Asha wouldn't say what she already felt was true.

Asha's bottom lip trembled. "He's been drugging me."

"Where is he? Where the hell is that motherfucker?" Ingrid yelled as she entered the station and hurried to the magistrate's desk. She was in such a tirade that she hadn't realized the small group seated on the bench staring at her.

"Ma'am, lower your voice and calm down," the uniformed officer warned.

"Nah, I ain't calming nothing until I confirm that one, y'all locked up the psycho that broke into my daddy's house and tried to kill him, and two, make sure his black ass don't get bail," Ingrid threatened. "My daddy is down the street, fighting for his life. And, last . . . I wanna make sure y'all add attempted murder charges."

"First of all, ma'am, charges can only be upgraded by the district attorney." The officer sighed. "And again, please lower your voice."

"Where is the whack-ass DA then?" Ingrid folded her arms. "Lemme speak to whoever that is."

"He would be at the courthouse. This is the police station," another officer volunteered as he stepped toward the desk. "If there's nothing else, feel free to leave."

"This is some bullshit." Ingrid turned around and saw the four sets of eyes that had been staring at her. "Oh, hell naw."

Devyn jumped to her feet. "Aye, they told you to leave, so I advise you to keep walking."

Ingrid came within six feet of Asha but paused when she saw Nigel.

"Keep it moving." Chase pointed to the door. "We didn't send for you. Don't start none, won't be none. It would be a damn shame to get that ass tapped in the police station, but I got time and bail money."

Ingrid's eyes went back to Asha. "How dare you sit your ass up in here and cry. You got some nerve."

"You got it twisted, Ingrid. Your daddy is the one who should be locked up. I'm going to make sure it happens when I file charges. He's a sexual deviant, and you're both fucking sick," Asha spat at her.

"Charges for what? You're the one who broke into his crib and had him assaulted." Ingrid looked her up and down.

"Like father, like daughter. Your daddy was doing the same thing to her that you were doing to me," Nigel spoke up.

"You shut the hell up, Bear. Ain't nobody talking to you," Ingrid yelled. "Don't act like it's my fault that your big ass couldn't stay awake. I'm surprised your little kitchen ain't burned down . . . yet."

"Girl, I will . . ." Nigel took a step forward, but Devyn jumped in front of him.

"You'll what? Put your hands on me again?" Ingrid taunted.

Chase stood up and before knocking Ingrid to the floor, smiled, and said, "He don't have to. I will."

The officers rushed to help Ingrid off the floor as Chase sat back beside Asha with a satisfied look.

"Get your hands off me. Didn't you see her assault me? Arrest her," Ingrid yelled as the officers dragged her out the door.

"Jesus, Chase, did you have to hit her in here?" Devyn whispered.

"Where else was I gonna hit her? Never point a gun at somebody if you're too scared to pull the trigger. She wanted to act up, so she had to get smacked up." Chase tilted her head.

"Asha Bailey?" the officer came back in and asked.

"Yes?" Asha answered.

"Can you come with me? We need you to answer a few questions," the officer stated.

"Sure." Asha nodded as she picked up her purse.

"You want me to come with you, Ash?" Devyn volunteered.

"No, I'm fine," Asha whispered.

"We'll be waiting right here for you." Devyn hugged her and watched as Asha followed the officer.

"I'm gonna see if I can get some information on Ben," Nigel told them.

Devyn nodded and sat back in her seat. She wanted to kill Sully. What the hell was wrong with him? How could he even do such a thing? Drugging Asha? Why? It was all too much. To think that something like that could happen to her best friend was frightening. They would've never thought that he was capable of something so deranged.

They sat for what seemed like hours, hoping that every time the door opened, Asha would walk out. Finally, she emerged. She wasn't alone, either. Devyn was shocked to see her by Ben's side, his arms holding Asha close to him.

"You good?" Nigel smiled as the couple strolled over to them.

Ben gave Nigel a dap and a hug. "Yeah, man, I'm good. No charges filed. Asha gave her statement, and they let a brother go."

"Thank God," Asha sighed.

"What about Sully?" Devyn asked.

"Oh, I most definitely filed charges against his ass. They'll be hard to prove, but I'm at least gonna try. He has a concussion and a bruised rib, but he'll be well enough to be arrested once he's discharged in a few hours," Asha told them.

"Serves his ass right." Chase nodded, then motioned her hands toward Ben and Asha, still embracing each other. "What's up with all this?"

"This is us, I guess." Asha smiled as she looked up at Ben.

"Damn right it is." Ben leaned down and kissed her.

Devyn clapped and leaped for joy, thrilled at not only the unexpected connection, but also the PDA Asha was allowing to happen. Devyn had never seen her so comfortable with a guy before. *I knew she had a crush on him. That's why she was pushing him so hard—that damn Asha.*

"I'm starving. How about we go get some food," Asha suggested.

"Actually, Chase and I already cooked. Dinner at our house," Devyn smiled.

"Oh, hell no." Asha shook her head. "We'll pass."

"I think you'll be surprised at what they prepared," Nigel laughed. "I promise if you don't enjoy it, I'll treat everyone to dinner at Sage."

"Now, *that's* an offer no one can refuse," Ben laughed. "Let's go eat."

Nigel took Devyn by the hand, and Ben took Asha's.

"No way. Nope. This ain't gonna work at all. Y'all both are boo'd up, and I ain't. This must be fixed immediately." Chase announced as she followed the two couples out the door. "Ben, Nigel, come on. I know y'all got a brother, cousin—somebody. Ben, I know there's some single bus drivers over there at your company."

Epilogue

Asha

Three Months Later . . .

"Excuse me, I have to take this," Asha whispered to Mrs. Phillips and Glenda, one of the casting agents at The Walton Agency. They'd been waiting for Dionne and Journi to return from the tour they were being given. Asha stepped out of the office and across the hallway into an empty conference room. She closed the door before answering.

"I take it congratulations are in order," the voice on the other end said. "I heard things went well."

"They did. The girls blew it out of the water. We're just waiting for them to get back to Glenda's office so she can give them the good news. They're being offered a contract."

"I suspected that's what was going to happen."

"What can I say? They've been trained by the best," Asha bragged.

"Well, let me know if I can do anything else."

"Actually, there is. I'm working on an amazing fundraiser in October for Breast Cancer Awareness. It's going to be a formal dinner, followed by a fashion show featuring the Pivot models, of course, along with breast cancer survivors." Asha explained the concept she and Ben had finally agreed on.

"Sounds wonderful. What do you need from me? Certainly, you're not asking me to participate, although I'm not opposed to that idea."

"You know that ain't happening. But, along with your generous cash donation, I was hoping you could reach out to some design houses and get them to sponsor and maybe provide attire for the survivors to model." Asha pitched the idea she'd been sitting on for the past two weeks and prayed it would work.

"I guess I can see what I can do. I'll let you know in a couple of days. I'm just excited things are working out so well for Devyn and Pivot."

"Thanks to you," Asha commented. "I don't understand why you can't just—"

"No, I'm not ready. And please don't tell me she knows about any of this. The call to Walton, the VIPs at the launch . . . You can't tell her anything about it, Asha."

"Scorpio, she doesn't know, but she should. At some point, she has to find out." Asha shook her head. Keeping the help that Scorpio had been giving Pivot was killing her. To Asha, it was a blessing, but she knew if Devyn found out from anyone else other than Scorpio, there would be hell to pay. Asha and Scorpio had been going back and forth over the dilemma.

"She will, in time. Just not yet. I don't want her to think I'm helping her out of guilt for what I did. That's not what this is at all. I believe in her and what she's doing. Devyn is smart and talented. She probably didn't even need my help, but I love her and want to do what I can to support her," Scorpio said.

"I get that, and I know she will too. We all want her to succeed: me, you, Chase, Uncle Julian. That's all any of us ever wanted. It's what her mother wanted." Asha continued, "You need to tell her."

"Maybe you're right. How long will you guys be in town?"

"We leave the day after tomorrow. We're gonna do a little shopping and sightseeing tomorrow, then head out the following morning," Asha replied.

"I can't believe you all drove a damn RV. I would've bought the plane tickets, Asha. Jeez."

"That wasn't necessary. Besides, it was a fun drive."

"Well, I'm actually back in town. Just got here today. I'm heading over to the new mansion my hubby purchased. Then I'm hitting the club tonight. Why don't we plan to meet for lunch tomorrow? That way, she and I can finally have the talk."

"Lunch tomorrow. Just let me know when and where." Asha was relieved that the longstanding beef would finally be squashed. They could then address the tea that was just spilled. Everyone knew that Scorpio was leaving her longtime husband, R&B superstar King Douglas. Their divorce proceedings had been pending for months, and from what Asha saw, Scorpio had been living the single life for a while. "Hubby? I thought you filed for divorce? Wait, does King even know you're coming?"

"Nope, I don't have to tell him when I'm coming home. Besides, I wanna see what's so special about this crib he built somewhere called 'The Manor of Harrington Oaks.' Honestly, I'm just nosy. Besides, filing doesn't mean we're divorced. We are still married."

"You are. Well, I need to get back inside," Asha told her.

"I'll call you tomorrow, Ash. Congrats, again," Scorpio said and hung up.

"Sorry about that." Asha apologized when she returned to the office and took her seat.

"No problem at all." Glenda smiled. "Mrs. Phillips here was just raving about Pivot and the importance it's played in Journi's and Dionne's progress. She isn't the only one who had great things to say. Pivot comes highly recommended, and I must say, we're impressed. You probably don't know this, but we've had our eye on your company since it launched."

"Really?" Asha nodded and crossed her legs.

"Yes, and I don't know if your schedule will permit, but we'd love to sit down with you and Miss Douglass to discuss a contract with Pivot to work with a few of our newer models." Glenda smiled.

"I'm sure Miss Douglass and I can accommodate a meeting before we leave. Thank you so much." Asha remained calm, suppressing the excited scream that she wanted to release.

This is it. We did it. Securing a contract with an elite agency was something they hadn't even considered, and now, it was happening. *This is just the beginning for us. Scorpio truly looked out. This is bigger than we ever imagined, and our lives will never be the same. I can't wait to tell Devyn and Chase.*

Devyn

Of all the hotels she'd ever stayed in, and there had been quite a few, the Westin was Devyn's favorite. She loved the upscale comfort of the accommodations and the friendly service. One thing she truly adored was the way it smelled. No matter which location she stepped into, she was welcomed with the familiar, refreshing signature White Tea fragrance. It was easily one of her favorite scents and instantly relaxed her. But now, as she sat in the hotel lobby, despite the familiar aroma, the last thing she felt was serenity.

"Dev, baby, you need to chill." Nigel looked up from the cooking show he was enjoying on his phone. The closer he got to the launch of Culture Cuisine Meal Kits, the more obsessed he seemed to become with celebrity chefs.

"I'm fine," Devyn lied.

He placed his hand firmly on her knee. "Then you need to tell that to your leg that's been shaking for the past twenty minutes. Everything is going to be all right. You said this is just one invitation of many for them: Either it will be yes or no. The only thing that matters is that they do their very best."

Devyn nodded without saying anything, hoping the pep talk she'd given Dionne and Journi before they left the hotel had been effective. When she'd received the same words of wisdom from her mother, they'd been inspiring and motivating. She now knew exactly how her mother felt: proud of the hard work and dedication that resulted in the opportunity, yet fearful of the possibility that it may result in disappointment. Like a parent, Devyn was well aware that rejection was a part of life and came in many forms, but she did not want them to experience it. Not yet, anyway.

What is taking so long? They should've been back by now. How long has it been? Maybe them not being back yet is a good thing? I really should've just gone with them for this audition. Why hasn't Asha at least called with an update? Devyn stared at her phone, making sure she had a signal and checking the time. She realized only an hour had passed since Asha, Mrs. Phillips, and the girls had piled into the SUV provided by The Walton Agency and headed to the meeting. It had been Devyn's decision not to attend in an effort not to be a distraction from Dionne and Journi. This was their defining moment, not hers. She wanted them to shine. Now, she wished she had taken a risk and tagged along. The suspense was killing her. The fact that an agency of Walton's caliber had reached out to them was huge—an opportunity of a lifetime within itself. Even if they weren't offered a contract, at least they'd be on the radar.

"You're still sitting down here?" Chase walked over and asked.

"I asked her if she wanted to go get something to eat, but she doesn't." Nigel shrugged without looking up from his phone this time.

"I'm not hungry," Devyn said.

"But I am," Nigel responded. "She'd rather sit here and shake with worry while my stomach beats me in my back."

"I'm gonna beat you in your back if you don't hush." Devyn gave him a warning look. "We can go get food when they get back."

"When they get back? Dev, you know that could take hours," Chase told her. "Let's just go grab something close. Where's Ben?"

When the agency contacted the girls for the "go-see," Ben offered to drive everyone up in the RV he'd been dying to put on the road. The thought of being in the same vehicle with everyone was a bit disturbing at first, but Asha convinced Devyn that it was only a four-hour drive. It was cheaper than buying plane tickets for everyone, and it would be fun. Luckily, she'd been right.

"He went to do something to the RV. I don't know. He just said he'd be back in a little while," Devyn answered.

"I shoulda went with him. At least I coulda got some food," Nigel mumbled.

"Oh God, fine. Let's go eat." Devyn stood, knowing that if she didn't agree that the two of them would continue to complain. "Wherever we go, I don't wanna hear you talking about how much better the food would be if you cooked it."

Nigel grinned. "I won't make any promises, but I'll try."

"I'll order an Uber while y'all pick a place," Chase told them.

"Let me hit up Google and see what pops up," Nigel said.

"How about you go and ask the concierge for a recommendation?" Devyn suggested.

"Good thinking. I'll be right back." He gave Devyn a quick kiss, then headed toward the front desk area.

"I hope everything is going all right," Devyn sighed, looking down at her phone again.

"It is. If those girls aren't anything else, they're prepared. You worked them to death this past week, their portfolios are flawless, they look amazing, and Asha made sure they're polished. They're ready, Dev," Chase assured her.

"I still can't believe this is happening. It's crazy. Walton never reaches out to models, let alone inexperienced ones. These girls have never booked a show or been on a damn set. I'm kinda wondering if I'm dreaming, honestly," Devyn told her.

"It is kinda odd, but I ain't questioning God's favor, and neither should you. Let's just take our blessings as we get 'em," Chase laughed.

"I know that's right." Devyn's tension eased a little. "I'm all nervous, like they asked me to come in."

"Does that mean you're interested in jumping back in the game, Devyn, dear? I mean, I'm sure Asha would have no problem mentioning that while she's there. Lemme send her a quick text." Chase reached for her phone.

"Don't you dare, Chase," Devyn laughed and grabbed at her arm.

"D?"

Devyn froze when she heard the voice. She hadn't heard it in years, but she instantly recognized it. The shocked look on Chase's face also confirmed who it was before she even turned around to see. Her body rotated in slow motion, in contrast to the quick pace of her heartbeat.

"Oh shit," Chase whispered.

"Devyn Morgan." Tremell smiled at her.

"Devyn Douglass," she corrected him, still stunned by his presence. He looked the same, only a little older, a little flashier, if that was even possible. Instead of a bald fade, he had tiny starter locs that looked like blond pieces of macaroni in his head. There were so many platinum chains around his neck that Devyn could hardly make out the team name of the jersey he was wearing. His jeans were too fitted, and his jacket, which he didn't need in the eighty-degree heat, was too big. She had no idea who his stylist was, but obviously, he needed a new one. The entourage he had with him didn't look any better.

"Oh, my bad, Devyn Douglass," he repeated. "How you been? You looking good, D."

Is this really happening? Is this dude really standing here talking to me like we're cool? Nah, he can't be.

"We were just leaving." Chase pulled Devyn toward her.

"What's good, Chase? You looking amazing, as usual." Tremell looked her over.

"A'ight, babe, the concierge says there's a bomb burger joint not too . . ." Nigel stopped and looked just as shocked as Devyn was to see Tremell and his crew.

Tremell looked Nigel up and down, then said, "'Sup?"

"Yo," Nigel responded, then turned to Devyn and Chase. "Y'all ready?"

"We are," Chase told him, then looked over at Tremell and said, "Nice jacket."

As soon as Devyn went to leave, Tremell touched her arm. "Dev, wait. Please."

Devyn quickly snatched away from him, and Nigel moved closer. Tremell's large security guard did the same, and the two big men squared off.

"Stand down, big guy. I ain't the one," Nigel cautioned.

"What you wanna do?" Tremell's bodyguard crossed his arms in front of him and stood with his legs slightly apart.

"Chill out, fellas, this ain't even like that," Tremell spoke up. "I'm just tryin'a holla at Dev right quick, that's all. Just for a moment, please. Ain't nobody asking for trouble."

Devyn looked around and saw the small gathering of spectators standing nearby, some of whom were now recording what was happening. The last thing she wanted was to be the center of another media spectacle with Tremell.

"It's fine, Nigel." Devyn touched his shoulder. "I got this."

"Dev, you sure?" Chase asked, just as ready to rumble as Tremell's posse was.

"Yeah," Devyn nodded. She looked at Tremell and motioned toward the hotel bar, "We can talk over there. Alone."

Tremell instructed his crew to stand down, then followed Devyn toward the far corner. She leaned against the wall and folded her arms, waiting for him to talk.

"You wanna sit down, grab a drink?" Tremell offered.

"No. This isn't two old friends catching up. I don't even want to hold a conversation with you, Tremell, to be honest," Devyn snapped at him.

"Damn, Dev, it's like that? I thought we were past all of what went down," Tremell sighed.

"Past all of it? Tremell, what the fuck is wrong with you? What the hell are we past? The fact that you humiliated me in front of our family and friends by leaving me at the altar? Or are we past the fact that you used that most painful moment to make a fucking video, with one of my closest friends, to promote your own career and assassinate mine in the process? Not to mention, you did all of this during a time when I was suffering from a debilitating illness and the death of my mother." Devyn unleashed the years of pent-up emotions she'd been holding in. "I lost everything while your ass was on top of the world, and you think I'm just supposed to move past it? Fuck you, Tremell."

Don't cry. Don't cry. Don't. You. Dare. Cry. Devyn said the words repeatedly in her head, reminding herself that she promised the last time she cried over Tremell would be the final tears she would ever shed behind his ass.

"I'm owed that, Dev, and I'm sorry for all of it. I should've been man enough to tell you I was having doubts about the wedding. But everything happened so fast. I didn't know how to handle it. I should have apologized. Real talk, the only reason I made the stupid video was that I was mad about how you swung on me in the church, and Scorpio was pissed too. It was wrong of both of us," Tremell admitted. His apology was too little, too late, but hearing him admit he was wrong was a little satisfying.

Devyn shook her head. "You weren't the only one who had doubts, Tremell. I did too."

"I didn't know that, Dev. All I knew was how important the wedding was for you, your mom, and everyone. When I told Asha that we might need to wait, she was dead ass against it," Tremell exhaled.

"Wait, when the hell did you tell that to Asha?" Devyn asked, surprised by what he said. *He's lying. He has to be.* Asha never mentioned Tremell having cold feet, before or after the wedding. "That doesn't even make sense because Asha is the main person who didn't want me to marry you."

"That's what I know. But the day I picked up my tux from the designer, she was there, and I mentioned it. She pretty much told me I didn't have a choice, and this wedding was going to happen, no matter what. Then she started rambling on about how life was too short, and she and I were going to have to be there for you. We needed to care for you and make sure you were good. I understood what she was saying, but, Devyn, I couldn't."

"What do you mean, Tremell? You make it seem like Asha knew something was going to happen. No one even knew I was sick, not even me." Devyn's eyes bore into him, and she was now uncomfortably hot.

"I'm not talking about your being sick, Devyn. I'm talking about your mother. Asha knew she was terminally ill; she knew she was dying."

She knew she was dying?

Devyn couldn't breathe. Her body betrayed her mind, which instructed her not to fall. Tremell's voice became distant as she closed her eyes and collapsed into his arms as he caught her before she hit the floor.

The Drama Continues in

Private Property 2: *Closing Costs*

coming soon . . .